COYOTE

Richard Thornley was born in 1950. His first book, *Zig Zag*, was published in 1981. As a ten-page film project, *Coyote* was awarded the George Orwell Memorial Prize in 1986.

BY RICHARD THORNLEY

Richard Thornley

COYOTE

Comprising a Final Bid
from the Maggot, Sundry Tricks,
and the Passing of the Soul
through Death

VINTAGE

Published by Vintage 1995

2 4 6 8 10 9 7 5 3 1

Copyright © Richard Thornley 1994

The right of Richard Thornley to be identified as the author of this work has been asserted by him in accordance with the Copyright, Designs and Patents Act, 1988

First published in Great Britain by
Jonathan Cape Ltd, 1994

Vintage
Random House, 20 Vauxhall Bridge Road,
London SW1V 2SA

Random House Australia (Pty) Limited
20 Alfred Street, Milsons Point, Sydney
New South Wales 2061, Australia

Random House New Zealand Limited
18 Poland Road, Glenfield,
Auckland 10, New Zealand

Random House South Africa (Pty) Limited
PO Box 337, Bergvlei, South Africa

Random House UK Limited Reg. No. 954009

A CIP catalogue record for this book
is available from the British Library

ISBN 0 09 947771 8

Papers used by Random House UK Ltd are natural, recyclable products made from wood grown in sustainable forests. The manufacturing processes conform to the environmental regulations of the country of origin

Printed and bound in Great Britain by
Cox & Wyman, Reading, Berkshire

For My Family

'Coyote – the Major Trickster Figure in myths of the North American Plains Indians . . . his dual role also places him in tales of entertainment where he appears mischievous, violent, erotic or merely foolish.'

Man, Myth and Magic, volume two

CONTENTS

CHAPTER ONE

A Dropping out of Thin Air

His sister Ann was ten when John Gay was born, and eleven when their widowed mother died. So then she found the ragman and she invited him and his first woman to live in the bottom of the house. John was wet-nursed by the ragman's woman until she upped and left the ragman one day for a better life, taking her nipples off to the house of a cousin who had nothing to do with boiling water.

The Gargantua came to the basement a week later. She was polite to Ann, but Ann took John back upstairs and cared for him herself.

Each morning, before John awoke, the ragman was off wheeling his cart around London, picking clean the dens and finishes, snaffling discarded finery for Gargantua to wash. As long as daylight lasted the ragman sat in front of their house and offered these clothes for sale. Some articles, he said, had a life of their own, some clothes stuck to nobody.

When he was left to himself, John breakfasted in the ragman's cellar. He carried down whatever scraps were in the kitchen, and he gave them to Gargantua who let him eat from the pot of thick soup which simmered forever sleepily on her stove. While he ate, the half-naked woman circled the cellar in a brutish shuffle, pushing pieces of cloth into the tubs of boiling water. She had a wide dumpy face, like a collyflower, embroidered with spidery veinburst; and her arms and breasts were blotched purple by scalds. She had no teeth. When she was thinking, her lips smacked as she sucked them in against her gums. John watched her carefully. She was a great, moist monster.

Besides the house, their mother left them many friends in the theatre. Ann became an actress. John was at first wild with excitement but quickly became bored with the plays in which she appeared.

Through boyhood he went instead with the ragman to watch the great Clown Grimaldi, at the Sadler's Wells and at Covent Garden. Grimaldi was the most popular man in London. He was friendly to

1

everybody and was admired by everybody. John liked his trickery; but of all the stage characters, John loved the graceful airy Harlequin.

The ragman never went to see Ann perform. John thought that he should do so, and said as much, but the ragman nodded indifferently and looked at John as though he were mad. Ann told John that he talked down to the ragman, and that the ragman could tell that he was being condescended to – which must annoy him, since he was, after all, the nearest thing to a father they had.

Thereafter, John did not talk to him at all. He *invented* parents, and the people he chose always responded to the affections of such a spirited and handsome boy. But John would quickly tire of them, and Ann was left to explain away the cruel change in his behaviour towards them.

Of *himself* at the age of ten, John Gay had no very clear idea; but he was sure that when he breathed the air went straight from his mouth down into his stomach. Often it gave him terrible pain. He tried, then, not to breathe deeply, but when he did the air attacked him. It swept down in a violent invasion, and he imagined hordes of tiny English soldiers rushing up to defend his gut from the waves of air. They would fight to drive the enemy back across the Channel. There were charges and clutter and stamping and artillery. The battle came and went and was at times a pitched stampeding. This was what caused the pain. As he had pictures of the pain, he came to understand it. He didn't fear the pain. The fear was before the battle, when the air was marching into place. Then his lips went cold and his hands went sticky. That was fear. He grew up fearing fear more than fearing God, although during the worst of the pain he made God a lot of far-reaching promises which he tried to keep.

And the air was his enemy.

He tested himself slowly and then he took his vengeance on the air. He leapt at it, he struck it and he unbalanced it. The air was vanquished. He had triumphed.

Ann had always refused to shield or to succour her brother, to become one of his invented parents. But what a conscience she had suffered over her refusal. John played havoc over that conscience. He knew from

2

very early on that he could perform, and he had the gratification of discovering that he could hold at least one person in his hand. His first self-awareness was of his ability to twist Ann so that she would concern herself with him. He had discovered that she was accessible to guilt.

As John grew older he remained as inconsciently avaricious as he had always been. He was plaintive and inconsiderate. There was perhaps something wrong with him. He was, Ann assured herself, not so much bad as simply not growing up into adulthood.

She once took John with her to the Westminster Gas Plant. She led him along a wooden platform which was roped below the roof of the furnace room. He was giddy with fear and excitement, and only after several moments did he dare to look down into the depths of the hot, dark cathedral.

Below him, thin underworld creatures sprawled along the walls beside the huge piles of coal which dwarfed them. Smears of filth lay strangely over the pale glow of mostly naked bodies. The men were still, like dead white maggots in a bucket. Sometimes one of these maggots would curl suddenly, and tighten, and break the silence with a groan which introduced a long and unsatisfied retching. The coughing started and ended abruptly, more contained than the operation of a machine. As John peered closely over the railing he saw that the men themselves could not claim authority over their bodies, which bent and exploded uncontrollably, as though they had been prodded by an inquisitive needle in the hand of some gigantic urchin.

He looked for Ann, but she had disappeared on into the gloom ahead. Feeling suddenly powerful and destructive towards the trapped men, he picked up a lump of coal and dropped it over the railing.

He could not see it fall, but it landed in a pool of water on the floor of the chamber. One of the great furnaces was splashed and it hissed a contemptuous annoyance. The men were not disturbed.

He was bored. He executed a precise and careful pirouette, and he entertained himself with a series of attitudes until Ann should return.

Beneath his feet the platform stirred and began to tremble regularly. A tall man, of some bulk, laboured towards him. As he passed he told John that now he would see, sir, now he would see the men rise. The platform shook, and trembled, and rested as the man disappeared towards the centre.

3

A moment passed. John heard then the cheap wail of a tin horn, which echoed round the building. Beneath him the maggots stirred and grouped. He heard splashing and saw that these men were rolling themselves in the pools of black water that lay about the floor. There were three, four, five sharp clangs, and the whole chamber soared into fiery illumination – the doors of the furnaces fell open and hung tight-jawed in a dumb gape while the fires spewed sheets of flame, roaring with their hunger.

The men shrank back against the walls to escape the heat. The air was solid and heavy and difficult to draw in, and it left a thick unwholesome coating on his tongue and throat.

He looked along the platform. The bulky gentleman was mopping his brow with a large white neckerchief, and beyond him Ann struggled to loosen her bonnet. John felt as though he would faint, his limbs were reluctant and his mind sank into a torpor. He called to Ann, but she could not hear him and she could not save him. He searched for the familiarity of pain but there was no pain. He wondered if he would go to Heaven, away from the heat and the fires at which he stared. And below him the hairless, emaciated men edged forward to replenish the inferno. Two pair shovelled the food into each glaring mouth, while a third pair serviced their fellows by dousing them from head to toe with buckets of water, that they should not be destroyed by their closeness to the flames. This simple gesture of care, set against the enraged appetites of the furnaces, shocked him and filled him with confusion. When the doors were slammed shut and the chamber was dark again, each dim white figure separated from its companions and lay exhausted in solitude, abandoned to the impersonal cough which flitted from man to man.

Ann and he left the building and walked silently away from the river, up towards Covent Garden. Ann was to act in *The Smuggler and the Jew* and he parted from her at the stage door.

From the rise at Four Ways he looked back at the city and saw it lit by pinpoints of gaslight. A thousand thousand fireflies hung above the dusked buildings in a splendid beauty. All that he wanted to do was to dance, like the graceful Harlequin.

Ann once told him of a dream which she had about him. John was a shabby little figure on a beach, hopping from side to side in a victory dance, with a collection of human heads flapping at his waist. He was fragile, thin and half dead. In place of his own head he wore the smiling skull of a bird. He had pecked all the humans to death but their faces were still fleshy, although their expressions were sad.

CHAPTER TWO

A Finding of Feet upon the Boards – Titou Gouffré

Grimaldi was by now manager at the Sadler's Wells and John Gay attached himself to the company, hoping that his skills would be noticed and called upon. The actors were friendly but he could not accept their friendship. Their bravado and their bonhomie frightened him. He found them wasteful and impure. The master himself was weakened by illness and remained distant; there was an air of indecision about the theatre and an uneasy gloom. The cause of the trouble was Grimaldi's bitterness towards his son, who steadfastly refused to wear the mantle which his father had prepared for him. It was a private battle and nobody dared to meddle.

Young Joe was well on his way to becoming a reprobate, but John admired him for his resistance to his father. 'I am not my father,' he would say, 'I will never be my father and I will never have his fame. I cannot be recognised for what I am and therefore I don't care how I am recognised.' When Gay told him that he was orphaned, young Joe exclaimed at such good fortune. The times had changed, said Joe. There was no longer the natural sympathy between the audience and the actors. The audience were not warm and they could not be tempted to warmth. They wanted to maintain their distance. They would not be clownishly seduced, they would be touched from behind the wall and blessed only by a statement of beauty.

Gay believed that he might achieve a statement of beauty.

Late into the night he practised in his room before mirrors, concentrating a posture, refining his attitudes and movements. Five concise quickening movements; and the somersault – into stasis. One, two, three, four, five – and the emergence. The attitude, the disturbance – and the revelation.

He tried hard to do what little was asked of him in the theatre and gained some attention from the actors. In front of his mirrors he drilled himself nightly. He worked harder on himself than he had ever done and he was rewarded by a feeling of perfect isolation.

Grimaldi regained his health. In the late Spring, of this year 1824, the Sadler's Wells was to mount a new production, a new pantomime. The company was not strong, owing to illness and injury, and Grimaldi was reluctant to risk the importation of an expensive name, perhaps clinging to the hope that his son would rise to the occasion. Gay agonised over whether he should assert his own claim.

One morning, when the actors sat discouraged, he felt himself engulfed by a strong fury of righteousness, as though he would be dragged, irrespective of his will, to the centre of the stage and there to lay down the law.

He fought within himself to regain control over this vertigo, because he wanted to be clear-headed in his exhibition. He wanted to ensure that he would give of his best. If there had been mirrors on the stage he would have advanced with confidence. Once catching sight of himself he would have performed in perfect containment. But as his upheaval quietened he saw clearly that he could not perform in front of Grimaldi. The master sat on an upturned tea-chest, snapping his fingers at the dearth of genius. John could not dare to be judged by him.

The moment passed and he was seized by melancholy. He slipped away from the stage and in the quiet emptiness of the dressing-room he sat forward with his head on his arms and cried at his timidity. He had served himself badly. He left the theatre unnoticed and went home.

When he came to his bedroom the mirrors confronted him with a silly emptiness and he turned them to face the wall. He lay on the bed and gazed at their backs, the dusty frames and the expanses of dirty, yellowed paper, suffocated by a feeling of dry old filth. He turned the mirrors round again, and when he lay on the bed he stared at the reflection of his window, through which white clouds were chased amongst a pale blue sky.

He fell asleep and he awoke suddenly somewhere in the night. It was as though he had been interrupted when he was about to speak, and yet now on his awakening he had nothing to say. The night was thick and black, but he could not bring himself to light a candle. The blackness was a parent who would be angry if disturbed. He lay still, in a light perspiration, scared that his body might make some involuntary movement, which would be like a scream. In due course he heard the ragman's preparations for the day, and he was scared that the ragman might come and find him. The ragman left, and he was thankful.

He lay this way until dawn, which itself came like a dreadful and immodest nakedness to the bed of dark, peeling back the covers. He noticed that his hand clutched tightly at the shirt between his legs to protect him from violation. Troubled by this image he kicked away the blanket and stood weakly on the floorboards. He was glad to have broken with the bed and he looked back at it with disgust. He was surprisingly clear-headed now, his mind raced like a fly-wheel, unattached to any sombre responsibility. He went to the sitting-room and took pen and paper and wrote his resignation from the Sadler's Wells.

It lacked in purity. He read it through and did not understand what he had written. After much crossing out and arranging of the sentences, he had: 'I am leevin the Sadler's Wells. John Gay.'

He tried 'I am leevin the Sadler's Wells. Gay.' And he tried 'I am leevin the Sadler's Wells. John.'

But these experiments with his own name so unnerved him that he fell back on: 'John Gay is leevin the Sadler's Wells, thank you.' He took the note back to his bedroom and sat on the bed until Ann had risen and left the house. Then he dressed reluctantly and walked to Islington at the time appointed for rehearsal.

Grimaldi was in a tremendous agitation with the actors and would not be approached. Gay felt at that instant such a tremendous hatred and shame that if he had stayed near Grimaldi for another moment he would have struck him and kicked him and gone berserk; he didn't know what he might have done. When a hand clapped him on the shoulder he spun round in blazing anger to defend himself against the intruder, whoever it might be; be it even young Joe, who looked at him and frowned, and laughed, and frowned again as though not sure what to make of the boy.

'Whoa! Heigh!' He said. 'Come back, John, come back now. Steady, John, steady. What the devil's in you? Come with me, John.'

Joe led him from the stage. His breath showed that he had been drinking but he was in no state of intoxication. Gay was on the point of weeping but had nothing left to weep. He handed Joe his note. Joe scanned it and thumped him affectionately on the back. 'I will show you something,' he said. 'You will find better ways than I, but I will show you something. I think, though, that you had better settle yourself with this, John. You should soften your devil.'

Gay was handed the small flask of brandy and he recklessly took a large swallow and hardly kept his stomach from rising to his lips. He spluttered, and sipped more moderately at the flask. Grimaldi's voice rang from the stage, forbidding him or any other actor to drink in his theatre.

Joe's voice bellowed back: 'Mister Gay is no longer one of your actors, sir. I have replaced him.'

Gay had drunk very little, but there arrived a pleasant screen between himself and the world. He observed Joe go up to the stage and talk with his father. Grimaldi was by turns dismissive, resigned and good humoured towards his son, who suddenly leapt from the boards and marched to the back of the auditorium, while the great man folded his arms and waited. Joe reappeared, and introduced to the stage a Monsieur Gouffré.

That day at Sadler's Wells Gay was in no fit state to challenge the man he watched; and even on the previous day his challenge would have been neither competent nor understood.

He could not believe what he was seeing. This ugly, hairy, squat thing, this Frenchman – this Gouffré – was possessed of or by a demonic ability. No sooner had the Monsieur reached the stage than up the vertical flats he scampered, without ropes, in an instant. Faster he went up and down, without contrivances. A freak of Nature, or Nature itself, this man gave no opportunity for Gay, the actors, or Grimaldi to rein in their astonishment.

The Monsieur went off again, like some nightmarish scuttling beast, immediately along the balconies of the theatre, up the pillars and across the roof of the building. Gay ran forward to the empty orchestra in order to follow his tour. He descended the other face of the proscenium with the same careless speed, and then he stood back on the stage, hunched and smiling wickedly; soiled breath and dribble poured from his cesspool of a mouth. Apart from this hideous panting there was dead silence.

Joe stared across at his father with a slow smile crossing his lips, while Grimaldi's mind strove to master its own discomfiture. The great man finally chose a derision with which to defend himself.

'Well,' he said. 'Thank you, your royal highness.'

The actors laughed, as they would surely have laughed at John Gay when given their cue.

Joe snorted his contempt. The Frenchman shrugged. Grimaldi clapped his hands and the actors walked to their positions.

'Are you with us, young Gay?' Grimaldi asked.

For Grimaldi there was no mystery, there was mechanics.

Gay did the Spring season at the Sadler's Wells. He played the tiny parts almost without thinking about them. He was not required to hold the stage; he wondered if he had ever been so required by anyone other than himself, and by anything in him other than his vanity.

The Frenchman found employment elsewhere, as a 'turn' at the Gardens. Each night, after his slight débuts, Gay ran across London to see the Frenchman's miraculous display.

CHAPTER THREE

*A Mysterious Defiance of Air – Gay's Entrancement by Titou Gouffré –
A Public Member's Billing and Cooing – The Appreciation of Science
over Emotion*

The Frenchman did not make the slightest improvement to his act.
There was no grace in the frantic movement, no statement of beauty; he
showed no desire to be adored by his audience.

Gay imagined what would happen if the Frenchman, at the apex of
his scurry, should come unstuck and fall to the ground. There he would
lie, on his back, with his arms and legs scrabbling feebly at the air.
People would point at him and would gather around him. Levers would
be sent for, and when he had been levered over he would dart off again,
ferocious and defiant, uninjured by his great fall.

Such a man was not so much an insect as an angel. He sought
nothing, neither affection nor appreciation. There is nothing to life, he
seemed to say, not even my supreme skills show that there is anything
creditable to life. Life is just a pointless scramble over your filthy heads.

Gay believed him.

The performers were not admitted to the general crowd, and Gay
was not allowed to approach the dressing enclosure. In vain he pleaded
for his status as an actor, but he was labelled a nuisance and threatened
with removal from the Gardens altogether. As a last resort he claimed
that he was instructed by Mister Grimaldi to convey a message to
Monsieur Gouffré. He was embarrassed at the shoddiness of this
fabrication, and a great oaf of a man laughed in his face. Nobody ever
spoke to the Frenchman, but if Mister Grimaldi would do so he had his
opportunity since he was in with the Frenchman at this very moment.

As soon as Gay knew that young Joe was present, his desperation
vanished. He stood back and passed a message through with one of the
errand boys, and within minutes Joe emerged and beckoned him from
the crowd.

He was overjoyed to see Gay, as they made their way through the chaos of the backstage. The Gardens were not so much a theatre as a circus, and there was an utter confusion of jostling, arguing, clamouring performers. Every half minute or so, the thin clear voice of a boy would find its way over the hubbub. Well-chosen for its piping incongruity, the voice would recite the latest order of performance, seemingly unperturbed by the disputes.

Joe's overjoyment bobbed and sank and bobbed. Gay asked him if he was well. He said that he had just woken up, he slept irregularly and had just been caught on the thirty-ninth wink.

He had not watched the Frenchman?

Certainly he had; he watched Titou every night, without fail. He watched Titou every moment of the day. Titou was not to be missed, Titou was a magician, a blessing; you will see, you will see. He is sleeping now, until we leave. He sleeps like a child. Come with us, John. But later, after he has slept, later.

That night and many other nights.

Gouffré's member hovered, almost perpendicular to the rest of his hairy body, purplish and heavy veined, washed and rubbed after the previous engagement. It was a prodigious, stallion cudgel, thick and long, uniformly tubular to the end. A masked lady entered the small, packed salon.

All of the ladies wore masks but Gay understood that their identities were rarely a secret; quite often the more capricious or reluctant ladies entered in the company of their husbands or lovers, and so their names were immediately known. The masks themselves were beautifully designed and finished, and were highly appreciated by the company. The designs were exotic and fanciful, in utter contrast to the nether business which they perhaps served to dissociate from the lady's image of herself. Now Gay saw the head of an Egyptian Empress, a plumed Amazon, now a bejewelled Minerva, an African Goddess or an exquisite Oriental Frailty whose mirrored tassels trembled in the gaslight. He was anywhere but in London.

The body was quickly unclothed, for it wore very little. The salon was warm for there was a heat arising from the audience, who sat as in a Parliament, in rows banked one upon another. This lady – this Indian Chieftainess with her splay of peacock feathers and ivory-toothed fringes which clackered delicately around her satin-covered cheek-bones – she took an unreasonable amount of time to shed her robe. She was game, but skittish. She sighed as though displeased with the programme. She retained her stockings. Many of the ladies did the same, not wishing to sacrifice their modesty by an undignified *rehabillement*.

She settled her knees on the cushioned pedestal and leaned forward to rest her arms on the banket. Two wagers were offered and accepted, but the wagering was subdued, the common feeling was that the lady's skittery be a flirtatious fraud.

She was greased, and so was Gouffré. Her pouch hung like a heavy peach from between two thin borders of chestnut-coloured privet. A single white drop clung to the base of the peach, betraying some lasciviousness behind the attitude of haughty sufferance.

There was competition among the ladies to accommodate Gouffré; they were enthusiastic in asserting their capacities, hence the wagering amongst the spectators. There had been injuries, through vanity or greed or excess of frenzy; there were carefully put-about rumours of a death, but the Fleet Ditch had of course concealed any possible proof and these rumours only excited the ambitions of the trialists.

Gouffré approached the Chieftainess and commenced to peg his way between her reared buttocks. The room fell silent. There was a high, stifled tension, which was exacerbated by the creak of corsetry and the rustle of silk and taffeta over restless spectators.

It was of minor interest. The lady was duly proved and pleasured to the full. She provided a tasteful little *évanouissement* before recovering herself and demanding a glass of wine to celebrate her triumph.

Gouffré was not acknowledged; for although he was much talked about he was merely an instrument and a French instrument at that. And yet he would be dutifully caring unless exhorted to be otherwise. He would separate the lady slowly and encule her at her bidding. He would withdraw at any point of demand, come it from herself or from any of the witnesses should a measurement be required to satisfy a wager. Once the lady *was* impaled, he would pause to allow her to adjust herself for comfort.

With relaxation the ladies sought further occupancy. They searched out unused space within themselves and insisted on its being filled; for they were anxious to be touched as deeply as possible, they were anxious to feel and to be goaded into displaying the extent of their feeling. Only then, and after further anointment of the trap, would Titou introduce an unhurried friction, which consistently disarmed the ladies' overbearing hospitality. Their resolve would be undermined by the surges and ebbs of sensation, which started to weave its magic within their haunches. There were tears of self-abandonment as Titou entered each time between the proffered globes to replenish the interior, and there were sobs and exclamations of beautied sorrow as he eased back along the cessy walls. He planted, from time to time, great tracts of seed along a plump white back, with childish amusement and with no diminution to his vigour.

At the end of the night Titou emerged into the Long Room, where he ate voraciously and drank a glass or two of good wine. By that time, the Finish was living up to its name.

At dawn, the Long Room was the last resort for John Bull, when with glazed and reddened eyes he rounded on his own melancholy. His nameless victims lay around him in a state of déshabille, their fine clothes sopping in wine and vomit. The most beautiful woman sprawled insensate across the sticky floor, her white calf gloves and burgundy gown bruising by the second as John Bull pissed *à cinq* over her torso, struggling to hold a bottle to his lips. How the creature hated beauty; how he strained to piss his loathing for himself out upon the whore. His burning, swollen face was split into a grimace of pleasure, his unflapped britches were damp and stinking, his belt was waxed with bile and smatters of regurgitated poultry. His whore steamed beside his boots, and John Bull became angry at her lack of devotion. He scrabbled at her dress in a terrier fury and with his riding whip he flogged her back to consciousness, and she smiled at him with stained and lackadaisical lips. He upended the bottle and the gin washed over the side of her face and trickled past her mouth and nose, and he was happy. He staggered back from her and belched and leered and felt full of himself, and looked around the room for his Ugly. The diseased or crippled Ugly, his, to escort him home; now; where was she, the hobbling crone, the one with sores and black rotting gums, where was she? Such an Ugly was *de rigueur* for fashionable Bulls this year as they rampaged through their merry-making.

Gouffré ate, and watched. His top lip curled in contempt, or was it only to allow him to pick a sliver of fish from between his teeth? The English Bulls hardly seemed to entertain him; there was no finesse amongst them, within them there was only an ungenerous, dullard exasperation at their own stupidity. Soused in alcohol, this English creature lumbered misanthropically through its existence like some absurd wingless bird, falling over its own feet and kicking itself in disgust.

Gay could not imagine that Gouffré would be pained by its predicament. Gouffré was surely puzzled that the creature could not manage to enjoy itself no matter how irritably it thrashed the empty air from side to side, and no matter what morsel the sharp beak stabbed in vengeance for its senseless palate. Gouffré would be more sympathetic towards the aristocrats, with whom he had just performed in his own peerless fashion. He would appreciate their refinement and their sense of decorum, for he understood the mingling of artificiality and pleasure.

It was strange that amongst his massive following at the Gardens he had become hailed as 'the animal'. Perhaps it was not strange, for he was outside a commoner's inane terms of reference. To commoners he was brutish and marvellous as he scampered easily over their heads. But they chose to love Grimaldi; because Grimaldi pampered them, Grimaldi cared for them, Grimaldi gave them what they wanted. Gouffré was careless. Gouffré did not flatter them, Gouffré was a true mirror.

It was Joe who made certain that Titou received due remuneration for his services in the salon. Gouffré took pleasure in his pleasuring, and did not set any value to Joe's concern that he should not be exploited.

Money, Gouffré believed, had its own natural and secluded breeding ground. When he needed money he would take whatever lined Joe's pockets and would sit in for a while at the Finish, and would gamble at dice. He slipped through the crowd to the gaming-table with the stealth of a young boy who knows the stagnant pool wherein the frogs might spawn, and he plucked his spoils gleefully from off the green baize surface. Invariably winning, he would beam and buy wine for the table he had left, and would return to Joe the amount he had borrowed.

Throughout his life Joe had lost money at the tables, and here was another reason for him to be concerned for Titou. 'It cannot last,' Joe warned. 'No man can play in such a way upon his resources. No man can live so purely. To live fully, as an open channel between destiny and spirit – it cannot be done. He will be hated or exhausted. He will be pushed or he will fall or he will burst into flames. And then he will need someone to care for him, perhaps someone to ease his way into the world.'

Gay wondered if Joe would care for him.

'Me?' Joe snorted. 'Heaven no! The money will care for him.'

Young Gay emerged untouched from these debauches. He found them ridiculous and he hated the sound of female pleasure. He himself disliked being embraced. He disliked mouths and lips; the wetness of lips and the moistness of hot breath, and the vacant – sometimes violent – search of kisses. He detested the stupidity and the intrusion. He detested the demand for response, seeing the lack of cleanliness not only in the gesture but in the motivation. When other people kissed he could accept it as a sign of recognition between them; but who had ever recognised *him*? And whom would he recognise?

He was calm in Gouffré's company. He was more at ease with Gouffré than with Joe.

Gay was convinced that Gouffré was a man of science. That Gouffré was, to himself, a carefully considered experiment by God. While he observed no religious customs he was, Gay felt and noticed, supremely exact. Gouffré was precise with himself. He would not attempt to assert himself, he would not be baited or allured; there was about him a great discipline of self and a bewildering awareness of others.

Of course Gouffré was goaded and reviled and insulted more than most – as any man would be who had emerged from a Catholic and Republican country to achieve a status in England by sodomising exalted women and impersonating the common housefly. But his persecutors achieved courage only when they were several in number, and Gouffré had the remarkable ability to consider each separately and remove each sting with some little self-deriding gesture. He did not make friends, but he managed to divert enemies by producing something from himself which left them satisfied with their contempt for him. He felt himself beneath contempt, and above praise. He dispensed, most exactly, with himself.

Gay felt propelled towards the isolation within which Titou Gouffré conducted this experiment. Gay imagined that he would find a place where he would achieve a similar, happy precision; where he would stand astride both time and place and be able to represent himself completely. He wanted Gouffré to help him. They would, in their revelations, be utterly different but they would share that strong unhampered purity. This was the only thing worth living for, this beauty which he might perfect in isolation. To perfect himself as a statement, with whose beauty he might confront the world.

This was possible. This was all possible. Gay dreamed it, saw it with his own eyes. Six statements. Himself, Gouffré, and four others. Six was the perfect number. They would have to find the four others. It was a stroke of luck that Gouffré had come to London. But how had he thought to come to London?

Gouffré sometimes jabbered at Gay, but he was impossible to understand. Gouffré took deep breaths of the foul London air, with pleasure. It was a good place, in his thoughts he had wanted to come to London, and in many of his dreams he had seen John Gay.

CHAPTER FOUR

Their Circle – Titou's Defence of the Rights of the Dead – His Scientific Demonstration of Superstitious Falsities

By the end of July, London no longer wanted Gouffré. During that month there started a murmur about plague. Within three weeks the theatres were ordered closed and the salon was deserted as its habitués decamped to their country estates. Not only did Titou Gouffré lose his employment but he was in danger of losing his life, since it was considered that any plague was indubitably an imported French spite against the true liberty of the English realm. The overheated mob took up a patriotic view-halloo and savaged several suspected foreign agents.

Titou took shelter with Ann and her brother. Gay too was without employment, and although Ann was offered a joint holding in a small company of actors who were to tour the south-west of the country, she elected to stay in London. The four of them – Gay, Ann, young Joe and Titou – were thrown together by this strange hiatus.

Joe spent the night at his lodgings but would arrive at the house early in the morning, having nowhere else to go. Like a patient witness, he would settle himself into a chair and brood politely for the rest of the day.

Each evening after dinner, Gouffré and Gay walked him home across the northern limits of the city. It was part of their exercise to turn right at the smallpox hospital and go aways up the Malden lane. Their custom was to draw lots for which trees they should climb – and there amongst heat-limpened leaves, on sturdy oak branches with bark thick and gnarled as elephant skin, they stood separately and watched the day decline from the Park across to Paddington. Joe and young Gay shared a trance-like appreciation of the falling day, that time when the late fluster of the birds ran quiet and the crimsons, golds and reds rioted across the open heaven. Their absorption by this splendid time was challenged only by the demon Frenchman, who appeared sporadically amongst the topmost branches of various trees and then disappeared, like a pernickety squirrel who was disappointed at the slow tempo of vegetable growth.

Calmed by his meditation, Joe had no need of further company. They left him at his lodgings and ran back eastwards silently through the Park twilight. At this time, in this quiet and steady rhythm of running, Gay felt at one with Gouffré, skipping lightly across the great solid surface of the world. He ran in a dream, hearing only the sound of his own heart as a pulse of creation. He drew behind him a vacuum into which fell all the haphazard fragments of an impure world. He ran on earth but he might as well be running through the heavens, invisible yet trailing brief mortalities in his wake. A picture of the ragman swung to and fro across his mind – the ragman's dour tread and the ceaseless pushing of the cart in front of him, the piles of clothes being pushed from here to there and back again, each footloose day.

Gay decided that he would never come back. His skins would shed themselves and burn like so many sparks in the darkness through which he passed.

They came one night, after leaving Joe at a later hour than usual, upon the strangest scene, which would for ever stay in Gay's mind as the trysting place between himself and Titou. They had left behind the great new houses on the east of the Park and so were entering the area between the villages of Saint Pancras and Camden, when they found themselves surrounded by a heavy and cool mist which had sprung from nowhere to drape itself around them.

Gay had thought that Titou was in front of him, but he was shocked when at a sudden thinning of the mist Titou's voice fell upon his ears with deep resonance, as though both of them had their heads inside a large and empty wine barrel.

The air was very clear now. The landscape in front of Gay was treelessly flat yet dimpled into a poxed complexion, and above the earth were small sapphire fires, wavering and rippling like infant phantoms escaping the clutches of the night. No sooner had Gay fixed one dancing flame in his vision than it would extinguish itself and spring up again in a different place, mocking his senses exuberantly.

Gay wandered towards the festival, open-heartedly to embrace the darting spirits. But as he advanced, Titou ran past him with a scream of rage. From a dark pit in front of them two men emerged with shovels. Titou screamed monstrously at them. Immediately they threw down their shovels and took to their heels. Titou replaced the earth, and grabbed Gay, and together they ran home.

Gay drank wine. Titou talked at him and Ann translated: that the dead should not be disturbed and yet that they could not die. Gay did not want to know about the dead. Titou was insistent: Gay should know, Gay *must* know. He must know that Evil went beyond death, that Evil was sought even beyond death. It must lie undisturbed – Titou was insistent. Gay offered the beauty of the flames, the joyous indigo dance of the spirits; and Titou sneered and laughed at him.

Gay talked to Ann, telling her of his dreams and hopes, of what he wanted from performance, a troupe perhaps, until she tired of attempting an explanation for Titou.

'But what are you *doing* with these plans?' she insisted. 'You know that we have some money put by.'

'Joe has money,' he said quickly. He stood and stretched. He did not want to talk; he would rather have drawn or painted his ideas, he would rather have danced them than surrendered them to words. He carried off a few steps in front of Ann but he became self-conscious and aware of his shortcomings.

'You will be a fine-looking man, John. You *are* a fine-looking man. And still young enough not to know it, which is more charming.'

He had always suffered from her irony, and was never more wary of it than at that moment. She went to bed. He sat in moods of despair and protest and drank quickly until he could hardly see, and then he awoke dragging sleep like a hard and heavy shell.

Gay wondered for a moment where he was, but he did not care. He was comfortable and cushioned by darkness. Away from him, on the floor, a small night-candle burned on a pedestal of books. Titou's voice carried from the darkness in a low drone of confidential encouragement, which was punctuated by sharp slaps as though Titou were marshalling a reluctant donkey. Gay would have fallen back to sleep; but Titou summoned him by name and, before he could move in one direction or the other, Titou's white and naked hindquarters shunted into the candle-light. Gay did not know what was intended of him.

Titou's knees shuffled to either side of the pedestal until his arse was on a level with the candle, some inches away. He sank down upon the floor and farted, and then, half-raising himself, he tucked his testicles up in front of his top-thighs, bent his right hand into the shape of a cup and smacked it into the divide between his buttocks. On a level with the candle he farted once more and a screen of blue flame danced around the wick. Three or four times with his hand he stoked himself and repeated the illumination; thereafter his arse gathered its responsibilities and charged itself, like an obese bellows, with a jerking sob of suction between each expulsive sigh.

The blue flames, Gay's 'spirits', had lasted but a short while and now there was a sad, mechanical emptiness to the exhibition. Titou, who had no view, continued in his explanations. Gay curled under his shell and went to sleep.

CHAPTER FIVE

Perdition: the First of Gay's Headaches – A Celtic Maggot Takes Shelter within his Head

A week later, Ann summoned him.

'I must tell you', she said, 'that I have found a friend.'

She had found a *good* friend, a man. Not for marriage. She had no intention of getting married. There was too much compromise in marriage. And sometimes – she chose her words carefully – there was an unhappiness which became inextricably bound into the nature of a marriage. The man, her friend, was married in such a way.

'Do you mean your lover?'

'I mean my friend. He is a companion. I love him . . . accordingly.'

'But will you live with him here?' Gay was alarmed.

'No! I do not want him, totally. And he does not want me totally. We are not like that. He is a generous and dear friend.' There was a blush rising to her cheeks. Gay did not know what she wanted him to say. 'I thought that you would be happy for me.'

He said, 'I *am* happy for you.'

'But you are not interested.'

'Who is he?'

'John, dear John, it means more to me than anything, but I can't tell you. It is a secret and we want to keep the secret to ourselves.'

'Then what is the point of me being interested?'

'Oh, John, you are impossible! Can't you see how I feel?'

'Not absolutely.'

She growled at him.

'So I may take it that you are sympathetic; you may take it that I am happy. Now I must go to my meeting. Titou is coming, will you come with us?'

He could not refuse her.

On their way down the street they met up with Titou and Joe, who were full of some scheme or other. Titou was impatient; he argued with Joe and took a sizeable purse of money off him. Joe chose to remain behind, which choice Gay would have made had he been in possession of any powers of decision.

Titou and Ann set a fast pace. Gay lingered, trying to place what Ann had told him into some kind of order, worrying at her announcement and the changes it might herald, wondering what he was supposed to do.

He lost sight of Ann and Titou but he knew that they were heading eastwards. It was the end of the business day, the streets were crowded, everybody seemed to be on the move. He could not think clearly. He remembered the name of the meeting hall and gathered several confusing directions on how to arrive there.

When, finally, he reached the Lamb and Flag and went upstairs, the room was but sparsely decorated with people. There were in fact more banners than people. It might have been better to die by the sword than by hunger, but the many absentees were still more scared of the rumoured plague. It was on this subject that Ann was addressing the meeting, she reported what she had observed in the city.

Gay did not want to distract her attention and so he edged on to a chair near the door, a most uncomfortably low-backed chair. Anyone wanting to avoid an excruciating cramp would be well advised to stand and speak rather than to sit and listen. When she had finished speaking Ann took her place on a bench. There were three benches and, Gay supposed, a certain pecking order which decided their occupancy.

There followed immediately some very fiery oratory from a man who could not have been many years older than himself, yet who had a tremendous mastery of fine phrases which served his depiction of the various governmental plots and machinations which threatened to obscure and prevent a progress of social justice. He was warmly applauded, which flustered him into a choking cough, as though he had by mistake swallowed more of his own words than he had intended. He drank a glass of water and called lamely for perseverance in the fight, and then he sat with his arm dangling over the top of the end of a bench. He had perhaps an interest in the theatre, and Gay looked to see if he was the one who held Ann's affections.

Her face gave nothing away; she was explaining something to Titou

23

who sat by her side with his arms and legs crossed resolutely, as if to shackle his mind to the concerns around him. Next to him there sat a young girl whose face under her white cap bore absolutely no expression save that of a vacant serenity, if such a thing is possible. She had the whitest skin, her features were perfectly formed, and yet her whole character suggested that there was nothing of substance in her at all. Childlike herself, she resembled a child's plaything, a rag doll with porcelain face, incapable of a smile or a tear. Gay did not know what she might or might not mind, but she paid no attention to his staring at her, and he thought that he might stare all night without her receiving any impression of his rudeness. It seemed as though she was unaware that she was alive.

When the meeting broke Gay sprang from his chair and crossed the room. Gouffré took him by the arm and talked excitedly; he looked for Ann to translate his words but Gay seized him by the shoulders and declared passionately his theatrical ambitions to Titou. He did not take his eyes off Titou and he did not hesitate. When he finished he grabbed Titou's hand and clasped him firmly.

He glimpsed Ann's cursory smile. She patted him lightly on the arm. 'I have told Titou all of this. He understands it perfectly, the six statements of beauty, all of it and more. Not only does he understand it but he has chosen to act on it. There is a third member to your troupe.' Ann was not pleased. She was agitated. 'I don't know what he knows, or how long he has followed her. He says nothing about her except that she is a witch, which I take to mean that she is important. He is incapable of offering any more reasonable form of flattery.' She glared at Titou.

He curled his lip and did not understand. He hunched his shoulders. He raised his eyebrows. 'Pourquoi pas?' he said.

'Well that is as may be,' Ann allowed.

'It is so much more than that!' Gay cried.

'Oh don't be so childish!' Ann turned her back on Titou and led her brother firmly back across the room. When they were outside, at the top of the stairway, she faced Gay. 'This is something about which I feel very strongly.'

'How should Titou and I interfere with you?'

'Will you listen! Now! Will you stop and listen? The girl who was sitting next to Titou is simple. She has been sent from her family in

Wales and has now ended up being engaged as a seamstress to a woman who keeps a house. Both of us know what that means. She has not yet been initiated into her intended occupation. She is an innocent, John, she is a child. Well, Titou has bought her.'

'But Titou did the right thing to buy her, surely?'

'You are quibbling. You understand what I mean. He has no rights to her at all, and he will *not* take advantage of her.'

'No,' Gay agreed uncertainly.

'She has been bought as a whore. Wouldn't you agree as to that being Titou's intention? What other use would he see in buying her for you?'

'For me?'

'You will not touch her, John, and nor will he.'

Gay did not want to touch her. He made no sense of Titou's action. And yet the strangeness of this dealing – and Ann's strident, almost hysterical admonition – teased his interest.

He watched the girl carefully as she followed Titou out of the meeting room. There was about her a loosely connected beauty, which must have grown with her as a child and which she would reclaim and inhabit fully when she became a woman. She was between worlds, and for this period when she had no sure footing her beauty made no commitment to her, choosing instead to dart uneasily around her, alighting haphazardly on limb or feature. He saw now that she had attempted to overcome childhood. Her efforts had met with some success but they had left her without replacement. There was nothing in her for him to touch.

They stood about while Ann went back into the room to obtain newspapers and settle what business she had. Gay did not know what part the girl would assume, but he felt that her being there and her being chosen by Titou consolidated the pact between them. She was something shared; he now thought more steadily of 'we' and his aspiration seemed less fanciful.

Titou shouted up at him. He was embroiled in a dispute at the servery and Gay hurried down to see what was the matter. Titou had asked for a length of cord. The server didn't have any cord for foreigners. After negotiation the server fetched a coil of light hemp rope from the back, enough to string up a dozen foreigners. He sold a length to Gay.

'Elle a voulu m'échapper.'

In the street outside, Titou tied the rope around the girl's waist. He handed the leash to Gay, who passed it over to Ann. She walked on ahead while he walked next to Titou, whose eyes never left the girl.

'Voilà notre fortune,' Titou murmured.

After they had gone a half mile or so, Gay forgot that Titou was with him. Titou's company never weighed heavily. He was the most independent of men. He never sought attention or felt so uneasy with himself that he demanded an interchange of thoughts, observations or trivial civilities. Gay was able, in peace, to skim his own thoughts across his mind. He was occasionally interrupted by Titou's spitting – Thurrup, Spat – which prevented those thoughts from sinking Gay into a serious frame of mind.

There were a great many mysteries abroad; Gay felt as though he had been released from an unwarranted and jaded lethargy, and in his sprung excitement he could hardly catalogue the challenges to be met.

Thurrup, Spat –

If first he and Titou might understand each other completely; which would come through action and their formulation of movements, from the start. He, Gay, had come through the pains to dance; he had not yet realised his worth, but he had been held back. He had been held back by himself and by others, he had not dared. But now –

Thurrup – and twin green pinpoints glared at Titou. He laughed. The dark shadow of a spit-stained cat twisted away. The bleached face of the girl flashed back at them through the dusk, stark even against its mantle of white-gold hair. 'Tu vois, elle comprend, j'sais pas qu'est-ce qui va se passer, on verra tout, tout; je l'ai achetée, je vais en profiter, eh, la sorcière . . .'

Titou muttered on, rubbing his hands together.

With him, Gay would dare all; now he would search for the power, uncover it and claim it, draw it inside himself. He felt its presence even now. It was in the air, thick and weightless, feinting. With the smell of burning pitch. Leaping and swirling.

Gay recognised where they were. They were in Paradise Row, not a quarter mile from home.

But he and Titou were running wildly. How was this? They had passed his sister and the girl. He did not remember passing them or touching them. He had jumped over them in one great leap, and he remembered at the same time looking back at them joyously and seeing them very clearly. How was this? They were quite unmoved by the feat. They did not see him. They walked on quite unguardedly, as if they supposed that he and Titou were behind them and that there was nothing to fear from the rear.

But he and Titou were sucked into a dark alleyway. He lost sight of Ann and the girl. He was moving very fast through the blackness and then suddenly he was brought up short. He stood still. He was not breathing deeply, as he should have been. He was breathing calmly, as though nothing had happened. It was as if he had been let drop. There was still some force drawing him forward as into a vacuum, but he was sealed off from it. He was sucked up against an invisible barrier, pressed against it, and then pressing himself on it.

He turned his head and just at his shoulder were Ann and the girl, as if they had never been anywhere else. He turned back. They were at the end of the alleyway. Not twenty feet in front of him, out in the centre of Cropwell Road, Titou crouched as though he had been thrown from the alleyway and had somersaulted out into the road, avoiding injury.

Gay pressed against the barrier. Titou's face was white with fear and misery. He shuffled painfully from side to side, like a broken-backed dog trying to discover why it could not stand. His face was twisted and bent by a wavering orange torchlight. He was as imprisoned as Gay. His body was hidden by a tongue of filthy black smoke.

He re-appeared, crouching helplessly. His face turned towards the alley. His top lip was curled high and his mouth was in a hideous smile. He looked not at Gay but at the girl, in terrible and pitiful hatred. His lip and nose stiffened into a rigid, loathing sneer. Victoriously he reared up from the ground.

'What *is* happening?' said Ann, pushing at Gay's shoulder. 'What is all that shouting? Where is Titou?'

Gay looked at the girl and he knew evil. She was unconcerned. Her expression was insolent. He wanted to splay her and stab inside her.

He was disturbed by the loud noises in the street. Titou was moving away from the alley, treading gently from side to side, so expertly balanced that he seemed to float over the unevenness of the ground.

Gay found himself released from his imprisonment, and he walked dreamily, placidly, out of the alleyway.

The frontage of houses and shops gave directly on to Cropwell Road. It was by now quite dark, yet two hundred yards away all was torchlight and furore. In between, and obscuring his view, there was a large black mass shifting uneasily – a herd of animals, Gay saw; cows or bullocks, jostling and venturing forward between the buildings.

'They have taken the wrong road. Titou will not drive them back on his own. Go with him, John.'

'I cannot,' Gay said. '*She* will.'

'She will not. Go and help him.'

There was no such simplicity, Gay knew. It was neither his place nor his time. Titou had halved the distance between himself and the animals. He swayed from side and side and they were wary of him. Behind the herd there was a smashing of glass and a shouting; from its midst a bullock trotted out quickly and stopped, feeling itself isolated in front of Titou. For a moment their bodies remained stationary; the bullock leaned forward, sniffing the air then tossing its head as if it was embarrassed at its trespass. Titou was almost up to the herd. Gay had never before noticed his dress, the raggedy clothes flopping around the muscular body which needed no embellishment. Titou stopped and he clapped his hands together sharply. The animals began to turn, edging uncomfortably back into each other.

From the background came a pistol shot, muffled and then clattering down the road. Another bullock came out of the middle of the herd as if compelled to represent its fellow creatures. In a flash Titou was on to it, with astounding strength seizing it by the horns and dragging its head and shoulders down to the ground. He lifted the horns and with his forehead he butted it on the nose. Panic-stricken it lurched away from him and ran into the shadows.

Titou clapped quickly, weaving from side to side of the road, darting at individual members of the vanguard, scuttling halfway up the fronts of the houses to scream his scorn at the beasts. There must have been a dozen Titous rampaging through their senses. Beside Gay, the girl began to choke – he ran forward to get away from her; and then all he could hear were Titou's claps and the angry pistols like a mad game of noise played against the stone walls.

28

Gay started clapping, and he sang and shouted, and he smelt the thick heady smell of burning hair. Titou was in the middle of the road ahead of him.

At once the herd separated, the animals squeezed themselves sideways as if trying to disappear. From the middle came a huge blazing beast, screaming in pain, charging desperately with maddened eyes to outstrip the fire which scrambled up his haunches and his back. Gay fled to shelter in a doorway. The flaming animal passed him trailing smoke and the stink from its burning flesh and hair. It carried itself on past the alleyway and then with a mighty screech, as if the throat had blistered dry from emptying the boiling lungs, its legs collapsed and it ran its twisted head into the earth. It somersaulted, the sparks abandoned it like fleas and it rested halfway to the ground, its hip impaled upon the front railings of a house.

Gay turned back but the herd was only a few dozen feet away and running towards him, a wild Hydra shooting out heads in every direction. He saw Titou riding the angry monster, hopping from back to back like a tingtong marionette trying to reach the wings of his paper theatre. Gay bolted to the safety of the alleyway. He took Ann and pushed her down into the darkness. The girl made to follow her, but Gay seized the coil of rope from her hand and, as the first of the herd charged by their narrow opening, he shouted for Titou and arced the coil high out into the air above the stampede, fishing for Titou's salvation.

As Titou went past he was settled with his knees gripped around a thick black neck. He saw Gay and he lunged up at the rope and grabbed it and slapped the coil down around the horns of his beast. Together they rushed on. Titou made no attempt to save himself. The girl was dragged from Gay's side, her body jerked into the air and was then drawn along the railings, sliced open until it dropped in pieces against a basement wall.

A shock of pain, like an arrowhead, smote at Gay's ear and he collapsed.

Simultaneously Titou went to ground with his beast. His arm rose momentarily above the bobbing, rushing backs and then there was no more sign from him.

After the beasts came the men, breaking what the beasts had not

29

broken, looting what they could find. They did not find Ann or her brother.

Ann paid for a neighbour to stand guard over Titou's body. Gay could not rest for the pain within his ear. The pain had its own pulse, slow and repulsive, which battled the feverish rhythm of Gay's heart. Many times during the night Gay rose and held a candle up to his shoulder, peering into the mirror, but he could see nothing in his ear. Neither could Ann. He embarked upon a restless sleep, wide-eyed, with his jaw fallen open and the pain ebbing heavenwards.

He went out before dawn with Joe and the ragman and his cart. There was no trace of the girl's body. Titou was in one place, on his own, trodden and speared and gored. They put his body on the cart and took it back to the house. Titou's eyes hung horribly down the sides of his face. Joe opened the sockets and squeezed the eyeballs back inside. Ann boiled water and they cleaned the body. Joe said that Titou would not have a priest and so they buried him the next day in the Saint Pancras burial ground, in his beloved London. Gay never saw Joe again. He heard that Joe went out of the country and was rumoured to have gone mad from his drinking.

The Maggot burrowed slowly until it rested up against the inside of Gay's temple. It took account of its new quarters, curled snugly, and slept.

Many nights Gay awoke and searched doggedly through the darkness for Titou. He went after Titou but the Maggot refused to parlay. Gay persisted, he willed, he begged, but there was only silence. He lay receptive, for hours on end, open to the slightest murmur; but there was no murmur. His visions were his own, mustered up and batted away into infinity and ignored. He wondered if they had done the right thing in interfering with Titou by pushing his eyes back into his head.

CHAPTER SIX

Mister Edmond Parsloe – Gay's Ascent – An Offer of Employment in the New World

A time shaken; the seasons back to back, the years somersaulting. One, two, three, four, five – and the stasis. A handful of years jettisoned across the green baize. A pair of drab, low years, and then the three ascending to middle royalty.

Edmond Parsloe found Gay. Parsloe, the respected player and Ann's lover.

'Eyes?' said Parsloe. 'My father had both his eyes put out by accident on stage during a sword fight. Lack of eyes ended his professional life, which in turn ended him. An actor cannot live on his imaginings. My father was perhaps imagining when he should have been concentrating.'

Of course Edmond was married, and he was at the same time with Ann, perhaps in love with Ann. Granted that Edmond had, some years ago, married a surprisingly uninteresting widow with two children and a little fortune. So the world loved where it might and bedded where it could.

Edmond Parsloe was a well-established actor. He had made his debut in Grimaldi's company, but had been possessed of the good sense to leave the great man's shoes under the great man's bed for somebody else to pick out and attempt to wear. Parsloe had made his own reputation. On the stage he carried a powerful and imposing authority; once off the boards he was a secretive and formal man – often fragile – who considered carefully the demands placed on his person and then refused most of them. He saw no point in – and did not care for – the vagaries of self-examination; it would have surprised him to admit that he was most content in fostering John Gay's ambitions. He had never thought of doing so.

Edmond, by nature, played very carefully and very successfully, and in this fashion he played Gay. He did not force himself on the boy, he did not look for authority or friendship or response. He waited until Gay broke surface, gasping for air and floundering: and then he gently suggested in what direction Gay might swim; and when Gay had found his feet Edmond provided him with the private parties and stages for his dancing. The boy danced all over London in a hundred scattered roles.

Parsloe had been warned many times by Ann of the boy's selfish character, but Gay's talent had more than carried him through and Edmond felt neither undue obligation nor that he had been exploited. Edmond saw that the boy would not be satisfied. He trained Gay for the Harlequin; that suit fitted him to perfection and he returned to the Wells in triumph.

'It is enough', declared *The Times* in this December of 1829, 'that Mister Gay's Harlequin should simply stand still. The Sadler's Wells would not lack for an audience. We wonder if his feats of acrobatics and skilled trickery are not the irritations of mere embarrassment on the part of the actor at his abundance of grace. In stasis he is splendid and heroic. In movement he holds a cracked mirror up to Nature and unites its myriad reflections. The airy spirit of the Harlequin is obtained most precisely.'

Gay was now a most precise young man, applauded and admired and secure in his employment unless he injured himself, which was unlikely since the performance was well within his powers. He watched himself carefully and was pleased with what he saw. He formed an attachment to no other body. He had no great respect or disrespect for women, he found them no more or less interesting than men or food. He was not vulnerable nor was he predatory. He politely disengaged himself from any attempts on his containment. He was discovered handsome, found vain, and considered unpleasing. He was alone but not lonely.

Gargantua's steam warmed and soothed muscles which had set overnight after Gay's performance. When he left her kitchen he was itchy with sweat. He walked back upstairs slowly, testing the reach of his thighs and the balance within his back, projecting a line which led from his coccyx, along his spinal column and up through his neck until it burst out above his forehead. It was as though his body were attached by an invisible cord to the hand of a puppeteer, far above him.

At the corner of the first flight of stairs he stood, and he dropped his shoulders, freeing himself from a yoke of tension. At such a moment his mind was a perfect blank. He continued his climb up past the sitting-room to his bedroom. He slept here infrequently. Usually he took advantage of whatever heat might be left in the stove on the floor below.

He stripped off his clothes and rubbed himself with a rough linen towel. He picked a clean shirt and concentrated on his breathing. The anticipation raced through his body and settled on his stomach in a dull, persistent nausea.

He bent his right leg at the knee and stretched the left out sideways. And down; and up. Now with the left leg bent and the right leg stretching. Down; and he straightened.

He could not concentrate on the exercise. In an effort to discipline himself as he walked out of the bedroom, he first placed each heel and then rolled forward on to his toes, tightening his balance. He descended the stairs on the balls of his feet, examining the pressure on his knees. At the bottom of the stairs he removed his hose, shuffled across to the privy, lowered himself and shat.

Returning to the bedroom he stood by the door and shook out his limbs, one by one. He flapped his feet and hands as if to disturb a light covering of snow. With his head thrown back he leapt nimbly before the mirror – an attitude. And then another attitude; and another; and another.

An hour later, at midday, he left his sweat-soaked shirt with the ragman's wife and started the walk towards Islington, carrying his box of make-up.

A keen north-easterly wind cut down into the borough, hardening the ruts on Corporation Row and preserving the silvery-white spangles of ice which glittered underfoot. Gay – muffled, hatted and warm – walked past a line of new houses which had been incongruously deposited opposite fields of coughing sheep. He picked his way carefully up Saint John's Street, fearing to turn an ankle on terrain more suited to goats than to actors. He might, at the junction with Goswell Street, have begged on to a stage-coach for the final few hundred yards, but he observed the discomfort of the bucketed passengers and the insecurity of the horses, and he followed them on foot, listening to the curses which the stinging air whipped from the postilion. Momentarily, he stood stockstill and laughed. The sound was lost to him and so he turned his face into the wind and tried again. He heard no bitter edge in the tone of the laugh. This satisfied him, and he walked on. He had not found any sudden absurdity in the world; rather it had simply occurred to him that he had not laughed for some time and was in need of practice.

He followed the coach into the Wells courtyard. A dozen or so ducks sat at the top of the river bank, embedded against the cold wind, their heads folded back on their plumage. They were remarkably stubborn, braving not only the elements but also the irritation of the Wells management, who had been much concerned by the amount of dung which was trodden into the floor of the auditorium.

From March to November they had employed a girl as duck-herd, but the degree of incompetence was so great, and the chorus of billed protestation so disruptive to rehearsals, that the management had replaced her with two boys, whose job it was to wash down and sweep the approaches to the theatre as darkness fell. By December, this tactic had merely caused considerable numbers of the audience to fall on patches of ice. Some concession was made to the ducks and they were now cast as essential to the rural charm of Sadler's Wells. A small dog was employed, and this tirelessly bluff animal trotted up and down the length of the two-bar fence, never missing an opportunity to bark himself off his feet at any careless, splay-toed intruder. The ducks regarded their sergeant-major with quiet contempt, for the stupid beast refused ever to profit from the warmth of the theatre and steadfastly ignored the scraps of food that were thrown down by coach travellers – although his little eyes twitched with the pressures of temptation.

This midday, the ducks were furled and stowed behind the fence, while the dog stared bleakly into the wind, a small ribboned medal – with which he had been presented at Christmas – hanging from the rope around his neck. Behind him the coachdriver was tying a travelling case on to the back of the coach and a young lady was being seen off by friends. The other passengers waited impatiently for their uncomfortable journey to the provinces.

Gay had very little notion what the rest of England was like, and he had no interest in travelling to find out. He imagined that most of the people there eked out an unenviable living. He had met one or two prosperously dressed ambassadors from the hinterland, and knew immediately that he would not survive in the burgeoning industrial centres of which they were so proud.

However, in the depressed economic climate, the Wells was forced to cast a wide net for sponsors. There had been one delicate evening when all the major actors were commanded by the management to meet with a Mister Lloyd of Lloyds Banking House in the Green Room. Gay had begged off.

Lloyds Bank did pledge some support, but the present production of *Mother Goose* was indebted to Barclay's Brewery as its main sponsor; Gay's dance with his prima ballerina was preceded by a rousing choral tribute to the efficacity of Barclay's beer as opposed to Hodges' Blue Ruin. It made no great dramatic sense, for while Pantaloon and his rustic mob slept off their Barclay's booze, Harlequin and Columbine presented a magnificent *pas de deux*. The moral should have been obvious.

But, there again, the dancing of Missis Searle was far from magnificent this year. Gay was obliged to wheel her round like a heavily laden tea trolley while she, no doubt feeling the pinch from her years and her costumes, attempted to ingratiate herself by leering impudently at friends in the audience. And she smelt. Lord, Gay no longer knew which was the worst of the evils — her mouth, her armpits, her feet, or, God perish the thought, her groin; God perish the thought of it. The woman was a quagmire of ghastly, oozing stink. He was haunted by visions of Missis Searle bursting through her hose like a mass of rotting offal. It was not a subject for jest.

He had hoped that tonight of all nights he would not have to endure Missis Searle. This New Year's Eve they were to mount a benefit performance for Grimaldi, who was woefully decrepit.

The theatre would, of course, be anxious to greet the old lion. Edmond had been invited to resurrect his Lover alongside the resident Mathews.

Gay stood beside the dog and absent-mindedly watched the departure of the coach. A hackney turned into the courtyard, quite possibly transporting Missis Searle. He hurried into the theatre.

Afterwards, in the mêlée on stage, Gay was introduced to a Mister and Missis Hamblin. They were Americans, owners of the Bowery Theatre in New York. Edmond was with them and they praised his performance. They arranged to meet the next day. Gay would have stayed longer in their company but he was tired and cold. As soon as he could decently do so he slipped away and went downstairs to his dressing-room.

He closed the door and the January draught slid underneath, sluicing his ankles. He laid his coat at the base of the door, shed the heavy Harlequin costume and rubbed his naked skin, fast and thorough, with a linen towel. Then he dressed and removed his face.

He went along the corridor. He knew that he had, tonight, mastered his performance. Grimaldi had noticed, had spoken to him, and had thanked him. Gay felt tired and empty; if not depressed, then lost. He wanted just a moment's peace.

As he napped in the warmth of the Green Room, his consciousness was conjured forth only by a thin persistent whistle through the air, at which the fog lifted, and there was a smell of burning hair, and there was a large black bird plucking pieces of flesh from his hips, working its way up his body until it loomed frightfully over his head, peering with lustful eyes at his temple. The bird carried off Titou, Edmond and young Joe, and it left Gay half awake with this dream as the Green Room door slammed shut on the old year.

The next afternoon, Parsloe and Gay were offered a contract to present the pantomime *Harlequin, Mother Goose* at the Bowery Theater in New York, for the next Christmas season. Passage would be paid for Edmond Parsloe and John Gay to portray the principal roles of Clown and Harlequin.

Of that New Year, 1830, Ann always remembered one morning in February. She awoke late and suddenly. Edmond was with her, his breath musty across the bolster, his eyes narrowly open as they usually were when he was sleeping. Edmond did not trust easily. She knew that he was not happy but she could not forgive him her own unhappiness. Whatever reason he might give her, she knew that he would go to America to escape all reasoning. He might consider the money, he might rise to the occasion because he was provoked by John; he might say that he needed a greater challenge in his work, that he believed in the possibility of some rare creation – but Edmond would go, would run, because his wife had told him that she was bearing their child. His wife would present him with a child and he would say that he was obliged to honour a theatrical contract.

She parted the curtains and looked out at the wintry half-light. Beneath her, her brother emptied the slop bucket into the drain at the back of the house. Some part of Ann worried in the old way for John, perhaps after all she should be grateful to Edmond for agreeing to lead the production. Poor Edmond; he was too old to start playing the Clown. He would surely only have ever risked this flight of adolescent ambition well away from London. John would run him ragged.

Her brother remained stationary, apparently marvelling at the white coarseness of the frost. He suddenly shook himself and leapt backwards in a somersault. The Maggot flexed, and hungered, and turned to face the air. It seemed to Ann as though some part of time had escaped her; for John was standing perfectly, anciently still, with his head slightly inclined to one side and a fingertip touching his temple.

A poignant attitude – one much appreciated in a stage Harlequin. And very suited to a white background.

The drain was habitually vile with stench. But it ran past the ragman's window, not her own; and the ragman's life was from the beginning a disaster of filth and children and hopelessness, and would be to the end, fixed so. As for her own life: loss and anger, everything which had slumbered next to the warm body of the man in her bed. To be reflected upon, with a fingertip at the temple; thus.

A baby girl, Elisabeth, was born to Edmond on July 25th. Ann did not see him after the birth; Edmond did not accept any engagements in the theatre.

Ann stood as part of a small circle outside the house on a fine October's morning, waiting for the hackney. When it came, the ragman shook Gay's hand and wished him good fortune, and Gay laughed and held stiffly his sister for a moment. He leaned out of the window and they looked at each other and waved until the carriage turned south to meet Edmond at Blackfriars.

Ann received several letters from Edmond. She had only one from

John; from Deal. It was a letter from a small boy – it talked of his excitement at the voyage and his presentiment that he and Edmond would triumph in New York. He was walking away, turning back to shout spitefully: 'I'm going now. You had better watch out, I'm going now, and I'm going even further! And you'll never see me again, so there!'

CHAPTER SEVEN

The Crown Hotel at Deal – A Testament and Blessing from both the Actors

A cold drizzle filtered gently through a muslin sky to polish the quayside cobblestones. The dominant smell was not of the sea but of fresh horse manure; the sea itself rolled sullenly in a flat wallow of grey water, flapping its belly against the empty berth.

Their ship – the *Moravagine* – had put out from Deal Harbour at noon. But this was not important, nor even ominous. It was explained to them that any ship due to sail on a Sunday would put out a day early, the better to preserve its crew from dissipation and leisure, the better to rescue its captain from an iniquitous Sabbath pilot's fee. The actors would have time to celebrate their departure in some style at the Crown Hotel, and would be fetched out to the *Moravagine* as soon as the pilot boat returned. A boy would be sent to collect them.

So Gay and Edmond left their baggage with the agent and walked up to the Crown Hotel to await the return of the pilot. After dining they sat by the fire in the snuggery, where they were advised by the hotel-keeper that they would be expected to provide their own bedding for the voyage, a detail which took them by surprise. They paid him and he had parcelled up – and portered off – the necessaries; and spirits and fortified wine, for it appeared that Captain Foster would not uncork his cellar without gross profiteering.

Not content with dipping into their pockets their victualler then proceeded to tax their nerves with fabulous exaggerations, 'Great Maritime Disasters I Have Known'. Until finally Edmond decreed that he wished to be left in blessed ignorance, he did not wish to hear anything more gloomy about the sea, with no offence intended but he had had quite enough of dark mysteries and scarifying nonsense.

The thoroughly morose hotel-keeper was unperturbed by Edmond's outburst. Indeed he quite understood Edmond's misgivings and sought only to put his mind at rest. If he might just offer one more piece of advice: the most common mistake committed by an innocent seafarer lay in his leaving behind him on dry land the most dreadful storms for his prospective heirs. Having observed several instances of domestic dispute, the hotel-keeper had gone to the trouble of obtaining a registration as clerk-assistant in the notification of wills, testaments and codicils. He hoped that the courageous travellers had left their affairs in order. As God had created him he was a born optimist, but he had heard of several occasions when a voyager had returned like an unsuspecting phantom to find his family marauding upon each other for the spoils of his estate. Had either of them neglected to clarify his will?

It was too ridiculous for Edmond, who burst out laughing at the persistence of this wheedling Dealer.

'How much do you charge for leaving us in peace with pen and paper?'

'It never occurred to me', Edmond's head rose, 'that dying would carry with it so much self-doubt. Arranging my affairs should at least leave me free for the rare pleasure of uninterrupted sleep, but I seem to be unwrapping all the ingredients for a nightmare. It cannot be unreasonable to assume that my stepchildren will have some provision from their own father's money, and therefore that I should bequeath my possessions to my own Lizzie. However, should I die, her best opportunity in life will come from the help and affection of her half-sisters. I do not want to offend them by sowing division within the family. I have never particularly liked them but I should not encourage in Lizzie such an independence of feeling. So I should perhaps include them, or is that simply bribing them for their loyalty towards her? And is that, in itself, wrong?' His chin jutted weakly as he leaned forward to retrieve the second quarto sheet from the small pile of writing in front of him.

Edmond had made a half dozen versions of his will; he was consumed by the seriousness of the matter. At times clear-headed and determined, at times dithering and incapable of resolution – for one hour and a half he had been sentencing himself round and round in circles, striving to pen his family into bequests, dispersing of himself liberally only to snatch at qualms. Gay had never before witnessed him so stricken and careful.

*

In the last four months, Gay had seen Edmond perhaps a dozen times, and Edmond had on each occasion been tired, harassed and forlorn. Gay knew that Ann suffered considerably from Edmond's absence, and he recognised the same angry hopelessness in his friend, but he could not breach their obstinacy towards one another. Edmond believed that he had made a choice and that he should stick to it. On one occasion only, when he was pent up with confusion and misery, did Edmond exclaim that the choice had been made for him by his wife, that he had been gulled into sacrifice; but on that occasion he stopped short, and Gay observed a spiral of guilt threading its way through his self-pity.

At their last meeting, called to finalise the arrangements for travel, Edmond had been buoyant. He had done his duty, he said, he had done more than his duty: he had ordered the household, he had cared for his wife and family, he had brought them through the turmoil of the new birth and was passing on to them a firm routine. His wife had fully recovered and his continued devotion to home and hearth would only succeed in confining her to lethargy. He was proud at having learned how to order a house but he recognised that he was depriving his wife of the one field in which she excelled. He was, he admitted, obnoxiously vigorous and bossy, and they would all no doubt be glad to have him off their backs. 'It has been a time of achievement. The baby has been achieved and I have achieved fatherhood. It is a great change. It has been an experience. I am glad that I have seen it through and that I can go to New York with pride in myself.'

Gay wondered.

In the coach on the way from London they had been applauded for their pioneering spirit. They had quite successfully entertained themselves and the other sheltered passengers. It had been, admittedly, a cramped stage; but Gay could not help noticing how Edmond would at the slightest opening for jest or playful severity touch whomsoever he might be addressing. This was not in itself indecorous or impolite. But it was not usual. Gay had not before seen this trait in Edmond. Edmond was not a toucher of people.

As night lengthened its reach into the snug Gay became certain that the business of will-making meant nothing to Edmond, that all the various equations and dilemmas and solutions served merely as an excuse for him to anchor himself to the pen. Edmond's mind was hardly concentrated on what he was doing. His expression was blank and abstracted, his eyes followed the course of the pen as they might follow a balloon on its way through the heavens. The scratching of the nib was the only sound to be heard in the snug, leaving aside the occasional snap from damp logs. The sound of the nib had become vaguely irritating to Gay and yet Edmond had his head cocked as though he was succoured by the blithe rhythms of the instrument.

When Edmond interrupted his pen, at intervals of twenty or so minutes (as before, with his question on the matter of purchasing loyalty), his queries and observations were only whimsical. He did not like to speak but spoke because he was embarrassed at not being alone. If Gay answered him or tried to draw him out, Edmond's attention would not so much lapse as draw back in defence of his right to preoccupation. The conversation would wither, there would open a well of expectancy over which Edmond would drop an eidered 'Indeed', 'I see', or 'I think that you may be right'.

He was not himself.

The hotel-keeper poked his head round the door, confidently hawking a choice of late-night refreshment. Edmond smiled and refused the suggestion of a last supper on earth. Gay would have some ham and sweet biscuits, but not before he had walked out. He wished for a change of air.

Securely wrapped, Gay stepped away into a somewhat warmer night, thickened and stilled by a fog which immediately sided with him.

The fog was strangely tepid. Gay stopped, his senses sharpened. He looked across at the flat shades of the nearest building, observing the weightless depth of the fog, its permeation of the stones.

Although he could not make out the extent of this street, and had forgotten or not noticed the situation of the Crown Hotel, he was reminded of Cropwell Road and the night which had been so thickly curtained by dark and hurtling beasts, Titou riding the blurred torrent to his death. Years ago.

He sucked at the air, expecting someone or something to appear, but the street was empty, enclosed within this still, amicable presence of

42

fog. Titou disappeared to his death, he would not be disturbed; there was a smell of death, a nearness across the water. Gay's head throbbed painfully.

When he entered the snuggery, Edmond was curled up on a pallet. Thus abandoned, Gay moved a chair to the fireside and wrote to Ann whatever came into his mind, prompted by the patterns of flame, and the sparks which clung briefly to the sooted chimney, and the shadows which hopped to and fro across the ceiling.

Edmond awoke sharply, even before the knock. He awoke urgently with the echo of a familiar cry in his ears. He got to his feet, halfway groping around him – not understanding what he should do in these new surroundings but quite prepared to blame his wife for the disorder – and then he perceived that there was absolutely nothing for him to do. He sent his baby and then his wife a good morning; he opened the curtain slightly and saw that it was not yet morning, and he wished, with pleasure, his baby a long and calm sleep.

Then came the knocking on the outer door; and Edmond wanted to be irretrievably departed from England while his child slept, at a time when he would not be more inquisitive about her.

He made noise enough to disturb John. He crossed from the snuggery to unbolt the outer door as quietly as possibly so that the hotel-keeper would not be disturbed and there would be no palaver of breakfasting. He wanted no procrastination. Even as he walked to the door he calculated how much they owed the Crown Hotel.

A boy stood with a lantern. Edmond promised that he would not be kept waiting.

John stood asinine. Edmond left money on the table next to his scrawlings. He cast an eye around the room to make sure that any small belongings were not being left behind and then he joined the watchboy. He took a deep breath. Gay offered him a biscuit.

It was remarkably cold in the pilot barge, and wet. Wet everywhere, clinging and worming its way through the skin to the bones. Edmond huddled into the darkness, hiding himself from thought, shutting his eyes, determined not to make a fool of himself in front of the seamen. Bend your backs. Break your oars. Macabre chants, and choppy water grasping for the side of the boat; water throwing itself across the boat and collapsing like cold iron. At the wolf-grey dawn the interference multiplied; he could see now prancing arcs of saltwater moments before they gaily seized on him, pattering him glibly with derision. His eyes met impenetrable stares from the rowers whose broad shoulders and thick calloused feet must be coated with an oil different from his own.

The mist evaporated, and they came on to the deep-water anchorage where the *Moravagine* lay. They climbed from the pilot boat to the deck, each one roped under the arms and across the chest. Edmond went immediately to his stateroom.

CHAPTER EIGHT

Mister Rennah Wells – The Reverend and Missis Venn – Mister Willibrord Van der Hertz – Mister Philip Schultz – Monsieur and Madame Chenevix – Mister Phillip Cox – Mister Joseph Dork – Misters Francis and James Trench – A Shaking down of the Good Ship Moravagine – A Boggling Occurrence to the Captain

Apart from Edmond, all the passengers remained on deck; from where they failed to observe a receding English coastline.

The occasion was not momentous. Emotions were over-inflated and had to be cut loose to wander back to the befogged jewel, after which the passengers strained so blindly. But it was best to be swayed by some sort of emotion, to indulge in some muted but suggestive display of breast-beating, to wrap oneself in pensiveness, nostalgia, gloom or apprehension. For those without such camouflage were likely to be seized upon by one of the Venns or, as in Gay's case, by their perturbing acolyte Mister Rennah Wells.

The leaving of England would be a private moment, Gay had thought. Perhaps prayerful, perhaps merely solemn. Possibly it was this Churchish connotation which inspired the Venns to set about guiding their little flock through the hazardous matter of voyagery.

The introductions had been made very quickly and Gay did not remember who was whom. This same incognisance afflicted the most part of the passengers. Not so the Venns. The crook did not sleep in those four hands. The Reverend and his wife alighted upon a name as if such correct perching alone would guarantee them charge over the hapless individual's innermost trepidation. Politeness dictated that they should meet no severing rebuff, but politeness could not begin to dislodge Mister Rennah Wells, who seemed capable of recalling but a single name. 'Mister John Gay, yes sir indeed.'

'Mister John Gay!'

'Mister John Gay.'

'My Lord, Mister John Gay.'

Thus, thus, thus and thus did John Gay suffer the misfortune of being pinned to the mast by his own name, this Mister Wells being so embarrassingly eager to elicit his sympathies. He remained on deck just long enough to register this imposition on his scattered emotions, and then he went below.

The actors' stateroom was tiny and crowded with smells of linseed, tar and damp musty wood. Gay squeezed into the top berth and fell uneasily asleep. He awoke with a violent headache, clamped tight by the heavy stink of pitch and paint and buffeted by the deep resonance of a male voice which led its mewling congregation through a morning hymn on the other side of the door. The singing stopped when Edmond, clad in his shirt, threw open the door and demanded to know where he might find the closet.

'Perhaps they were shocked,' Edmond conceded. 'Perhaps such a thing would shock them even in these circumstances. But I don't think that they were shocked. I saw only Venn's vanity. He was not shocked; he was angry at the disturbance to his power. How entertaining the mealtimes will be.'

Edmond appeared but briefly and sickly at the first luncheon. Gay was seated on the opposite side of the table from him and several places away. Edmond was seated amongst the more ponderous members of the company – the delicately mannered French pair, the Venns and Mister Cox. He ate slowly and methodically, as if eating was in itself an untried experience. He diverted all enquiries, giving the barest information and politely returning the business of self-revelation to the very certain Reverend or the very sincere Cox. The food, which was carried in for them from another part of the ship, was simple and wholesome and Gay's offer of wine was gratefully accepted by half the company, each of whom pledged to reciprocate the generosity. Mister Wells suggested that a rota should be established but it was assumed that each person would recognise their social obligations. Considering that they were for the most part unknown to each other and confined to a single, bolted table on two bolted benches in a room some thirteen yards by eight yards, this first forced intimacy was not as taxing as Gay had feared; and there was a great amount of amusement and disarming foolishness caused by the swaying of the ship, which subverted any but the most fragile decorum. Gay felt not claustrophobic but light-headed

46

and even frivolous. He was aware of many glances darting around the table and much suppressed laughter. There was a sort of madness in this little prison, a sense of how ridiculous they all were; as though instead of sitting at this pretence of a habitual Sunday luncheon, their legs danced to a lively tune beneath the wooden benches.

The calling together of the two ends of the table seemed a proper way to conclude the luncheon. Mrs Venn straightaway joined Madame Chenevix on one of the two heavy sofas, both of which bore the marks of considerable usage. Edmond departed quietly to his stateroom; and when Van der Hertz proposed a turn around the deck Gay was silently grateful for the rescue.

They did not get far. Gay moved gingerly from the hatch to the rail. The *Moravagine* was not carrying full sail and slipped nonchalantly through a bashful sea. Once again Gay could not discover within himself the meaningful loneliness which he had expected. For although the waters stretched away on every side, the ship itself bore more resemblance to a market street at that busy hour when the traders hurried to prepare their stalls for the day. Gay, with absolutely no knowledge of boats other than what he imagined from the term 'ship-shape', was aghast at the filth which littered the deck. On first and on second appearance it seemed as though the ship had been expelled haphazardly from England with a cargo of detritus. Ropes straggled around a cauldron of steaming pitch and several panels beneath the gunwale were missing. Those sailors who were on deck walked, leapt or crawled amongst piles of crates and haybales, boxes of hens and hillocks of frayed fibres, stepping around pools of what looked like animal excrement. In all it appeared that the ship was in no sort of order whatsoever, was indeed in the process of being constructed or dismantled, what with the hammering and the wrenching and the casting of matter over the side into the water. Gay could, by standing on the rim of the hatch, see his own and Edmond's new chests, dumped and forgotten beside the foremast – most of their possessions, the new Harlequin suit from Smalley, the plates of himself and Edmond from Oxberry's engraver, and a large proportion of their finest clothes all serving as a flimsy stepladder and likely at any rough wave to tumble and slide overboard along with all the other debris, if they were not first hurled over by some sailor who had no idea of their value.

Gay grabbed at a passing shoulder. 'Those boxes', he pointed, 'must be stowed.'

'Yassah.'

'Boxes. Under. Inside.' Gay reached into his waistcoat. The man took the coin, pranced away down the deck and spat on his hand and put his finger into the cauldron and picked up a brush and made no further progress towards the mast. As Gay's anger rose, he was himself aware of being the object of some attention.

He turned to Van der Hertz, who pointed him back down the ship towards the mate: up to whom Gay climbed and complained.

Gay was informed that the chests would be stowed by nightfall, that the hold was at the moment taking in water, but that their adherence to this course would enable satisfactory repairs to be made in a very short time, and that it was the Captain's business to pay off his men at the end of the voyage, and that most passengers would find it more comfortable below decks while the ship was being shook down, and that there was a danger of injury for those unaccustomed to a preparation for sea.

'Is this ship not ready for sea?' Gay demanded.

'No, sir. Not in my judgment.'

'But we are *at* sea, we are sailing. Are we not?'

'You might say that we are afloat and heading in an agreed direction.'

Gay was not sure whether he was being fooled with; the mate's composure offered no clue. 'Is it by pure good luck that we are not sinking?'

'Not, sir, to my way of thinking.'

'Are there other ways of thinking?'

'Likely. But my way of thinking carries an authority; which is why I must ask yourself and the rest of the passengers to remain below until you may move around in greater safety. Gentlemen – please keep to your quarters!'

As Gay followed the direction of the mate's cry he saw that the passengers – Van der Hertz was being joined by a half dozen other men – did indeed constitute a hapless and dithering group, clutching on to one another like a procession of blind, bent and semi-legged beggars emerging from the cellar of a hospice.

Gay found no difficulty in retracing his steps. His stage skills served him well. He rarely had confidence in the precision of other actors and did not now rely on any steadiness from the planks beneath his feet.

The salon was quiet. The passengers moved cautiously and privately. Wells lurked, ready for conversation, but Gay felt suddenly drowsy in the warmth of the cabin. His cheeks stung and his vision was cloudy. He looked in on Edmond, who lay with a book propped open on his knees, not encouraging any other company. Gay quickly slid into a deep unconsciousness, immune to the noises from the deck overhead.

They spent most of the next three days in a stupor of sleep and dream. When they emerged into the salon at meal times they found the other passengers similarly heavy-limbed and puffed with drowsiness, the conversation gentle and not pursued, the faces sometimes remarkable but their importance quick to fade as in the dream continuing.

Gay did have his moment of homesickness. He went on deck when they were much nearer to France than to Cornwall, the sea being a very pale cold blue and uniformly wrinkled, the sun cloaked by the edge of the world. And then it was not so much a homesickness as a dismay at the wide unoccupied ocean.

He went up once again, at night, and it terrified him. It was the water, dribbling soundlessly about the deck; its estrangement from the great bulk of ocean which bedded the hull of the ship, deep and black and unscathed. He did not feel in danger but he was unnerved by the massive solemn impersonality.

Of Mister Rennah Wells, Edmond said with some dislike: 'He is so full of himself, he has a slipperiness which I detest. He fills me with revulsion.'

'He is worse than the Reverend?'

'Yes. No. Perhaps. I do not want to think about it.'

Edmond's book. Edmond claimed that it was a most interesting book. He spent a very great deal of time with it. Pages twenty-six and twenty-seven were well-thumbed and dirty around the margins. There was no sign that the rest of the pages had ever been turned.

Edmond was conscious of a twitch about his right eye. He silently conversed with himself, almost constantly. He fought not to go to sleep, for if he did so he awoke again immediately with a sick and sad sense of nothingness and a fear that his mind was working at an involuntary and mad pace. He decided many times how he should feel about being parted from his wife and baby daughter but his decisions could in no way keep sealed the feelings of loss which boiled up from inside him. He curled into a tight ball and lay for hours in that position, with one finger inside the book, ready to seize upon his reading as a defence should there be a knock on his door from any prospective inquisitor.

The purpose of the Captain's luncheon, it seemed to Gay, was to make clear to the passengers how entirely superfluous and disruptive they might be to the running of his ship.

Quite impervious to the possibilities of social intercourse, the Captain chose to lecture them as soon as they had assembled in his cabin – they being the six occupants of the private staterooms and thereby assumed to be suitable vehicles for communicating the Captain's will to the men berthing in the salon.

The Captain's will was that they should keep themselves to themselves. They would be allowed on deck for one hour in the morning and one hour in the afternoon, good weather allowing. In bad weather the mainmast hatchway would be battened down and they would be obliged to provide for themselves. There was a small pantry in the corner of the salon, next to the wash-closet. He expected that the *Moravagine* would meet some weather between their present position and the islands of the Azores, due to the imminence of the solstice.

He would not on any account tolerate any kind of religious service above decks, since such services in his experience sowed either division or maudlin sentiments amongst the crew. He himself officiated at the very simplest Sunday prayers, and this served the spiritual needs of his sailors. Any further religious observance was left to each man in private communion with his God or Creed.

If there were fighting amongst the passengers, those involved, irrespective of right or wrong or provocation or revenge, *anyone* involved in any fracas would be taken out of the passengers' quarters and confined in the old shot lockers above the keel of the ship. Such a measure would apply equally to men and to women; he was sure that his remarks would prove unnecessary, but he urged all the ladies to behave with the utmost modesty and caution, for their own welfare. Too often, and only sometimes unintentionally, they were the prime cause of trouble on a long voyage; and they would be well advised to keep to their own staterooms, to choose some private recreation, and to avoid involvement with those berthed in the salon. On no account was any lady to have any contact whatsoever with any member of the crew other than himself or the first mate.

He had, said the Captain, not the slightest desire or duty to take any responsibility for the passengers other than to carry them as part of his cargo, as safely as he could, to New York. Any other responsibility he handed back to themselves, trusting that they would behave accordingly. As a seaman he had made many crossings, on several of which he had been hard pressed to differentiate between the behaviour of animals, slaves and passengers. Therefore, on receiving his own command, he had decided never to carry slaves and, as a matter of course, to provide the severest warnings to his passengers, no matter what station of life they claimed to uphold on dry land. Most seamen behaved badly on land, and, conversely, being at sea proved a great trial for many landsmen out of touch with their element and having nothing to fill their time. There should be no gaming, no libertinage, nor cliquery; nor any victimisation of any man. Nor any philosophising, nor any politicking. Nor any drunkenness, nor dancing, nor selling of possessions nor offering of credit.

And so to the luncheon, once the Captain had bombarded his guests. He remained quiet at first, as though considering whether he had done himself justice in his delivery. And certainly there was no return of fire. The Captain replied to the Reverend Venn, who asked after his own cargo and was assured that those bundles of pamphlets were safely stored. Then the Captain raised his voice and led the charge of his cargo.

A greater part of the forard hold was taken up by printed matter of one sort and another, there were many cases of books and judicial reports. The main ballast consisted of a great number of sacks of Portland cement, a newly manufactured product which had caused considerable problems in loading, what with the weight of the sacks and the pernicious dust which they were obliged to isolate from the delicate bales of linen and lace. Much else was as usual for such a voyage: a consignment of seed drills, hunting rifles, several grand pianofortes, cases of tea and spices and silks, half the lower middle deck was taken up by thorough-bred stallions. Apart from the Reverend Venn, the only other traveller accompanying his – ('wares', Gay thought, is what the Captain was about to say) – his works was a Mister Vanderhertz, who had supervised the taking on board of a great number of thin sheets of rubber, for which he was convinced he would find a market in the Americas. There was also aboard – the Captain stared down the table; his speech slowed – a fire-engine, powered by steam, a fire engine . . .

The Captain sat staring blankly towards the end of the table. His fork lay across the plate, his hand held the fork, motionless.

Gay did not know what could have happened. The Reverend and his wife were eating confidently. Edmond had long since ceased showing any interest in the gathering.

'A fire engine . . .' Gay filled the silence. 'That is extraordinary. What inventive mind would conceive of taking a large kettle to a fire?'

The Captain had held court for so long that everybody else had forgotten how to speak, or else thought speaking to be out of place along with philosophising and offering of credit. Knives and forks clinked against plates, the Reverend took a sip of wine.

Gay thought, the Captain is dead. The man has just died of some cerebral attack. He has passed on. And now we are left with his ship and his laws in the middle of nowhere.

Gay stared at the Captain, who did not move in the slightest nor show any sign of life, but was struck dead.

Gay did not want to be the one to uncover this fact. He carried on eating, watching the Captain's glassy stare from out of the corner of his eye.

What would happen now?

Gay felt propelled towards a wild laughter. How long could this go on? What would happen? Would the Captain topple face forward into his cucumbers? Would the ship leave the water and wing its way up to Heaven at the Captain's command? Would the Reverend's wife seize the opportunity to dance naked on the quarterdeck? What on earth would happen next? The man was certainly dead.

To Gay's left, the Frenchman slapped his hand down on to the dining table. Gay thought, ah, now we will see, there will be panic, decisions will have to be taken.

'Vous m'excusez.' The Frenchman coughed. Everyone looked at him. He seemed to be choking. Now, Gay thought, he will die too, will he? Is that the comedy? Oh and are we all poisoned! Gay glared at his plate.

'A new application of the steam engine,' the Captain's voice resonated, 'which will become common on ocean-going vessels if the problem of explosions is solved.'

Gay's head swivelled.

What did happen?

CHAPTER NINE

Gay Prowls – Edmond Pines – Mister Rennah Wells Pollutes

In the confines of their stateroom, when they had returned forard, Gay questioned Edmond carefully. Had he perhaps noticed a gap in the sequence of time? Edmond had noticed one long yawning gap, which had lasted from the moment they entered the Captain's cabin until the moment they left. He had been at one point struck by the Captain's misogyny but had been lulled by the realisation that the man was more generally misanthropic.

Had Edmond thought him demented, perhaps? Or subject to visitations?

'Who,' said Edmond, 'who in their right mind would ever want to visit him? I cannot imagine that anyone would admit to being at home should *he* come to visit *them*. And he is not colourful enough ever to become demented, although he might perhaps become murderous should anyone ever be foolish enough as to tell him how plain and tedious he is.'

They, and presumably the rest of the passengers, were at this moment interrupted by the sounds of a furious dispute between the French husband and wife.

Neither Monsieur nor Madame Chenevix appeared in the salon for supper. At that gathering the Reverend spoke highly of the Captain; Missis Venn agreed demurely, her eyes hardly rising above the level of the dining-table.

Edmond retired to bed before Missis Venn; and Gay, in the company of Van der Hertz and the pasty Dane (Schultz), gave his opinion that a man with great responsibilities was apt to let his mind wander when he was tethered amongst novices who knew nothing of his problems.

Schultz, it seemed, knew something about the sea and the route that the *Moravagine* would be taking. Van der Hertz prodded him for information.

Gay's own mind wandered. He found himself lethargic and was irritable with himself. Schultz had rummaged inside the chest beneath his berth and had fetched up a chart, which he had spread over half the table. They joined Van der Hertz in guessing at the *Moravagine*'s whereabouts. Schultz deferred to any opinion, but Van der Hertz paid more attention to him than to the others, Gay noticed.

He was, though, bored with noticing; and the steadily sliding lamplight – to and fro, to and fro, across the table and back again – exacerbated his ennui. What he wanted to do was to run, to feel himself moving; through his legs and his ribs and his shoulders to shake himself into feeling alive. In this surrounding it was impossible. He was not used to impossibility. The surrounding imposed. There would be at most in this salon some mental life, some discussion.

The Dane, he decided, was a man without hope, undermined by some experience or other and now without faith in himself. The ruddy-faced farmer would be unwilling ever to say a bad word about anybody, he would march enthusiastically in any direction, hailing good fellows and working honestly. The Dutchman's mouth, heavily curtained by thick mustaches, would never utter an ill-considered opinion. What might Gay learn about rubber?

Edmond was arranging their stateroom. Had arranged and was not over-anxious for his opinion of the arrangement. Was still arranging. Gay took a bottle.

Edmond remembered a tremendous exhilaration, the residue of which cosseted him when he awoke. He lay in his berth, light-headed, with the feeling that he had to get out of his stateroom. A witty mimicry of the passengers from John had greatly amused him – he must get out and see for himself. He had not drunk so much for several months and it had done him no harm.

He was delighted to observe that any enquiries about his health bounced off him without disturbing him. He was struck by the pale beauty of Madame Chenevix, who was impeccably dressed and coiffed and emerald-eyed and stretched taut across some barely concealed emotion. Edmond perceived women as being at their most beautiful when they were unhappy; he was capable of great sympathy in the presence of a strained beauty.

He roused Gay for a timely stroll around the deck, at which he successfully introduced himself to the sight of the ocean and the abrasion of its winds.

He held lively conversations at luncheon; at dinner he had several of the company laughing.

When he went to bed he slept for seven hours; but he awoke suddenly in the early hours of the morning, weighed down with sadness at what a hollow fool he was. He prayed for the baby, crying quietly into his pillows.

Edmond remained morose.

And yet, suddenly, Edmond bewildered Gay by throwing himself out into the salon society with all the charm that he could manufacture.

So there were two very fine days – luncheons, afternoons and dinners – when the salon was entertained by Edmond's soliciting each man into expressing openly his hopes and plans for enterprise in the new continent. Indeed it was as though they were introduced to one another again, this time in the spirit of some communal adventuring. The brothers Trench had very little idea what they should do in the Americas, but Mister Cox had no idea how he might alone transport his saplings and would need help to establish a farming and fruit business in Boston – after which town Van der Hertz sought information. Mister Dork had been to London to seek finance for the expansion of a concern which had achieved some success in the south in the making of a nut sauce or butter – some madness which his local banks refused to countenance, but which a Mister William Lloyd of London had found much to his taste when spread underneath a coating of Shropshire plum jam. Such a small world. And did perchance Mister Cox grow plums? No, he grew Pippin apples. Ah well, and the world was somewhat larger.

Mister Wells farted. It was a misfortune which the salon accepted. Mister Wells was untamed from top to bottom. His long legs spread in every direction when he sat down, he was the most tripped-over object on the ship. The man was well above two yards high and would only move about the salon in a painful condition of bent-ness, looming frightfully. He was further pained by timidity and never announced his

56

arrival, so he did often scare unsuspecting lower mortals. The salt winds had taken his hair and caused it to stiffen into a thickly sprung brush, which meant that he had to stoop still further in order to avoid becoming snared on the splintery ceiling. Evidently, since his adolescence, he had been restrained from exhibiting too much excitement for fear of causing unintentional injury to those around him. If he was to be a giant then it had been urged upon him to be a peaceful giant. The excitement was ruthlessly internal and the poor man could only, literally, give vent to his emotions.

At first, his gusting merely trembled amongst the acrid stink of pitch. When the *Moravagine* had been sealed to the mate's satisfaction and the upper deck was cleared, the funny smell was attributed by Mister Schultz to an excess of stagnant water in the bilges, which would quickly filter through now that the ship was running more into the wind and both taking on and expelling an increased amount of seawater. Then it was perhaps some infected atmosphere from the animals which were stabled further aft on the same deck as the passengers. But, no. The smell was too impermanent, and, Mister Cox announced after visiting the animals, the smell was simply too horrible to have come from anything living. It was a rotting stench, a decaying stench; most probably of putrefying flesh. Not unlike the smell of a gangrenous stump, hazarded Schultz.

To his great credit, Wells courageously confided in Van der Hertz, who confided in and so on even unto the Reverend Missis Venn, who was the last person to exclaim, 'There is that smell again! Will you not see the Captain about it?'

Wells' condition was accepted, a light gagging cough was deemed to be the maximum gesture of protest. But Wells was excitable, and did fart silently, and farted horrendously when he felt that it was his turn to reveal his plans to the company. He was, he blushed, very much drawn to the open air and large, open spaces. He had decided to take up the life of an artist. He was going back to the Americas in order to paint scenes of the countryside, which he would send to London so that everyone might have some view of the mysterious terrain. He hoped to thoroughly immerse himself in studies of the landscape, leading a simple and natural life, unnoticed.

'Unnoticed?' queried Edmond. 'Surely not. Not for an artist, that is not the life for an artist.'

As for being an artist, Wells did not know whether he could justify an acceptance of the title. He perhaps had more vision because he could usually see over the heads of other people. And he was not short of inspiration; he was every day inspired by some small scene. Would they be willing to see? He had started a drawing, last night, in his berth. Just a simple sketch.

He fetched them a piece of paper on which there was a representation, as from above, of the table at which they sat, with five heads, or tops of heads, intruding on the rectangle. The heads were, he explained, temporarily without shoulders.

Nobody knew quite what to say, the subject being so unfamiliar. Gay had never seen such a devotion to the details of hair – its patterns, its sweeps, its partings, its lacking in certain places, its wayward strands, its uneven curls, its untidy sense of direction. The head of Schultz was immediately placed, with its twin hedgerows lining the unplanted *colline*; but who was this, and this, and this? And who on earth was this figure with the unicorn-like protrusion jutting from the temple?

At Edmond's suggestion they each submitted their guesses to Wells' adjudication. Edmond got Edmond and three others; he was the only person besides Schultz to identify himself. ('Vanity,' laughed Edmond, later. 'I am ridiculously vain.') Monsieur Chenevix was the sole competitor to achieve the nap hand. The man with the horn was apparently Gay himself, victim to considerable artistic licence or slip of the pencil, or perhaps wearing a stage-cap of some sort. ('And that is being polite,' said Edmond. 'As an artist the man is a cack-handed imbecile, and from the way he eyes you I would attribute to him a certain shirt-lifting quality. His eyes are like dirty, prying fingers. Allow him a wide berth for his Art.')

Madame Chenevix translated for her husband. From what *maître* had Monsieur Wells taken his education?

Wells was embarrassed to admit that he had not served any recognised apprenticeship. He had accepted a commission from his stepfather to travel from Boston to see the Reverend Venn, and he had gone on to London in the hope that that city would shape his rougher edges. Wells' excitability rose. He was painfully shy and most ill-at-ease with his own blurtings. As a boy he had left England to sail with his family to the eastern edge of the new continent. He had been fortified by the spiritual teachings of his grampaw, and had left home to carry these teachings westwards into the new territories, the Indian lands.

'You have seen them?' Gay wondered.

'It was no doubt difficult for Mister Wells,' the Reverend Venn butted in, 'difficult to match his sensibilities to the romantic and savage nature of the primitive peoples. That is surely why he has taken it upon himself to retrace his own life – firstly to Boston, then through my own advocacy of spiritual disciplines, to London – in search of the modern scientific spirit. Which reasoning, *I* believe, if correctly guided, will fathom those eternal truths that have, in themselves, a universal moral bearing.'

Such impressive guff quite floored Gay. He had no idea what the Reverend Venn was talking about. The Reverend could not seem to let a simple sentence lie, but chose instead to elevate Rennah towards the fabulous.

'You went to London?' Edmond mused. 'How strange. I have spent my entire life in London without being aware of its propensity for moral rigour. What did you do in London?'

Rennah had not known what to do. He had not had the good fortune to meet with any artists. But he had one day been seized upon by a man of education, in the street, who asked him if he would consent to sitting for the measuring of his head. Having nothing better to do, he agreed. He left Doctor Sotheby's house with a copy of the measurements and returned later in the week with a copy of his head, done by layering plastered horsehair over a bowling ball. Sotheby then employed him to make other heads – nothing much artistic, Wells said, for he only had to follow the measurements. The customers who bought his heads didn't want nothing similar to their own families. Most often his constructions were of the Duke of Wellington, Lord Byron and Mister William Pitt. And some ladies of nobleness and beauty.

'As ornaments?' Edmond's innocent tone hardly disguised the sneer in his voice.

'As examples of human achievement, my dear sir,' the Reverend Venn assured him, 'to be looked upon and to edify a house with the sense of moral possibility. Just as our Church has chosen an unadorned cross as the living symbol of spiritual values. It is quite beneficial to have one of these great heads in the entrance hall of a house, as it is to

59

have a symbol of Our Lord in a chapel or private room. It encourages a reflection on virtue.'

Wells nodded slowly.

'It is for example,' the Reverend emphasised.

'These heads are most often placed in the nursery, from what I understand.' Edmond pursed his lips.

'As an inspiration to the children,' Venn nodded approvingly.

Edmond asked if they might now have the evening prayer, as it seemed as though most of the company would not retire immediately to bed and it would be thoughtless of them to expect Missis Venn to wait upon the conversation. The Reverend happily agreed. Missis Venn was fetched; her husband officiated, and he then escorted her back to their stateroom.

The Frenchies departed. Several of the men sat in silent reflection and the atmosphere in the salon was no longer buoyant. Gay was thinking, damn Edmond, damn Edmond with his insistence on his baby, damn his parade of suffering. Edmond tapped his fingers on the table and did not raise his head to meet Gay's anger.

Instead he tapped away and softly broke into 'Dee-hi-ho, Donny-oh Donny-oh'. Gay joined him in the first chorus; they arrived at a chorus of four after the second verse, but Edmond abandoned the song and quietly re-opened the conversation.

'The Reverend did not quite comprehend the value of your heads, Mister Wells, did he?'

'They didn't have no value, sir.' Wells was most respectful to everybody, but was almost in awe of Edmond.

'Or purpose? You see, I have a child and I cannot think of anything more sinister to place by her cradle than a featureless head. My child demands endless variety, she wishes to feel teeth and skin and tongues and hair. And I allow her to do so. How else is she to educate herself, or be encouraged to attempt her own education?'

Edmond, thought Gay, has become almost indecently personal. One does not wish to know about Edmond's nostrils, and I do not wish to know about education.

'See, truth is, Mister Parsloe, that it's something new.' Wells' American twang was as thin as his body, and had degenerated almost into a whine. There was a smell.

'So I have heard. That a person's character and intelligence bear direct relation to the shape and size of their head. Have you evidence?'

'Not me, no, sir.'

'But Doctor Sotheby?'

'I believe so. He's done this for a long time. Gotten to be well-known for it. People were always bringin' him heads.'

'How so?' Van der Hertz.

'There's business in heads.'

'They do occasionally have some importance,' Gay grinned. 'As in the phrase "a man should always keep his head".'

'Or keep his wits about him,' Edmond advised curtly.

'Skulls,' Wells stipulated. 'I only came across skulls – '

'And their duggery.'

'Well,' said Wells, 'that is true. Some people have a holy number of heads. One King Charles had at least six of them, as I recall, all of them belonging to different owners. Two come to us for private sale at nigh on the same time.'

'How was that resolved?'

'One was sold in France, and one in London.'

'And that deceit did not disturb your conscience?'

'Maybe.'

Edmond laughed. 'I don't think that it would disturb mine.'

'Nor even King Charles,' Wells grinned. Van der Hertz laughed. Wells looked around gratefully, and with a little more confidence he chose to explain himself to Edmond. 'See, Mister Parsloe, I don't hold with these ideas. I don't claim to know much about them, not having the right learning. I was held back when I was a child, like a dog, like a beast sometimes. I was something of a jackass and maybe I deserved it, getting myself ridiculed for my unnatural height. Truthfully I might be imagining such things, but I don't think so.' Wells' eyes misted over. He had the company wriggling and uneasy.

'You might well', Edmond snapped, 'be fabricating this horror of your own childhood. You might be permitted to do so. Such a fabrication would serve your own ambition in leaving you free to follow a self-serving course with a strong moral justification.' Edmond nodded. 'But I have been made aware of the disgraceful lengths to which some fathers, and mothers, will go in the training of their children, from the moment they become innocent babies. This *science*, this ornamenture, this exampling – it is not, thank God, commonplace, but it is not rare. The heads you made are placed in the nursery and the child is expected to attain to the example. Such a thing might be edifying, might be . . . I don't know what it can be . . . perhaps of value for reflection on virtue. But I fail to see what virtue an infant can nourish when its head is set within iron clamps and screws, its skull being tightly and horribly pressed into the proportions which are so fortuitously occupied by the mind of the Duke of Wellington! That is a form of torture which no artist would ever countenance; ever.'

Edmond walked to the closet. His eyes bulged as if the pressure of revulsion would never be drained by tears.

'I believe him to be a dangerous simpleton,' Edmond said. 'At best he is a clumsy and stupid idealist. However, I never find myself able to credit the best in people. Have you noticed how he speaks? He speaks like a bad actor or a precocious boy. He tried for the measured tone of an English gentleman and it does not fit him. I cannot think of a voice which *would* fit him. It is all very well for Venn to claim the pulpit to which he was born, but Mister Wells is an impostor.'

'That may be, but his words are possibly sincere,' Gay suggested.

'Ah, but he thereby wishes us to understand that *he* is sincere. He is very careful to suggest his innocence, and Mister Venn is only too happy to shelter him. Well I assure you that, at his age, Mister Wells is either sly or demented. No. He is both.'

Gay lay in the darkness and considered that Edmond's nerves were exhausted. The worst that could be said about Mister Rennah Wells was that he gave one a piercing headache.

CHAPTER TEN

High Seas – Edmond Impersonates a Bird – Which Falls out of the Sky – Chenevix's Gift – Gay Is Nearly Drowned

Hours later Gay awoke as if in the middle of a prizefight. His body was pressed close against the wall of the stateroom. His left temple had received a blow, but he was not injured. It required some effort to push himself away from the wall. He rolled over in his bunk, and lined his shoulders up against the wood, and pushed the bolster in at an angle to protect his head.

He wondered if the ship had changed direction. And was heading where? Back to London would be as good a direction as any. They had been at sea for eight days. It had not been an interesting time. Portugal was the nearest land. Gay went back to sleep.

'Ta-tum-tum tiddly-ya-dum
Ta-tum-tum tiddly-ya-dum
Ta-tum-tum tiddly-ya-dum
Ta-tum-tum-tum-tum.'

And a happy new year. Gay opened one eye. Edmond was holding on to both sides of the door frame. His clothes, Gay saw, were moist, and his face shone damply. This time, he whistled the tune, trilling like a throttled canary. Edmond had always considered that he had a talent for the impersonation of birds, but he was in fact ridiculous, the more so for hopping gauntly from foot to foot across the open doorway. He said, 'We are running, John, and running magnificently. You should not miss the sight.'

Gay asked, 'What does that have to do with the happy new year?'

Edmond laughed. 'It was supposed to be "Ladies of Spain", but the melody became unstuck.'

The *Moravagine* was running very fast before luncheon under stretched bellies of canvas, her spars snapping and cracking like a whip to a horse. The air was surprisingly warm, the aspect enthralling and the passengers each one sharing the excitement. Gay felt happy at the tremendous progress, not in terms of yards or miles, but that everything was perfect: the ship and the elements were perfectly balanced and functioning at their utmost, human and Godly design were complementary in execution. After luncheon there was a great deal of singing, an exuberant singing, a happy challenge to the usual monotonous chants of the crew whose spirit of drudgery had leaked through from the deck. At the afternoon hour, when the passengers were again released outside, there was a change in the atmosphere. The sky was a grim grey, the wind was colder and the waves arrived in a sturdy pattern. But the *Moravagine* continued triumphantly under full roaring sail. She swept through the seas, her ropes humming and shrilling. Gay held himself tightly to the rail, his hair being pulled back from his face by the wind. He looked back towards the mainmast. Edmond had removed his spectacles, but he saw Gay and raised a papal arm in joyful salutation and laughed, and the ship soared suddenly and Edmond disappeared.

Gay was, in a trice, hurled upwards from the deck and saw clearly how the ship was sliding away from him down a steep hillside of water towards the dark valley. It seemed to him that his body would not fall fast enough to regain the deck, that he would come down into the ocean and be borne away by a mob of water. But he was hit square across the thighs by a stretch of rigging, and he fell in company with the ship.

Then there was a stillness. There was a great tension as the ship's fall was halted and it was asked to rise again. The ship agonised at the pressure. Gay, lying on his back, saw the sails sag like aged skin. All magnificent force from above was paltry and haggard and spent; all power lay gathered beneath, bending the backbone of the ship. Gay started to scramble across the deck. As he did so he felt the ship begin to rise. Its mind made up, it rose faster and faster, the sails flapped and bloomed, the masts shuddered. Men swarmed up the rigging, over Gay's head, to help it.

He edged away, hanging on to the rail like a child riding in a swerving chariot, whipped and tearful at the madness of the driver. Schultz it was who waited for the following elevation and returned for

64

Gay; who, with Wells, examined Edmond's body and then set out for the forecastle to fetch the carpenter.

'It is not so bad,' said Edmond. The ship fell again. Edmond bit hard on the strap, sweat rose through the skin on his forehead. As the ship halted, steadied, and onerously assumed its responsibility for rising again, his face went white and a ratcheted sigh of pain escaped from between his teeth.

The cook and the carpenter conferred. Both agreed that Edmond's back was not broken. The leg was twisted – this much was obvious to Van der Hertz, who had been the first to reach Edmond as he lay headlong down the midshiphouse steps, with the right leg bent between the mast and the handrail. Unbelievably, the leg had not been broken, and the carpenter was not needed. The ankle, though, was severely out of place and must be returned.

They laid Edmond on the table. Van der Hertz, Gay, James Trench, Wells, Schultz and Cox all grasped the lip of the bench with one hand and stretched the other arm across Edmond's body, trying to keep themselves and him from being thrown to the floor. They were, all of them, with the possible exception of Schultz, quite frightened by the plunging of the ship. Their clothes were wet through, there was a wildness in each eye, but Edmond's injuries prevented any outbreak of panic. The hatchway was opened suddenly and a bundle of cord was thrown down the ladder.

'It will be a strong storm,' Schultz advised. 'We have to decide what we should do.'

Edmond was in no state to decide. The carpenter praised the cook's skill at setting bones. Rennah knew only about heads. Schultz knew about the customs on board a ship: the cook, it was, who usually served in the absence of a surgeon.

The cook felt along the sides of Edmond's knee and pressed his fingers around the ankle. Edmond cried out. Monsieur Chenevix stationed himself beside Edmond's head.

'He must be held,' said the cook. 'Do you feel this, sir? You must brace yourself.'

There was no answer. Edmond's eyes stared loosely at the ceiling. They were without expression.

'Vous pouvez commencer,' murmured Chenevix. 'To begin, if you please.'

The cook put one hand on the side of Edmond's knee, the other above the ankle. When the ship steadied he leaned heavily on the knee and pushed. At the next hiatus he repeated the procedure. He was most severe. It was as though he were within the safe confines of his galley, gluttonously wrenching at the scaled ankle of a chicken. Gay wondered at the strength of the human skin. Edmond's shoulders twitched but he gave no cry of pain. He seemed to have removed himself into a deep state of reverie. His breathing was slow and shallow.

Rather coldly, Gay estimated that Edmond would be unlikely ever to caper across a stage again. The ship rolled, and slid, and plunged. The cook straightened up. He said that he had done the best he could, and would have to leave them.

Gay saw that Chenevix, Cox and Schultz were waiting on his pronouncement, their arms resting across Edmond's body. From the top of the hatchway came the sound of hammering. Chenevix clapped his hands together. The ceiling swung quickly towards the lamp. Van der Hertz talked to Chenevix in his own language, back and forth they each jerked the argument. The lamp crashed against the ceiling.

'We are all to be roped,' Gay explained, to the darkness.

'I see,' said Edmond.

'You have only to call out. I am at hand.' Gay hesitated. 'How is it?'

'My back is most painful.'

'And your leg?'

'There is very little sensation. I do not wish to move my back. I am tired.'

'We must go through this storm.'

'Then we will. Thank you, John.'

Gay kissed Edmond's cheek and left him cocooned in the darkness.

A glass object smashed against the other side of the table. The salon reeked of brandy, drops of water dribbled steadily from the ceiling to the floor. Gay made his way down the salon, crawling along the boards, holding on to the bench with one hand, fighting off the settee which ran downhill at him out of the darkness. Someone, somewhere in the salon roped into his berth, repeated a prayer around and around, looping himself tightly in against a mainstay of God. The sea arrived in great lumps against the larboard side; the salon reared unhappily and wheeled away from the shock, swerving and bouncing like a drunkard against a wall. Gay felt an acute sensation of being surrounded not by danger but by ugliness, as if he, the other passengers and the ship itself were being cuffed playfully by a mad and vindictive giant as overhead the winds screamed with laughter. Schultz pulled Gay in through the stateroom door and shouted at him to lie in the upper berth. The ropes were drawn tightly over him; painfully; 'I cannot even move!' Gay shouted. Schultz ignored him and left.

Surging from the middle of sleep, Gay was suddenly and violently sick. He managed to turn his head so that the vomit swelled upwards and fell away down the back of his neck to the pillow and inside his collar. The ship was in God knows what position, cavorting on its stern or flopping on its side like a dying fish; there was only a vile cold misery, a shrieking and a berserk thumping, a stream of icy water spewing over his legs. Inside his head there was an incessant whine, pounding panic through his body. He retched continuously, writhing against the ropes.

Hallucinations. They were terrible. They were so fast and strung together endlessly. He was at one moment not at all at sea but instead was being ridden crackety-crack across the line of iron railings. And next as a figure of gigantic proportions, half inflated like a hollow and heavy and dismayed balloon, his skin stabbed and scraped by mountain peaks which rose sharply from the dark floor of the earth. And all the while the air, so far from being his ally, shouted at him from inside his head: It is gone! It is lost! There is no going back! On! On!
   And against these exhortations from the Maggot Gay's body felt as though it were cartwheeling, smacked back and forth by the ship which kept him from his home in the water where he would and should dissolve.

And this was it: the crash and the door flying open in darkness and the torrent leaping over him, rummaging through his clothes for his body, the water gripping him.
   Then the water left him uncovered; but was back again suddenly to

check on him. Then it wound away, rushing to check on someone else. The ship seemed not to move for a long time.

And then the ship lifted as though it were thrown. There was a final dead thump, a long crashing in the salon and the sea smashed in over Gay and high up against the wall in front of him.

He found that he had, against his will, stocked his lungs with air. The world was very silent. There was a pumping noise of restlessness in his ears but everything else was still.

The water subsided gently. Gay strained upwards against the ropes and found that he could breathe again. His ears cleared and he heard the sobs of the storm above him. The next lunge of the ship seemed almost hospitable.

He was sore, tired and impossibly cold. The noise from the wind was not so great, but the ship still lifted violently and flew, half-sideways, until it hit a block of water. The ropes had stretched and each time the vessel stuck fast the shock lifted Gay on to the wooden edge of the bunk. His back was a long ridge of agony; his shoulders were scratched and bloodied by a continuous scraping against the wall.

The ropes loosened and travelled several inches up and down his body, chafing at raw skin. Gay developed a fear that he might fall asleep and be hanged.

He freed his legs, the rest was accidental, for he could not hold himself against a downward swoop of the ship and was thrown into a freezing slop of salt water. He picked himself up and immediately ran headlong into the bunkpost, to which he clung. He could see nothing. He felt a fury of sadness at his own impotence and wretchedness. The ship swung and the water rushed up to his knees. His anger rose. He slid back to the far wall. He strained upwards for the door handle, and when the ship swung the door fell open and Gay looked into the salon.

There were pale grey points of light at the level of the water. Blackness arrived with a salvo of clangs, and then slits of sickly grey opened on the other side of the ship. At the same time a fountain of water poured down the hatchway steps and boiled around the benches. There was no other sign of life in the salon. The berths were all curtained off. The salon was desolate.

68

And then Gay understood. The sea had not trapped him. He had nearly drowned because *he* had trapped the sea.

When the boat tipped, he clawed his way back up the slippery floorboards and undid the latch at the base of the stateroom port.

CHAPTER ELEVEN

Safe Havens – Mister Van der Hertz's Business – Edmond Refuses to Be Cosseted

'And so let us give thanks for our deliverance. Let us be mindful of His works. Let our hearts rejoice. Let our voices sing out in His praise.'

Rennah Wells had been badly thrown about, Mister Cox had had many splinters of glass removed from his face. The Reverend had taken a severe chill, and there was an edge of outrage to his singing. The *Moravagine* herself was obliged to put into the port of Horta, on the island of Faial.

From within his ropes, Edmond had observed that the Reverend was not amongst those who applied themselves to clearing the debris in the salon. Furthermore, his wife seemed to have exhausted her inclination to play nursemaid and so the Reverend enrolled any spare passenger to listen to his woes. Edmond had spareness to spare. The Reverend spoke with dignity, but the subject of his speech was always himself. Edmond was greatly relieved when the *Moravagine* berthed and he could finally insist that his own ropes be untied. In truth he felt better and more cheerful than at any time on the ship.

Gay attributed this to the mysterious mesmery of the Frenchman; Edmond preferred to believe in the skills of the cook. But, having all his life hated bodies of water, Edmond was most delighted that he had managed to resist perhaps the worst that an ocean might throw at him. His daughter Lizzie would be proud of him when the tale came to be told; he was quietly proud of himself. And happy to be out of his gloomy stateroom. And would be happier still to put a foot on dry land.

Edmond thought it quite unnecessary for Gay and Schultz to carry him up to the deck. His leg was not strong, but he felt that everything was in its right place and would work quite well with slow exercise. He told Gay as much, and said that he did not wish to be swaddled. But when he loosened his hold on Schultz's shoulder he found that he could not support himself. His leg was painful but capable of withstanding his weight; it was the weakness in his back which undid him. Schultz ducked his shoulder under Edmond's arm.

'We have only to get across the quay,' Gay encouraged. 'There is a rooming house. All the passengers will stay there.'

Edmond looked across at a picturesque two-storey building set back from the waterfront, white and welcoming, sunlit. He was unused to the sun, his eyelids fell; he turned away and had difficulty in raising them again. When he did so, he was not sure that he hadn't fallen victim to some blindness or illusion, for the sea on the other side of the *Moravagine* was a deep crimson colour. He asked Gay to verify the impression.

'It is blood,' said Gay. 'They are butchering the whales on the other side of the bay.'

Edmond said, 'I am not going to stay in a room from which I can see nothing but blood. And what is that noise?'

'There are large gluttonous fish which feed on the gore. They are sometimes so maddened by their lusts that they tear each other apart.'

'No person in their right senses could wish to witness such an abhorrence.'

Schultz had visited the islands before and found some alternative lodgings at the Estalagem, which was situated beneath the fort and which gave a delightful prospect across the straits to the neighbouring island of Pico. Their clothes and bedding were brought ashore to be washed; the ship's holds were opened for them to draw on their luggage, all of which had also to be rinsed free of the effects of the storm which had intruded willy-nilly on all parts of the ship. Schultz warned Gay that their engraving plates would have been corroded by the salt. 'Look at us!' Gay burst out at Edmond in misery. 'Look at me! We have nothing, except for your stupid vanity and my stupid pride. We have nothing at all.'

Hardly encouraging was the conversation at dinner. Schultz returned from the *Moravagine* with the news that there was a problem about the cargo. The Portland cement in the stern hold had absorbed water and become solid. It had quadrupled in weight and could not be moved. The ship slanted noticeably. Captain Foster had never before encountered such a problem and was in two minds about the advisability of putting to sea with so much weight and at such a strange

71

angle of advance. The crew were labouring at the problem and the passengers would be sent for when the Captain was satisfied.

Edmond's door was open. He was lying on his bed, facing the window. As Gay watched, Edmond lifted each leg, in turn, out in front of him. He repeated the exercise several times, without any apparent difficulty. When Gay stood beside him he noticed that Edmond was quite pale, his brow furrowed with exertion or pain which he could only mask with difficulty. Edmond jigged his foot across the mattress. 'Agile of foot and spirit,' he announced.

'Edmond, should you not think about returning home?'

'I have thought about it, and I have decided against it. If I do not appear on that stage, John, then neither will you. They will not have you. That is the truth of the matter.'

'Should *we* not think then about returning home?'

'No, we should not. Thinking is not your greatest talent – '

'Be serious, Edmond.'

'Very well. I am certain that my leg will mend, and I have no intention of going back to London with my tail tucked between my mended legs.'

'And your back?'

'I will find out in New York.'

'Mister Van der Hertz, I have no wish to argue with you but I will tell you plainly that Mister Schultz is not a coward. In fact,' Edmond considered, 'he is someone in whom I would trust.'

Van der Hertz nodded. 'It is a great pity that the one action of fleeing his ship at Copenhagen should be enough to brand him as a coward.'

'But for that he has served in prison! And then to be ostracised in his own country!'

'Men will always seize on a weakness and take it as a mark of character.'

'It is fortunate that women do not judge in the same foolish way.'

'Doubly unfortunate then for Lieutenant Schultz that his wife should leave him.'

'She must think of her security.'

'Quite so.' Van der Hertz did not show much expression. He was, thought Edmond, quite impenetrable. He was most amiable, most

72

unperturbable, most correct without being meticulous or mannered, most disarming without any forfeit to his own composure. But that heavy, tragic-looking mustache. So very unfashionable.

'And what of your own romantic nature, Mister Van der Hertz? That should be a part of a man's nature, so I am told by Lord Byron.'

'Yes, I like the game, when it is played fully by both people. But I do not like afterwards, the compromise. It is not my intention to catch or to be caught.'

'Ah, how very clever. For what we are saying is that we do not want to commit our affections. And yet a woman knows no other way.'

Van der Hertz agreed with him. But they had misunderstood each other. Van der Hertz described it as incomprehensible that a woman should see no other way with a man than to get him to commit himself to her. Such a demanding attitude came only from a woman's fear, and such a fear was limitless, and it would almost certainly provoke her defeat. 'Would that not often be the case?' he hazarded. 'Might not a woman bear a man a child merely to force him to prove his sense of responsibility towards her?'

Edmond's blood rose. 'Such conceptions may happen entirely by accident. And then what is she to do?'

'There need be no accident,' Van der Hertz decreed. 'There will have been either stupidity, or calculation, or the surrender to an instinct which the man might not have shared.'

'Might I suggest to you that you have conveniently ignored the animal nature of man?'

'I have allowed for such a nature.'

'Then you are more capable of controlling yourself than any man I have met.'

He shrugged. 'I am not such a libertine; this is true. But you must allow that it is quite possible for a woman to be safe from the chance of conception.'

'With sponges and eelskins and such rigmarole, or with such constant attention to her lover that the act of love becomes only a mechanical slavery, at times exceedingly painful. No. What is demanded of *us* is devotion, and worry, and responsibility. And that is what is supposed to shape us from the bed to the grave. Even in the act of love *we* must keep our wits about us.'

'And that, my friend, is why I make romance my business.'

Word came that they were to board the *Moravagine* before nightfall, so that the ship might catch an early tide. Edmond found himself alone with Van der Hertz, who helped him hobble towards the quayside while Gay went on ahead to ascertain that their baggage was put safely aboard. Edmond had no further interest in mysterious conversation.

'What, then, is your business?'

'It is quite possible,' Van der Hertz replied immediately, 'to insert a cup, or cap, within the female vagina, and this would prevent the male seed from achieving conception. With a simple accustoming the article may be removed at will, causing little discomfort.'

He held out a piece of flimsy, light brown – what? Edmond supposed that it might be a fabric or newly lifeless skin.

'It is horrible to touch, and it is not pretty,' Edmond decided.

'But this rubber is strong and it stretches, and it harbours less disease than eelskin or pig-gut. It can be washed and worn many times.'

'And that is what you are taking to the Americas?'

'Indeed.'

'It is quite outrageous.'

Van der Hertz nodded seriously. 'I think so. Too much so for my own country.'

'But not for your own women.'

'On the contrary. They are the more practical and inquisitive sex.'

Edmond was aware of feeling rather ridiculous, standing on the quay next to the bustle of porters and seamen with a piece of rubber held between forefinger and thumb. He felt a little sorry for Van der Hertz, for he could not imagine how he might introduce his invention to the female sex other than by bedding a considerable percentage of the population, which would seem to involve a dismaying investment of time, money and effort.

Edmond handed him back his piece of material, and hobbled towards the *Moravagine*.

Mister Philip Cox had elected to stay on the islands, which provided soil good enough for the cultivation of his apples. The Reverend Venn was still not fully recovered but grasped heroically at the divine plan which commanded him to Boston. Mister Wells had drawn, James and Francis had remained entrenched. Edmond's heart sank. It was singularly depressing to see them all again, although Madame Chenevix had achieved an even more ethereal pallor by tightening her stays. Schultz went to see the ship's mate because the ship itself appeared not at all inclined towards the correct position for gliding horizontally across a surface of water.

CHAPTER TWELVE

Ailments – And on – Cultural Pursuits – And on

They put out at eight in the morning. Rather:

The ship dragged itself away from the island, chaperoned by two whalers in case the temptation for it to sink down into the bloody underworld became too great.

All day the passengers stood on deck, ready to abandon their sullen vessel which was by now built as much of hardened cement as of wood. It could not be said that the *Moravagine* sailed; she merely opted to use sail in order to move, taking what little breeze there was in the manner of an obese invalid waving a pocketful of white handkerchieves in order to attract the attention of a passer-by. Every time the ship's hourly bell sounded, Edmond roared, 'Another bell, another furlong. Nothing can stop us now.'

But Edmond's humour failed when at noon the next day the two whalers altered course and tiptoed southwards, leaving the *Moravagine* to waddle like a graceless débutante across the polished sea towards the new world.

It was tedious. My Lord, it was unutterably tedious. The tedium defied description. The monotony of the limp breeze. The great volumes of meat which were eaten. The listlessness of the passengers. The dull flat heat. Day after day after day.

They came together as a group for prayers each evening at six. The singing of hymns had died away but the Reverend Venn sermonised with some ingenuity, having a great repertoire of insights into the failings of mankind and their spiritual remedies. Gay did not concern himself with overmuch moral investigation but he appreciated the man's calm voice as it bolstered the creaking music of the ship's timbers. The Reverend Venn achieved a better state of health when the word of God was allowed to pass through his windpipe rather than being locked up within his breast.

His balm, though, could not salve the physical ailments. Rennah's legs and Gay's shoulders refused to heal. Their cuts and scratches swelled and split open without bleeding. On land the healing had progressed a little, but after four days at sea Gay could no longer bear to wear anything against his enflamed and raw flesh and was obliged to keep to the stateroom, either sitting or lying face down on his bunk.

There was a pair of wolfhounds travelling with the diminished contingent of sires on the lower middle deck; large, grey hunting dogs of magnificent proportion and dignity. Schultz claimed that there was a great healing power in the saliva of dogs. Wells had never heard of such a thing, but his ridicule was silenced by Schultz's description of ankle-chafe in a Danish prison. Schultz swore that a regular cleansing by the guard's dog had saved his ability to walk; and he repeated this assurance to Gay whose cuts, he said, would perhaps never harden in a state of constant exposure to salt humidity. Schultz obtained permission from the mate to walk the wolfhounds around the deck each morning, and he then brought them to the passengers' quarters and had them thoroughly tongue the open sores. Thus Gay came to be bathed daily by the spongy, pink tongues of the wolfhounds, a luxuriously strange sensation and one which revisited him over many years in any number of pleasing dreams.

Less luxurious, and considerably more odorous, was the layer of pig grease which Gay applied afterwards to seal his flesh. The healing, though, was remarkably quick; for which Gay was grateful, as he had begun to attract the attention of unnaturally large ants whose numbers below deck multiplied as the temperatures above deck climbed.

The ants horrified Madame Béatrice Chenevix. Gay did not really notice them unless she visited the salon, and then on seeing – on *feeling* – her repulsion, he was made aware of the dozens of probing, scampering, fiddling creatures; and then he saw with Madame Béatrice's eyes that no part of the room was ever still. When she shut herself away with her husband, Gay was no longer disturbed and could not make up his mind whether indeed the ants were not a blessing for their provision of some entertainment to relieve the insufferable boredom of this second part of the voyage.

The ants provoked a marvellous exhibition in the art of futile outrage from Rennah Wells, who set himself up to slaughter as many of the insects as possible and frequently used more force per capita than he would have needed to kill a chicken. During the course of his campaign he manufactured many ingenious instruments, viz: a sucking bellows; a miniature fire-mat; a tube for propelling leeches through the air; a grease-portalled salt chamber. Rennah was assuredly vigilant. When the sporting instinct deserted him – dehydrating an ant requiring 'hardly as much skill as scalping a papist' (M. and Mme Chenevix to bed previous) – Rennah delighted in smacking the palm of his hand explosively against table, bunkpost, bench and ceiling, or rolling the pad of his forefinger on the same, much pleased with his tamp of authority and the little mush of death on his skin.

But it was his dedication which impressed Gay – neither favourably nor unfavourably. The man became totally absorbed in his vocation. He had failed, not miserably, to establish himself as the salon artist. Now he plunged himself into retribution and was happily sanctified through the provision of useful office to the Reverend and Missis Venn. They were not fond of tiny impediments to the rapture which might be induced by the evening sermon, and they bestowed a modicum of respectability upon Rennah by turning a deaf ear and a blind eye to the slamming fists and corkscrewing fingers of the happy reaper.

'We shall', said Edmond, 'become utterly senseless.'

It became so hot that the passengers obtained permission to promenade in the late afternoon, when the sun settled like a red yolk ahead of the prow and the deck lay in shadow. The aft hatchway was thrown open, and as the air cooled so the sailors started to chip away at the hardened cement. It was a slow and unyielding task, as they did not have the right tools, and no sooner had they pierced the crust than the air increased the density and reluctance of what lay underneath. Listening to the tempo of the blows, Schultz concluded that there was but a token effort being made to clear the ship. It would be simpler to wait until they reached New York and then beach the *Moravagine* like a turtle to cut away its gigantic egg. It would be simpler still to beach the old barque, to strip out the masts and the insurance payment, and let it rot. Whereupon, Schultz decided, he might himself purchase the skeleton for very little money and supervise its repair.

Edmond borrowed a book from Van der Hertz and took it to his bunk. He was sick and tired of glutting himself on the endless diet of meat. Gay fished for hours and caught nothing.

The *Moravagine* lumbered on through a wrinkled light blue sea. Her passengers succumbed to apathy. Their living quarters hung in silence.

Gay thought, absolutely nothing. He was drained of all thought. He saw a pure white moon, to which he made love, and he was transparent and without substance.

'I have injured the ship,' Gay said brightly. He pointed, and Edmond saw what seemed to be a large mushroom growing from a split in the planking beside the bunkpost. Edmond poked his finger into the mound of thick grey paste.

'Wouldn't you say that these small black things were seeds?'

Gay looked closer and saw that the growth, although a grey colour *en masse*, was in fact a dirty yellow, speckled with dozens or hundreds of black points – none of them as yet with a life of their own.

Gay roused Schultz, who had no idea what the growth might be but observed that the entire surface of the wall behind their bunks was bulging in the most unusual way. Daylight would bring some explanation.

Edmond fell sound asleep but Gay wondered if, by some unique combination of lunar circumstance, he had not perhaps fertilised the *Moravagine*.

The passengers were asked to come up on deck while the crew lifted their belongings out of the forard hatchway. Each man claimed his baggage, which was then carried below into the salon. Several planks had by now burst open in Gay's cabin and the wall was oozing great blobs of stiffish mulch. A foul smell of fermentation was spreading through the passengers' quarters.

When the crew had hauled Mister Van der Hertz's cargo up to the deck, the mate reported that the cases containing the parts of the fire-

79

engine were seen to rise from their level. As if, relayed Rennah who had craned over the mate's shoulder, some monster was stirring in the depths of the hold, resentful of the weight which had crushed it.

'A literate monster,' Edmond announced from the door to the stateroom. 'It is a monster of letters, apparently.' He held out a handful of ooze. 'Unless I am much mistaken, these are not seeds but printed letters.'

It was true. In the forard hold the books were rising. They had drunk deeply at the storm and were now expanding in the warm humidity, forcing their way upwards in a pulp of prose. The complete reports of the British Chancery 1818–1828 swelled proudly. Tomes thrust. Almanacks strained. Novels flounced. And, in the vanguard, several thousand copies of the moral addresses authored by the Reverend Edward Venn had been disembowelled and were dying a mangled death, the gore of which had crusaded into Edmond's stateroom.

It was indecent.

Edmond was enormously amused by such a spreading of the Word. 'Where there is sin, there shall ye seek it out.' He smeared a gob of holy paste across the lintel.

'Hush,' Gay beseeched him.

They went up on deck, where the good Reverend was being comforted by Missis Venn as his sentences were shovelled into the ocean. It took the crew an hour or so to dig down to the level of Gay's stateroom, and the carpenter did not manage to repair the wall before luncheon. There was some discussion about refilling the hold, although it was obvious that the books would not ever submit. If they were denied their levitation, might they not then exert themselves laterally, pressing open the side of the ship?

Once the Reverend had retired to brood over his loss there was a great deal of merriment on deck, which entirely failed to amuse Captain Foster.

'That man,' said Edmond, 'is incapable of raising the corners of his mouth.'

'But he has a problem,' Schultz warned. 'The front of his ship is rising, while the stern is sinking. There is nothing that he can do about it. You will see', Schultz leaned over the rail and pointed aft, 'that there are three ports closed.'

'But they are above the level of the water.'

'In a sea they would not be so.'

'The water would come in.'

'No. They are certainly sealed. That is not his fear. But one week ago only two ports were shut, and so we can see that the stern has gone down in the water.'

'We are sinking then,' Gay deduced.

'Half sinking, half rising. And the degree of our unbalance will continue to rise.'

'As if we were not already lunatic.' Edmond was absurdly cheerful.

'But what will happen?' asked Gay.

Schultz shrugged. 'I do not know. But the reason that we are feeding better than on any other ship is because the Captain has sealed the ports, and the animals are dying because they have no air.'

'The horses.'

'Yes. It is better perhaps to preserve this knowledge from Missis Venn. The Madame is French, and besides she does not seem to eat.'

'She takes a great amount of paregoric elixir,' Edmond advised. 'She suffers from the migraine. Her husband is a fool. He believes that there is a fault in her mind. Whereas she is merely a night creature. His one aim is to animate her, but unfortunately she hates the light.'

'What?' Gay was caught off-guard by Edmond's gibberish. 'Have you spoken to her?'

'No,' Edmond grinned. 'This is a fiction on my part; one of many fictions I invent concerning Madame Chenevix. It helps to while away the time, at least until I am confronted by the necessity of learning how to swim.'

Schultz pursed his lips. 'This may not be necessary. It cannot be very long until we shall see land.'

'In any case,' Edmond continued, 'I would think about the art of swimming for no more than a minute, and by then I would have drowned. I imagine that swimming does not reward much mental application; unlike Madame Chenevix, in whom I could happily drown.'

Gay smiled; Schultz considered whether or not Edmond was mad.

The Catechisms, the Evidences, the Comments, the Meditations and the Refutations: by that evening a little more of the Reverend Venn's oeuvre had risen to the level of the hatchway and was pitchforked over the side of the *Moravagine*, where it spread like a trail of dough behind the ship.

Edmond walked as often and as far as he might, observing the continuous regurgitation from the hold. By the next day, the hold was leeched of Vennery and Edmond came across *Staircases and Handrails* by P. Nicholson, *The Upholsterer's Accelerator* by T. King, *Hints on Manures* by Lupture and *Maids, their Varieties* from the Old Arm Chair publishing house. Edmond read *Sea Weeds and Other Poems* by R. Robertson. He perused *Rectum Stricture* by E. Jukes and threw out *Remarks on Creosote* by J. R. Cormack. On the next day Edmond decided that Powell's *Undulatory Theory of Light* could not be dramatically rendered, but this sabbath ended pleasantly enough with C. J. Napier's *Remarks on Military Flogging*.

The following day dawned with Mister R. MacGhee's *The Nullity of Government in Ireland*, which hardly merited much attention. When Edmond found himself stuck for choice between *The Family Dyer and Scourer* and Wright's *Addresses to Persons Afflicted with Deafness*, he went below and ordered John to sit with him through a reading of *Mother Goose*.

Yet another serving of horse and crushed barley interrupted their diversions. Edmond winced at the pain in his back as he pulled himself off the sofa. He smiled at James Trench, who had emerged to collect the brothers' private peckings. God keep me safe, Edmond prayed; may God protect Lizzie and Ann and keep them alive and well and happy; and let God fetch this wretched ship to New York.

They were not far north of the Indies. Five ports were sealed and the *Moravagine* slanted gravely, her stern ponderous and her prow straining upward like the nose of a swimming dog.

They no longer moved. There was a tense dearth of wind, the atmosphere pressing heavy and hot. All around the ship the water was a piercing light blue, a luminously radiant satin. It was as though heaven and ocean had been turned upside down and the ship become glued to the ether. Crew and passengers stood about the deck, bottling their agitation and staring in disbelief at the great black fortress of cloud which loomed across the midday sky. The Maggot summoned every last iota of power, and Gay stretched out his arms and somersaulted.

At which, Rennah Wells licked his lips.

CHAPTER THIRTEEN

New York: Edmond Reports to Ann

REMARKABLE CIRCUMSTANCE, Tuesday last. – The ship *Moravagine*, out of London on October 15th, having suffered greatly in the gales off our southernmost coasts, was feared to be in great danger of sinking. Being loth to lose his ship, Captain Foster of the *Moravagine* steered her as far upriver as he might until the unusual amount of drift ice compelled him to beach the vessel before she broke up. Such a feat was managed *without a single loss of life*, and was the more remarkable for being accomplished without the aid of the Insurance Companies' relief schooner *President* which had been sent out on the previous evening to search for the stricken ship.

'A slight odour of rat.' Edmond folded the *Gazette*.

The tempest had slid quietly away to the west and the *Moravagine* had been no more damaged than when it had left the Azores. Book-ridden, cement-struck, diminished in horsepower, the tilted ship had at last wallowed into the Hudson River and dropped anchor off New York Island on the first of December.

A pre-dawn wind shrieked through the spars, the ship was covered from stern to prow in a thin rind of ice. Three passengers were rowed ashored in the yawl: Van der Hertz, to arrange for rapid accommodation of the passengers and the transfer of his cargo; Schultz, to ascertain and to report back to the Captain on the whereabouts of the shipping and insurance agents; and Gay, who so utterly hated the ship and the passengers that he insisted on leaving them at the earliest opportunity.

By noon, Schultz had engineered a temporary docking of the *Moravagine*. Van der Hertz and Venns were safely transferred to the Boston packet, and the other passengers were disembarked and lodged.

The *Moravagine* then put out again and sloped northwards, and Edmond sat in the Customs House at the Battery waiting for Gay.

'It doesn't matter,' said Edmond. 'Let us get to where we are going; let us get as far away from this . . . this *water* as we can.'

'I had no idea', said Gay 'that the ship would be fetched in so early. Where is it now?'

'Out again,' said Edmond. 'Nothing has ever moved that vessel so fast as a decent gust of chicanery.'

The *Moravagine* did indeed break up. Its disintegration was carefully supervised by Schultz, its bones were stored through the wet spring, its innards left to rot. Until all that remained was a rock-hard tombstone on the side of the Hudson River, with morsels of Christian verbiage leafing the undergrowth and judicial summaries paving the shoreline.

December 15th.

My dearest Ann,

You cannot possibly imagine my great joy at receiving your letter. There is no voice on earth I have more longed to hear, other than the untutored cries of my own Elisabeth which rebuke me many times each day. I cannot thank you enough for your trouble and your care in keeping watch over her well-being; discovering her as it were without being uncovered. She touches me at every turn and I am so utterly unable to reach her. My words have no meaning for her, my thoughts are stretched uselessly thin across the distance. Even my prayers are blown hither and thither, and scatter themselves God knows where. I have never felt so dismally misdirected, and I finished by reaching far inside myself for any small cry of love that I can find and willing it a safe voyage back to England.

And at last I am answered by your letter, and I am selfishly and gloriously happy. I must indeed be a most selfish man for I have thought it impossible that my infant should survive and grow without me. The very strangest emotion is that peculiar mixture of bitterness and pride at your assurance that she does so well in my absence. I did expect that time would stand still, that *our* time would stand still. For myself I have felt a lifetime of dark stillness these past two months. And now I fear that when I will return to rush the many wasted hours and days into one great burst of love, Elisabeth will look at me in a frightened way and will run in terror to beseech her mother for comfort and will plead 'Who is that man?' and 'What has he to do with me?'

As indeed, my dearest Ann, you yourself might ask.

I cannot explain. I cannot, without an overwhelming sense of dishonesty, listen to my own explainings any longer. I can say that you hold my heart, but the words lie flat and will not move. I do not know why we behaved so foolishly in London, and in such a way for so long. Our dishonesty was in itself so dishonest. I regret bitterly such a waste and I yearn for just one of our moments together. I have laid bare a pure stream of longing within myself. I am clear. I must be with you. What little there is of me must be with you, *is* with you. Or I must again cover myself up and be nothing but a pure actor. I love you. The words lie flat. They cannot move; and I do not want to move you, I would be ashamed to do so. The best that I can hope for is that you will understand what I know, and I am shamefully aware that this is as much to ask of you as it is to ask of Elisabeth her trust in me.

I suppose that, as I must approach her with caution and respect and a gaudy bauble to dangle between our eyes, so I must contain my tears in front of you and entertain you with a report of your kin and his company. How strange it is that you survey my daughter while I survey your brother.

I have already described a little of the sea journey to you and I cannot bring myself to recount any more. I would be a fool to preserve that unpleasantness in my thoughts when I will before very long be obliged to muster the resolution for the return voyage. Suffice it to say the obvious: we are off the wretched ship! We have survived!

And we have outlived the ship itself. She – I hesitate to ennoble that sluggard tub – *it* has been classed as a wreck and has passed on into the grave, shrouded in the mysteries of a devious claim on the pockets of the insurance company. I enclose a paragraph from the newspaper. The story is swallowed but not comfortably digested. It is however a tale of loyalty, for as I understand the matter the mate would have been held responsible for a thoughtless arrangement of the cargo, whereas now both Captain and crew have emerged with flying colours, albeit without a mast from which to fly them.

We were put ashore most stealthily, and such was the extent of our relief that nobody cared a jot for the fate – factual or fictional – of the *Moravagine*. Indeed we all burst ashore and scattered immediately in different directions as though in an explosion of antipathy for each other. There was a remarkable lack of farewells and absolutely no exchange of addresses. Never have so many unhappy attachments been dissolved so painlessly.

John had been put ashore earlier to arrange for our accommodation and so, needless to say, we were the last to be accommodated; and that due more to the capabilities of Missis Hamblin than to any rigorous scouting from the Harlequin, who had from the smell of his breath spent most of the morning drinking and dossing in a cellar bar, although he claimed to have been seized by astonishment at the coldness of the wind and the fierce blueness of the sky and the hollering style of every possible extravagance that might be found in America, and he assured me that he immediately *had* the tone of the society to be found on the Island of New York. There was a battle of chemistry between his rhapsodic wax and my own vitriol, which might never have ended were it not for the discretion of Missis Hamblin in reserving us rooms in the Broad Street Hotel; very pleasant rooms, although quite unnecessarily expensive for our purpose which was solely to indulge ourselves in sweet and lengthy sleep.

John was right in one sense at least. You can have no idea of the penetration of the cold wind in this city. It is shocking and persistent. It is a great leveller and makes the city quite barren. I have never before experienced such extremes of climate. I have in the last weeks been plunged into fog, icy water, dry and roasting inferno, and now this chill abrasion. I feel like a pinch of some ingredient in a savage recipe. I have been hung, salted, dropped, doused, evaporated, swilled, pummelled, seasoned, doused again, grilled and chilled and now pegged out like the skin of an old rabbit.

We were visited by Tom Hamblin on the first evening, when we were quite in a daze of exhaustion and still inclined to roll from one foot to the other. He is the most solid man and was not at all struck by the fact of our arrival in New York. He has in his time imported many actors from London and I have no doubt that he greets each one with the same bemused air, as if a little stream had deposited a pleasant surprise on his doorstep. We were, of course, quite ungrounded and keen to leap in whatever direction he proposed. It was somewhat disconcerting to observe that he had no proposal whatsoever, and he sat for a long while as though deliberating whether or not to throw us back into the sea. I brought him a little rudely to the question when we should open with the *Goose*, and he straightway announced for the twenty-sixth of December. Contrary to appearances, he knew exactly what he was doing, and I realised that I was a fool not to take account of our being in *his* city, in *his* country and in *his* theatre; so who would know better than he?

I apologised for having so condescended to him; he took the apology in fine heart and showed great consideration for our insecurities in promising that he would do his utmost to ensure that we would obtain a good audience. He had, he warned, yet to plot his campaign for imposing upon the town the significance of the art of pantomime.

The word 'significance' much impressed John, as did Hamblin's remarks on the need to educate the populace of New York. On occasions I feel that John's idea of the perfect audience would be to look out and see a hundred ranks of serried imbeciles marshalled to attention in front of him, their mouths gaping in admiration, their souls coagulating in a perfumed cloud just above the footlights. I don't know that John ever *considers* anything, least of all himself, but he continues to hold faith in himself as a revelation. It is quite strange. It may be a conceit, but he is not at all vain. If he has adopted an attitude of vanity it is only borrowed from my own character. He has absolutely no sense of the mundanity, the compromise, the falseness of the theatre – and he is extraordinarily irksome in his innocence.

'Well,' said I to Hamblin, perceiving the customary managerial problem to be but slightly hidden behind an insignificant significance. 'Well, sir; in my experience as a pearl I have been cast in front of many a swine. Given that they are somehow herded into the theatre, the matter of impressing them is up to us. Pigs, I understand, are reluctant to go downhill, and so we should be uphill. Perhaps you might issue to the newspapers an elevating history of our heroic rescue from the *Moravagine*. Courage, danger, feats of this and that; I am certain that we will attract an inquisitive audience.'

Hamblin guffawed and said that he would see what he might do.

Well, my dear Ann, every other mouth was intending to take a bite off that miserable barque. There was no reason why we should not attempt to do the same. Significance fits well into an obituary, but funerals only ever achieve popular attendance because the spectator has no need to purchase a ticket.

I need have no conscience about this unworthy pursuit of heroism, for Hamblin did nothing.

It has taken me quite some time to understand his, and our, quandary. And I cannot say that we are yet out of the darkness, nor that we are destined to take the lights.

John's estimation of his own significance fitted quite well with his appreciation of the Broad Street Hotel. I persuaded him of the foolishness of spending our money so wastefully.

On Hamblin's advice we decamped firstly to the house owned by a Missis Tidswell. Presumably Hamblin judged that we would all share her Englishness. Quite frankly, this Missis Tidswell was a vile and vulgar slattern of a woman who revelled in such imaginings of status as she could never have expected in Cheapside. She presided over the most grotesque hen coop I have ever had the misfortune to visit. She was disgustingly mannered and overwhelmingly persistent in her feeble opinions. I cannot find the insults to describe her daughters. There was but one parlour, into which we were invited on the first – and only – evening, and where we were subjected to an impertinent Tidswellogue on the subject of what was considered to be genteel in New York. John and I were invited to 'sit and take a long nine, as my speshul gemtlemen wiwl do'. Heaven knows what a 'long nine' might be, and it must have been a great many years since the Tidswell trollop had received as much as a 'short three', unless from someone genteel enough to push her head into a trough and have at her from behind in generous darkness.

John and I opted for the freezing air and a brisk walkaway in any direction whatsoever. Finally to the corner of Greenwich and Dey Streets. John caught sight of an advertisement for lodgings. Next morning our fleeing to Miss Manley's Boarding House. From where I now write.

There is something not at all in place along my back. I can sit only for short periods.

I must not dawdle. We are into rehearsals and so I snatch my precious solitude late at night. There has been little of note.

I am the world's most impoverished appreciator, and, whether it is because of the continuing cold wind or whether I have no interest in this town, I have noticed very little which might claim your attention. It is in general a consolation to me to feel that I am only here in order to work. I have no desire to pry into the habits and customs of the peoples.

As soon as we were settled we entertained Tom and Mary Hamblin and those half dozen American actors who are to make up the 'starring' company for *Mother Goose*. Miss Manley arranged for a large platter of spiced beef ribs and herself undertook a selection of baked pies and biscuits.

'I cannot bear these formal dinners,' John said. 'I do not care to be spirited and gracious. They are impossibly foolish.'

At which I informed him that we had travelled a great many miles in order to drag with us an old pantomime from a country where that entertainment was dying as surely as Joe Grimaldi; that our success depended solely on our ability to fool the Americans; and that the two of us both being second-rate imitators, we had better be prepared to do whatsoever was necessary to avoid being exposed as such.

I must say that we entertained quite capably, and were not called upon for any grand performance. With the Hamblins came Miss Elizabeth Jarvis and Misters William Rudd, George Downie, Peter Delaunay and Louis Cascarino – all with warm hearts and the greatest respect for us imitators. There was no semblance of the constrained London dinner party. In New York a great deal is drunk before dinner and the food is sampled carelessly. There is a much greater appetite for news of the London theatre, and a much greater desire to come to some immediate grounds on which to base a friendship. The conversation is unguarded and devoid of that supercilious examination which, in London, is supposed to establish one's membership of some clique or other. In short, the dialogue is fearless and without ironies. It is not a suitable setting for wit or disparagement and so I conducted myself somewhat authoritatively. John was rather overwhelmed and behaved to his *Times* review of last year, which all the Americans had read. He was considered a great talent, much was expected of him and he easily relinquished the unduly nasty title of second-rate imitator with which I had goaded him forward.

The actors left early as they were all to appear in a light comedy at the Bowery later that night. Hamblin had not discouraged them from drinking. I was surprised at his lack of discipline but they carried their 'Liquor' well, and carried John off with them back to the theatre. Hamblin stayed behind to talk with me.

'They have some prospects,' said Hamblin, 'and fine enthusiasm.'

We might have continued with a pleasant and general conversation until the end of the evening, for he is a cultured man and very steady in his opinions. He is not frantic about anything and talks in the easy manner of a farmer leaning on a gate wth his sown fields sprouting in front of him, almost soporific in his wisdoms.

I mentioned that we should start to rehearse and he, without any hesitation, offered us the stage each morning, and within a week through until four in the afternoon.

The next was a difficult point, as I did not wish to worry him and as I did not know how the matter would stand amongst our terms of contract.

'Who should study for Mister Gay's Harlequin?'

'Is he injured?'

I suggested that we might allow for accidents befalling John, or even myself. 'In that case,' said Hamblin, 'we might say Downie for Parsloe, and Cascarino for Mister Gay.'

He was so amenable that I had by now begun to suspect that something more essential was occupying his worries. I could not think of any problem that we had not touched upon. Hamblin started on a speculation as to what effect the closing of the river through ice would have on the price of foodstuffs and the gathering of news from Europe. I listened intently but could find no hint of how this might lead to his, or our, undoing. Eventually I asked him what concern there might be over the news from Europe.

'Oh,' he said, 'great concern. Or a great show of concern. We are many miles from Europe but we are mostly Europeans, and for lack of any further problem from the natives we fight according to the same ideals and national antipathies as the Europeans do.'

'And what is your concern?' I asked.

'Well, Edmond, my concern is simply that you are English.' I did not at all understand, and he elaborated wearily. 'A year ago your nationality would have been to your advantage, but right now there is a strong feeling against the English. You see that it is not shared by the actors, but it is in the streets and so it is in my theatre.'

'In the Bowery Theater?'

'The *American* Theater in the Bowery.'

So this was why Hamblin had not announced our arrival in New York.

You cannot imagine, Ann, what a perplexity I felt at this news. Having not so very long ago pursued a Christian war against the tyranny of Bonaparte, having exported to this country what little civilisation it possesses and whatever inventions the industrious English mind has perfected, we are now detested. I am quite prepared to believe that the lobsterish element of our society provokes some scorn and resentment, but this is not infrequent within our own land. I am prepared to encounter with some sympathy a revulsion for the crass, self-opinionated, imperious Englishman, but to extend this hatred blindly towards a whole race is undeniably insensitive to the many colours which enrich our people. The English have a great sense of self-mockery; there can be nothing in them which the rest of the world despises that has not already been quite well enough despised by the English themselves. Above all, it appears that it is the wretched Irish who have taken upon themselves the easy scramble towards the moral heights, upon which they now jump up and down in the most primitive, tribal, stupidity. Daubing themselves American they safely vent their spleen on English actors – that is to say, on English-men who are playing at being English. What on earth has an actor to do with his race?

I am angered and shocked to be held in question simply because I am English. I have never heard of such a thing.

Hamblin did his best to contain my outrage by pointing out that there was very little difference between the behaviour of the New York 'Rowdies' and our own pit-mobs at home. It was, he said, a strange compliment to the actors that they should be taken so seriously and that the theatre should become a forum for debate on the growth of a nation rather than a mere poultice which absorbed the excrescences from a settled society.

'What would you have us do?' I asked him.

'Why, nothing,' he replied. 'This town, if not the whole country, is ruled by rumour and politics and fashion. If you slide in on a wave then you will go far. If you swim out against it, you'll get buried. I reckon that you should carry on quietly with your rehearsing and not lord it about town. Believe me, there will be a time to be English. Just let me figure it out.'

I did not know what to make of his remarks, but we were quickly furnished with some insight into the state of the New York theatre, which I pass on to you.

John watched the second half of the main bill at the Bowery. The play was called *Whither My Children, or A Settler's Lament*, and it was roundly applauded by a full house. There were apparently gasps of horror when the wife of the embattled settler managed to drop her baby which, John conceded, had some excuse for a wooden performance, it being made of that material. He summarised the play as tedious, excessively sentimental, and acted as though off the back of a cart. The ensuing light comedy was batted across the footlights with a pugnacity that defied belief. It was, said John, like being seated in front of a very drunken bore. The jokes – such as they were – the comic situations, and even the lines were repeated several times; which had not bothered the audience in the slightest. There was a strongly partisan spirit in them that allowed the actors to do as they pleased, which consisted of each one dominating the stage as repetitiously as possible. Their performances were in themselves heroic, and they had been cheered accordingly at the end of the night.

At the end of the night I say, Ann; and hark to this. The theatre closed – as usual – at half past two in the morning! My heart sinks at the prospect of having to keep my eyelids from doing the same, when we are expected to flutter brightly at such a late hour.

Our second experience came on the following evening. Hamblin took a box at the Park Theater, which is in a tense rivalry with the Bowery. The Park Theater makes no bones about its Englishness, and if we are to become a part of this warfare I think that we should have been engaged there rather than in the American Theater.

They had engaged Blanchard to give his Coriolanus.

At his first appearance he was greeted with a disgruntled jeering, which was immediately drowned out by a counter-storm of cheers. His acting was of a high standard but he could hardly compete with the *voces populi*. Poor Coriolanus found himself neglected in every quarter. Those well-dressed members of the audience who might have been expected to offer their attention only treated the theatre as they might have treated their private club, often leaning forward in serious debate amongst themselves for several minutes at a time while Blanchard declaimed and gruffer voices gloried back with shouts of 'Jackson!', 'Jackson!', 'Live Free or Die!', 'Hurrah!', or 'Whose Flag!'

Amidst the chaos, an interval caught everyone by surprise and despite his best intentions Hamblin was noticed. A part of the audience cheered and he decided that it would be best if he left the theatre. The second act was constantly interrupted while a group of male voices bellowed a lusty anthem, and the evening concluded early with a hail of vegetable matter being directed this way and that – more suited to the great storm in *Lear* than to senatorial debate. There was a barging skirmish in the street outside, fists were thrown, and John flailed our way through with his Harlequin stick – the first time I have seen him carry his own character to such lengths.

Shakespeare might well have wished to hold the mirror up to Nature, but could not have counted on an audience being so out of love with their own reflection. Such is the New York theatre.

I did call upon Blanchard some days later at his lodgings, to commiserate with him. He finds the whole matter greatly disheartening, at one extreme comparing himself to Joan of Arc et cetera, at the other deriding Coriolanus for not having the common sense to take the money and run – which he, Blanchard, intends to do at the earliest opportunity permitted by his contract. To this end he has decided that his best interest in the play lies in his being hit hard by a soft vegetable, so that he may claim a violent injury and retire with full payment. He has perfected the art of lunging head first and most dramatically at collyflowers. But unfortunately the glare from the new lights at The Park prevents him from identifying a collyflower until too late in its trajectory. I did think that he had rather exaggerated the raging bull aspect of Coriolanus in his movements, but I now understand that part of a Roman psyche which searches head-down for wounds, all be they from a legion of humble vegetables. By the bye, when he does run Blanchard has promised to play Ariel and carry this letter to you.

And so everybody finds in Shakespeare whatever they wish to find.

He is a great genius. I comfort myself with doubting very much whether the history of a Goose will arouse so many emotions.

You see how I am forced back into cleverness. It is for the lack of an attachment to anything or anyone in this city that I write such nonsense. I have the greatest desire to cut and run, to steal my Elisabeth and persuade you that we might make a home together. Such is my wild presumption. I am not now disturbed by the prospect of 'cutting', but I am forced to admit that the 'running' will be but a gradual business. I have started to rehearse with the American actors, making them familiar with the pantomime; and Hamblin is supervising the construction of some new stage machinery for the tricks and illusions, which cannot hope to be as competent as in London. We will do our best. My back has a mind of its own which I am resolved to subjugate; the complaints are persistent and familiar, but the outcries are sudden and bring on a devil of a sweat. The strength is there but is somehow obstructed. I have therefore delayed any full-blooded exertions, viz. the set pieces with John, until the last possible moment.

Hamblin goes about his own machinations. I must get to my feet. Cannot sit any longer. Anon.

CHAPTER FOURTEEN

Maggot Takes Air

Gay tethered himself to the vacant cellar at Miss Manley's. He was not perturbed by the solitude. The only way to keep himself warm was to exercise, and he undertook any number of far-fetched improvisations in order to woo the silent, ill-lit and frozen chamber.

He was quite unable to seal his mind, however. It engaged him in a ceaseless chatter. He felt uncentred. He could not concentrate his thoughts nor hold to the importance of the Bowery Theater production.

He was dismayed to discover that, after all, he was to perform before mere, coarse people. Even after the voyage he had anticipated something more fundamental in the way of a challenge, something more stark, something demanding a divine precision. In his imaginings he had somehow presumed that there would be, from this stage, no dealings with people.

When he delved into the town of New York he was astonished at the constant hurdy-gurdy of demand. Nothing seemed sacred, nor even substantial. He saw everywhere a concern for self-establishment and in this there was not, nor would be, any interest for him. Unleashed, unclaimed, he was only delayed by these people and this place. The briskness, the worldliness, constrained him within a meaningless excitement. The air was never still, and it thus evaded his challenge.

'If Edmond were not with me,' Gay thought suddenly, 'then I would not stay here. There is more than this.'

He dreamed that Edmond was utterly bodiless. This was in New York where, on a street outside the window, all the other people were ghosts. He chatted easily with Edmond; in fact he quite dominated Edmond, he had not spoken so well of his ideals since he had aired them before Ann.

He awoke with a sickly fear, as though he had just destroyed every bit of trust which Edmond had placed within him for safe-keeping. But he could not help himself. His mind chattered on, offering a strumpetly consolation. Gay slammed his fist against the frame of the bed. In some last half-dream he reasoned that he had chosen to confide in Rennah Wells.

He was exasperated with these flits of his mind. He jumped out of bed, shook Edmond, and assured the hapless sleeper that he would see him home.

'Not just now,' Edmond grumbled. 'Thank you. But later will do.'

CHAPTER FIFTEEN

Edmond Continues his Report: the Moral Tones Set by Peale's Museum
— Mister Rennah Wells Rears his Head

You will be anxious for news of John. Forgive me for chattering on so. He has been left much to his own devices and has quite sealed himself away. He quickly established a refuge in Miss Manley's cellar, and I understood that he exercised there regularly. He seemed to enjoy the anonymity of travelling and is endowed with the naturally adventurous spirit of a vagabond. He is quite often incomprehensible when we meet at the end of the day. He reports New York as 'exhilarating' or 'rootless' or 'elixic' or 'exorbitant' or 'immodest'. There usually follows some small vignette — John is an excellent mimic, although quite unable to give a moral hue to his impressions. He entertains me in the most touching manner, rather as if I were an invalid.

Today John arrived in the early afternoon at the theatre with the news that Grimaldi was performing at a venue called Peale's Museum, that very afternoon. He could hardly restrain himself. He knew very well that it could not possibly be Old Joe, but conjectured that young Joe Grimaldi had established himself in New York — which was merely unlikely. John's enthusiasm however swept away any misgivings. It *would* be young Joe; and we were bound to find invention and experiment and verve. Young Joe was never short of friends or schemes, and he would be well placed to join us in the *Goose*.

I had chipped and chivvied away all morning at our rehearsal, and it had been the most slow business. I admit that my own heart grasped at John's excitement.

By the time we had arrived at Peale's Museum, John had of course lost the tickets. But he claimed that he had an acquaintance with the manager and went off to explain our mishap, leaving me to peruse the programme which was mounted on a board in front of the building. 'Old Joe Grimaldi' was well announced, alongside 'Mister Sutton and

Others', 'Calvin Edson, The Living Skeleton', and 'The Anaconda'. Only young Joe could have found himself in such company. Some weight lifted from my mind, as I was having little success with George Downie, whose comic sense and timing were more disastrous than young Joe's worst gin-sodden flailings. My own eyes wandered to the reverse of the advertisement and I was amused to see announced: 'At six in the evening, before a private audience, Monsieur Pierre Chenevix from the French Academy of Sciences'. The spell-binder from the *Moravagine*! What a hatchery this Peale's Museum must be!

It was a most shabby place. The seats were arranged in tiers, cheaply mounted on exposed wooden poles. There was but a quartet of musicians between us and the stage. The matinay audience was a motley crew, lounging over the empty seats, looking for the most part as though they had paid to escape the cold rather than for the privilege of witnessing a theatrical performance.

There was no overture. The orchestra struck up a merry tune and a number of glum women danced on to the stage, scattering themselves so as to give the impression of fully occupying the boards. They were jaded, badly painted, hollow-eyed and hardly capable of any animation. Like a troupe of malnourished cygnets they pranced half-heartedly in some wearily woven formula of sidestep, backstep, leg-cocking caper. Set against the effervescent jig played nonchalantly by the musicians, the effect was tragic, if not downright comic. I was hard pressed not to hoot with laughter, but this would have disturbed the equally gloomy appreciations of the audience, who sat with the most demeaning and forlorn aspects of lust glazing their faces.

I have never been much enthralled by ventriloquism, and such was the next 'turn'. Mister Sutton was quite capable of 'othering' the house and supplying the members of the audience with the most obvious secret thoughts, which occasioned a vulgar laughter. He performed best, during the final moments of his display, with his last dumbie.

This was a shrunken and emaciated object which supposed to impersonate a man of fifty or thereabouts, and which had been constructed, in the poorest taste, without arms or legs. This ugly-headed torso was given the most witty repartee and was constantly foxing its master. The performance was excellent, and we led the applause as Sutton left the stage. We clapped and laughed loudly as the dumbie continued to talk, its mouth moving in a perfectly human fashion with, I presumed, the aid of well-concealed wires or perhaps an arm reaching up from inside the boxchair on which it rested.

'I ain't long for this earth,' said the dumbie, 'but I like a good joke. A good joke lightens my day.' The dumbie then embarked on a lengthy pontification, which was crowded with homespun truths of such banality as to emphasise the grotesquery of its shape.

'Now tell me a good joke,' the dumbie insisted. 'Make me laugh and git the money back on yer ticket. I ain't heard a good joke in weeks. A man in my condishun needs to laugh. Since I was but ten years old I ain't had nuthin but misfortune. Misfortune guided me, Mother Courage shaped me, and the Good Lord done took away my meddlin powers.'

I realised suddenly that this was no dumbie, but a living human creature. As I did so, the head jerked back and the mouth opened in a cackle and then came down and spat a chewed wad out on to the stage. From the audience something was lobbed. The torso lunged forward and caught the object in his mouth. But he overbalanced, and he fell off the chair face down, with a mighty smack on the boards. The audience stood. A man ran out of the wings. Two of the orchestra left their places. They picked the torso up by the shoulders and replaced him on the box; to great applause and to the shouts of 'Yo, Calvin!', 'Alright man!', 'We hear you!' and suchlike.

Calvin's nose was wiped. When left alone on stage he started a long chew of the new wad, which he had obtained so painfully. With a mad grin he shouted: 'Forty-three years and I ain't done yet! Hallelujah! I am mighty grateful to y'all.'

The audience applauded. I was held in such a state of disbelief that any sense of reasoning had long since fled. I had no idea in what to invest my emotions, and I was perturbed by the easy transfer between piety and disdain within the audience. It was a most depressing spectacle and I stayed only to share John's disappointment.

'Here we go a-gin!' twanged the Grimaldi hallmark from the wings.

On the stage swaggered a man whom I had never seen before in my life. He was without agility, charm or intelligence. He had nothing but a big red nose and a baggy costume and a string of vulgar jokes about a string of sausages. He was, from mouth to toe, an utter impostor.

I have never seen John so beside himself with anger. I had not realised that there was such a deep and passionate loyalty in his nature. He stood and hurled his outrage at the stage, screaming the most pointed threats against the actor and the management which employed him. He summoned such a great torrent of rage that he would undoubtedly have been carried by it on to the boards and would have slaughtered the hapless fake, had I not been able to call upon the assistance of the Englishman who was sitting behind us and had we not together wrestled John out of the auditorium.

You have, Ann, sometimes expressed the view that your brother is a coward, a frightened observer rather than someone who engages himself. Well I would not be so sure. He is not, I think, new to his convictions, but has been slow to recognise them. (As, indeed, I have been.)

To my absolute horror the dregs of daylight revealed my assistant to be none other than Mister Rennah Wells, that pernicious and sham toolcutter of an 'artist' from the *Moravagine* – concerning whom I have already written to you.

John ran off. I could not tame him. He was bitterly wounded and stretched tight between fury and despair. Had I been in good physical condition I would surely have followed him, but he took off with his devil for company and left me in a state of alarm. Into which this Wells worked his mundane and doleful comfortings. He was quite accustomed to the deceits of Peale's Museum, it appeared that he visited the place on each and every afternoon. To my shame I allowed him to draw me back into the auditorium.

The orchestra was playing a waltzing melody, gentle and irresistible. Within a glass-fronted cage which had been wheeled on to the boards I saw a mound of curled and glistening skin, platformed near the top of the enclosure.

'Oh, magnificent beast!' my companion hissed. 'Supreme Beelzebub! On thy belly! On thy belly shalt thou go!'

He and the others of the audience broke into blusters of applause, which then set fast into a unisonal and urgent clapping, doubling on the tempo of the music. A small hatchway opened in the back of the cage and three white rabbits were shaken forward.

The scene on stage remained pastoral for several moments. The audience's applause fell away. And then with a remarkable spontaneity the tempo was summoned once again, each man bellowing lustily: 'Kill – Kill – Kill – Kill – Kill!' At which a thin tail-rope of snake lowered slowly from the platform; perhaps twelve inches. And a small bulbous head appeared, a tiny tongue frolicking at its lips like a little bird fluttering warily around a stone ledge.

Slowly, and most mechanically, the serpent stretched in a great and beautiful arc across the cage towards one of the rabbits. It opened its mouth and leaned forward and seized the rabbit's head. The rabbit was spasmodically engorged, twitching as its body was winched through the bleached and corrugated mouth, which finally closed over the rabbit's hindquarters, removing it from daylight and from life itself. It was a most terrifying and exact performance. The curtains were drawn, the orchestra disengaged at the earliest opportunity, and we were abandoned to the dark December cold. Mister Wells remained in a state of religious exaltation and, seeing him thus inhibited, I made good my immediate escape from that vile den.

Thankfully I had time only for the most superficial reflection, for when I reached Miss Manley's John had returned and was in a stiff humour. I fabricated some anger at the Grimaldi matter and he commanded that we organise a response from the theatre managers and have the poor actor banished from the stage. This will be the end of the matter, for John's usage of the 'we' is only ever royal in its bestowal of responsibility upon myself; his own insistencies are fully exhausted by the assumption that I will arrange for their fulfilment.

But I was shocked once again upon hearing that he had happened upon Peale's Museum as a result of his having packed his Harlequin costume and gone a-hunting around every theatre in New York, beseeching each one of them to employ him. I had no inkling of this desperation, nor of his low opinion of himself. I can only hope that the damage to his name has been minimal and that he does not take seriously his inability to obtain a single offer of work.

He has not paid much attention to my admonishment, and the day has taken too much of a toll on my moral sense for me to be smartened into sympathetic conversation. I have pleaded exhaustion. I am to bed with a headful of the world's woes. If I nightmare over Mister Wells, mutilated ministers or such I will leap off the mattress and finish this letter. But for the moment, sweet dreams.

I am up early. I want to finish this letter peacefully, before the day pours in and I am jostled away from you. It is again severely cold in New York and I cannot imagine that the river will melt for Blanchard. The cold is shocking and scours across the city. Our sky is a hard blue enamel shell. The light is unnaturally bright and stark; it stamps the most precise shadows on streets and walls. These streets forever head outwards in straight lines towards ocean or marsh, offering no shelter from the wind. There is an obligation towards transience which I feel keenly, which causes me to shudder. I would be at home in London, Elisabethed and Anned. I embrace you both with all my being,

Edmond.

CHAPTER SIXTEEN

Mother Goose – The Rehearsal of the Pantomime – Unnatural City and Theatre Politicking – Edmond Drawn in – Gay Drawn out – Coldness

The door opened and Gay entered the parlour, wrapped in a morning gown, thick with sleep, lips dry and eyes furtive: altogether a sad victim of celebration, Edmond gauged.

He said nothing.

Gay sat down on the settee and rubbed his legs and yawned. He put his elbows on his knees and peered out at Edmond from between his fingers.

'I apologise for the argument last night,' he said glumly.

Edmond folded his napkin and placed the letter to Ann inside his book for *Mother Goose*.

'Tomorrow,' he commanded, 'you will rehearse. We will begin at ten in the morning.' He stood up and drained his coffee cup. 'There will be no late arrivings. We will get on with our business.' He put on his coat and arranged his scarf in front of the mirror over the fireplace.

'Are you quite recovered?'

'I am well enough recovered to give you a run for your money. You would do well to show some application, John.'

He had not intended to be critical, and on reaching the top of the staircase he turned to wink encouragingly at Gay. But the boy was absent-mindedly picking at his feet. Hardly a boy any longer, thought Edmond; I am ageing.

'It will be a pleasure to work with you, sir,' he called lightly. Gay sprang up like an ambushed thief. He saw Edmond's smile and scratched his head.

'It will be an honour to work with you.'

Edmond hesitated. 'Whatever you see in me when we rehearse, John, it is to be kept a secret.'

Edmond gave an embarrassed half-gesture of a wave and started down the stairs.

So he is not recovered, Gay thought, and he doubts that he will do so.

Gay claimed what was left of the hot water. He fetched his razor and soap and he shaved. He was not feeling well, being worked on by the effects of the brandy which he had consumed during the night.

He had, not ten hours ago, visited a house in Chatham Street and had been utterly charmed by the domestic harmony which flowed from the character of Missis Rutherford. He had spent two or three hours with her, in the company of a Miss Jane Robbins, talking and singing to them both, describing Edmond and Ann, and presenting quite clearly the mysteries of anguish and love and the difficulties of conjoining two pure souls. Miss Jane Robbins had dabbed at her eyes with a handkerchief. Missis Rutherford was moved to offer advice in the most tactful manner. Gay had found himself with a surfeit of emotion and had been sympathetically escorted upstairs by Miss Robbins – for whom he donned his Harlequin manner and illustrated several pranks until she was helpless from laughter. As he had kissed her hand she mentioned her livelihood in a most apologetic and modest way, seeking to influence him neither by ardour nor by threat. He ascertained her fee and placed one coin on each eyelid as she lay in her shift on the bed, to the end of which he retreated and struck an attitude. After several moments she unsilvered her eyes and looked at him timidly, then laughing and wondering at his strangeness. She hoped that he would visit her again and not be put off by the taxes levied on her by Missis Rutherford. Gay ran back, unaccountably happy, to Dey Street.

The plot of Thomas Dibdin's *Harlequin, Mother Goose* is as follows:

Colin and Colinette are prevented by her miserly guardian Avaro from getting married. He wants her to marry the rich Squire Bugle. During the preparations for this loveless ceremony, Mother Goose is brought before Squire Bugle as a witch. Colin defends her and she escapes. She rewards Colin by giving him a goose that lays a golden egg each day, which he offers to Avaro in exchange for the hand of Colinette.

The greedy Avaro wants all the gold immediately and Colin unwillingly agrees to cut the goose open. Mother Goose rescues the bird from death. Colin, Squire Bugle and Avaro are condemned to wander about the world as Harlequin, Clown and Pantaloon; each of them contending for the hand of Colinette (who has been transformed into Columbine) until that moment when the golden eggs have been rescued from the sea-bed.

The settings are as follows:

A Village, a Church and Churchyard, a Bridge, a Stream and a Cottage.

A Thick Wood.

A Great Hall.

A Sea.

An Old Country Inn, interior and exterior.

A Market Town.

A Woodcutter's Cottage.

A Pavilion.

A Flower Garden.

A Square.

An Orchestra in Vauxhall Gardens.

A Grocer's Shop and Post Office.

A Parlour.

A Farm Yard.

A Mermaid's Cave with Sea.

A Submarine Palace.

Trick Clocks, Trick Tables and Chairs, Dials, Sunflowers, Statues; a Trick Balcony, two Trick Banks to a Steel Trap and Spring Gun, a Trick Beehive, a Banqueting Table capable of propulsion, a Trick Bottle with a Firework, a Pie containing a Live Duck, *Et Alia*.

There was no possibility of pumping great amounts of water through to the Bowery stage; there was no tank to hold it. Hamblin would allow a stream but the pumps could not be unfrozen, so cold it was outside the theatre. The Bowery was not well stocked with Egyptian Realms, *Femmes Suspendues*, or Fires of crimson, green and blue – which latter Hamblin was not prepared to import for the selfsame reason of having no ready water with which to douse any accidental blaze. The Star-Trap was rough and hardly ready, the Transformations creaked, and the Trick Balcony had already tricked Edmond once, causing him to fall heavily down on to a tea chest.

Edmond knew how to fall when he was prepared for danger; the Bowery sets required him to keep this sixth sense throughout. But because of the restrictions on diverting spectacle, John and he would have to work twice as hard to hold the audience. Wit, Edmond foresaw, would be better halved than doubled before the Bowery clientèle. Therefore the tumbling, the trickery and the knock-about would have to be quadrupled. Edmond set himself two additional propulsions through the star-trap and a brawl with John, as well as the mock sword fight.

The star-trap consists of sixteen segments of a wooden circle which are hinged into a part of the stage and through which the actor is catapulted on a counter-weighted platform. The force of propulsion itself exerts a great pressure on the actor's lower back, and should the trap not function, or be in any way blocked by a piece of stage furniture left carelessly overhead, then the actor is crushed up against a ceiling of wooden planks. Schultz and the carpenter from the *Moravagine* fitted the star-trap in the Bowery Theater. Edmond trusted them.

They sent the Lamenting Settler's Coffin thirty feet into the air on their first essay. On the second attempt the platform shot at an angle and the coffin was smashed to pieces underneath the stage. They succeeded in guiding a grand-father clock both in the correct direction and to a reasonable height; and on the next day they hired a street nigger, who managed sporadic elevations without ever joining the heavenly choir.

Edmond removed his spectacles and took the nigger's place. The pain at his launch was acute, but brief. He could do better by taking the weight of his landing mostly on his right foot, but he could not risk this unbalance on the way upwards for fear of losing his direction to the trap. He went once again and pronounced himself satisfied and immediately left the theatre. Schultz, who had noticed the cloudy look in Edmond's eyes, reduced the thrust of the platform. But Gay, who came through the trap into a double somersault, could not gain sufficient height and so the propulsion was later increased.

Mindful of a certain reserve between Miss Jarvis and Gay, Edmond on the first morning of full rehearsal had the principal actors walk through the pantomime whilst the supporting company underwent a performance.

Gay and Miss Jarvis both performed casually, but impressed the company. George Downie took the part of Squire Bugle/Clown while Edmond watched from the orchestra. Gay was gracious enough to compliment Downie, although the waverings of intonation and style of speech were so tortuous as to sometimes render the dialogues incomprehensible.

'George Downie is afraid of appearing foolish,' Edmond confided to Gay, 'and therefore he seizes at the heroic, part of which he assumes to be a Shakespearean oratory of his lines. You must provoke him, but do not bait him. He must be taught to enjoy himself.' Edmond then stood the company down for the midday refreshment, and instructed Gay and Miss Jarvis to practise their moonlight dance of the ninth scene.

'Without musicians?' Gay demurred.

'I think so, yes.' Edmond smiled. 'It will do us all good to see you work a little harder.'

Most of the company had brought their midday food with them, and settled to watch the dance. They executed several movements, faltered, started again in a frozen fashion. Then Edmond leapt on to the stage and seized Gay for a comic *pas de deux*, singing madly and making a mockery of their movements with wild exaggeration. Gay threw himself into the frolic, pinning Edmond into the female role. Edmond simpered and pirouetted and tripped lightly and swanned, the company laughing and applauding at the farce which was so unexpected and yet so well-known to Gay and Edmond – so very well-known and practised that Gay could meet Edmond's eye and nod almost imperceptibly, and they sang and danced their way across to Miss Jarvis, clowning into her. The tone of the dance changed: one or two more precise movements, a greater reach, a seriousness and a beauty from Gay which quelled the Clown and claimed the Columbine to match him. Miss Jarvis rose to the occasion.

He rehearsed with her again in the late afternoon. She danced above herself and was enthralled. They finished to spontaneous applause from the actors and sat to rest at the back of the stage. Miss Jarvis was called away by the costumier. She kissed Gay on his cheek and placed her hand on his knee to help herself rise. As she walked away across the stage she lifted her arms to adjust her hair. Gay stared after her.

'When you are ready,' said Edmond, 'I would like us to work our way through the scene in the flower garden.'

'I am ready,' Gay replied.

'Good. Well let us get on with it then.'

Gay approached Edmond at breakfast the next day. Edmond regarded him warily.

'I will not dance with Miss Jarvis today. She is too forward.'

'Oh,' said Edmond. 'Well no, you will not. She should perhaps work through her lines with Mister Downie. I am most impressed at her endeavour. You are well matched. Look to your own performance.'

Edmond watched him slope away. 'Oh for God's sake eat some breakfast and come to the Bowery this afternoon. I will have no more of this temper. We open in eight days and we are little more than a shambles. I will not have your personal misgivings interfering with my production.'

Edmond folded his letter. 'I have some news from Ann. She enjoys good health and sends us her warmest greetings. The Duke of Wellington has resigned from the Government. And I am afraid that young Joe Grimaldi is dead. From a fit of madness, after a drunken brawl. I am sorry. On New Year's Eve we shall pay tribute to him. I am sorry, John.'

Edmond walked to the Post Office, where he left another letter for Ann. At noon, he called on Miss Jarvis. He urged her to come to some arrangement with Gay. He made it perfectly clear that the pantomime could not hope for any success if she and John dabbled in any personal attachment.

At rehearsals they performed with the greatest skill, as perfect lovers.

Gay worked intently to disguise Edmond's weakness. There was no way of avoiding the star-trap, the fall from the balcony, the diving exits or the hazards of the banquet table. But Gay might take most of the impetus during the tumbling slapstick and, if girded with a wide support belt, Edmond would manage to hold Miss Jarvis in the pyramid at the final transformation scene.

It was not all such a serious business. Edmond invented and censored a mass of scathing repartee on the foibles, fears and snobberies of the

New Yorkers whom Gay mimicked. They were frequently incapacitated by laughter. Besides, said Edmond, if they were too serious they would freeze without female company.

The temperatures had sunk so very low that shop windowglass shattered of its own accord and lay mixed amongst the sheets of frozen water and urine which spangled the streets. Men, women and children were discovered frozen to death each morning, white frost carpeting their eyes, their jaws seized open, their tongues so delicate that they might be snapped off. Walking to and from the theatre was hazardous. Gay was almost crushed against a wall by a sliding coach. Edmond saw a horse impale itself on the spar of a bolster wagon as it thrashed in a frenzy of panic at being unable to get up off its knees.

The newspapers daily recounted some fresh horror caused by the cold. There was panic about the shortage of drinking water. There were fears that all water might be infected due to splitting pipes. There were solemn warnings about weeping out of doors and about the inadvisability of turning one's head too suddenly upon waking, lest the neck of the unwary sleeper had become fragile and brittle through accidental exposure to the nightly severities.

There was no shortage of fears. The city thrived on them. Edmond was astonished at the joy which greeted the news of the Duke of Wellington's resignation. An extraordinary number of people professed huge relief, as though the entire British Army had been forever on the point of landing an invasion in order to pillage whatever was sacred to the American way of life.

Hamblin laughed. 'If we are not menaced by the savage Indians, then we are menaced by the British. We Americans are always threatened.'

'As a pastime?' Edmond queried.

'No, that is too European. It is not a joke. We have had to establish ourselves. Danger is still the way of life in the West. Here in the East a good solid imaginary danger keeps every man out hustling for his peace of mind. You conquer one danger and someone invents another. That's what keeps us moving.'

Hamblin was a strange weave of absolute cynicism and enthusiastic naivety. Edmond had come to see that, while appearing to deride the middle ground by appearing to ignore it, Hamblin was greatly reassured by a predictable performance from a predictable actor. He had no time for Gay. He only admired Edmond inasmuch as Edmond could direct the company. When Edmond hinted that Hamblin might assume an overall control, the man did not engage himself.

Edmond was not used to taking such a large responsibility, and he had taken it without realising the extent of the demands. He was an actor; he wanted now to be free to act. He offered several slight complaints to Hamblin, expecting his assistance, but Hamblin poked him away almost jocularly. He had taken to dubbing Edmond with the nickname of Fast Eddie; Edmond had been in the theatre long enough to develop a thick skin, but it nevertheless irritated him to have to wear it. Between Gay and Edmond, Hamblin became Bumblin; the soubriquet was overheard by Miss Jarvis and there began a slight malaise as the actors considered their loyalties. It was reckoned that Edmond gave himself airs, that he was schoolmasterish and dictatorial.

Just before Christmas, Edmond confronted Hamblin in his office. Edmond confessed that he had made a mistake, that he had rehearsed the company too hard too early, and that they were bored and resentful.

'If you've got trouble,' said Hamblin, 'I'll fire the lot of them and pay you a month. Tell me what I can do for you and I'll try to do it. Don't expect me to double guess you. For Chrissakes speak plainly.'

'Take us through the dress rehearsals.'

'I'll be happy to oblige you.'

'And you must watch over the management of the stage for the first week. There are many opportunities for injury if the stagemen are not attentive.'

'I would do that for any visiting company.'

Edmond nodded. 'Finally, Tom, I have to ask you – although it is none of my business – how do you intend to attract an audience? How will the city know about us? I have seen nothing, I am not aware that there has been any effort made – '

'Here.' Hamblin pushed a sheaf of printed matter across the bureau. 'These will be in the newspapers tomorrow. Right now is the time to be English, and we've made the most of it. Edmond, I'll work you for the next three days and I'll throw a party on Saturday. You may sleep it off Christmas Day. We open to a full house Monday. We will, believe me.'

*

III

Edmond could only presume that Tom Hamblin was either well-liked or else was owed a great many favours by New York journalists. The announcements were prominently positioned. Several newspapers carried short exhortations to their readers to take advantage of the enterprise shown by the American Theater in the Bowery, and *The Constellation* and the *New York Evening Post* each devoted a half column to the arrival of the comic pantomime. The *New York American* – which habitually ignored the Bowery and showered its praises on the Richmond Theater – set about heralding the new character of English culture in the wake of the Iron Duke's departure.

Ann was mentioned as a lantern-bearer for the cause of reform which was finally triumphing in England. Edmond Parsloe and John Gay were loosely assigned prominent roles in 'a salon society which agitated as openly as possible in the cause of political freedoms', and *Harlequin, Mother Goose* was 'despite its great comic appeal, a brave attack on oppressive authority'.

'What nonsense!' Edmond stormed. 'How did Hamblin come to these fairy tales?'

Gay admitted to having answered Hamblin's queries about Ann, and Miss Jarvis had passed on every bit of the concoction which Gay had frothed out of his imaginings in order to entertain her and assuage her inquisitive nature.

Hamblin had his own reasons for believing them. The articles in the newspapers amounted to an open declaration of contempt for the outdated representations at the Park Theater 'and for those complacent souls who slake their thirst at the Shakespeare Tavern'.

CHAPTER SEVENTEEN

Christmas Eve – A Final Rehearsal – Edmond Piecemeal – The Re-Appearance and Fortunes of Mister Van der Hertz – Columbine Switches Horses – Colonel David Crockett – Toasts – Harlequin and Clown Unhappily A-bed

. . . and you will see, my dear Ann, that even were we not vain, our names would be taken in vain. So we shall go forward on vanity. And why not? Vanity is a magnificent crutch, although I fear that I will need crutches of a more substantial material before the approaching Monday. This matter of using your name has added insult to my injury. I can only apologise.

This is a country which swallows magnifications and false colourings, a plain truth being very undesirable and banished to the back of the stage. We are come out of the trap and hang in mid air, awaiting our fate.

By the bye, we are now indeed quite fêted. I leave most of the fluttering to John. I am only too glad to return to the parlour and lie flat down upon the carpet . . .

A Lord George Watters took it upon himself to host a reception, at which there were many people of quality.

'But is he himself not a fake?' Gay had demanded of Edmond.

'As much as you or I. But he is in society, and it follows that we will be in audience.'

Columbine felt herself to have been plucked and discarded, and therefore she swanned gracefully before the drooping shroud of Willibrord Van der Hertz's mustaches. Harlequin, on the other hand, was disconcerted by the blushes of Miss Jane Robbins, the only lady in the room who was clad in a high-necked dress.

On the morning of Christmas Eve, the *New York American* reported an epidemic of cholera in London and Paris. It urged the New York authorities to take every available precaution 'to ensure that our population is protected from this new plague, which will surely be brought to our city by those recently arrived from France and England'.

In the *New York Evening Post*, the Park Theater took several inches to announce that the English actors in that theatre's company had agreed to end their contracts, 'in no way wishing to risk the health of those generous and warm-hearted citizens who attend the theater'.

'This will rebound on them,' Hamblin considered. 'There are no newspapers tomorrow, and the rumour will be forgotten by Monday. Nobody wants to talk sickness at Christmas.'

Edmond barely managed to get through the Christmas Eve dress rehearsal. They played until six to the stink of paint and the silent glances of the seamstresses. Edmond was irascible and sweating profusely, but at the finish he ordered another run of the Flower Garden scene. Hamblin refused. Edmond insisted. Miss Jarvis made the first move to position herself.

Halfway through the scene Edmond broke off and pronounced himself satisfied.

There was for a moment a ghostly silence in the theatre; whether of disapproval, relief or fatigue Gay did not know. Edmond stood stiffly alone, in the centre of the stage, like a pariah.

'You will make sure', Edmond barked, 'that the balcony supports are tightly joined. And that the traps are oiled.'

Gay was about to rescue him from his isolation, but Edmond raised his head. 'I think, then,' he said gravely, 'that we are as ready for an audience as we will ever be.'

At which point, unexpectedly, George Downie walked forward with a bottle of champaigne.

'I have only two glasses,' Downie declaimed heroically. 'One of these I give to Mister Edmond Parsloe for his refreshment, and the other I raise on behalf of the whole company, to express our appreciation of him and to give him his health.'

As Downie raised his glass the entire cast and stage-men and orchestra and Hamblin himself burst into a heated applause, clapping and cheering, until Edmond could recover his composure and raise his head to still them.

'I am . . .' he faltered. 'I thank you all most sincerely for your help and your good hearts. I hardly know where I am nor what I should say. But I thank you all. I am honoured. I wish you a most happy Christmas. Thank you, most sincerely, for your kindness. I thank you all.'

The actors were anxious to be gone from the theatre. Not all of them were invited by Hamblin to the Coal-Hole festivity. The dressing-rooms emptied quickly, a pile of costume left on each chair to be washed before Monday night. Gay laid the damp Harlequin suit over the back of his chair and took his evening clothes down from the rail. Edmond remained sitting in front of his mirror. Gay said, 'I have never before come across that custom of salutation at the end of a rehearsal.'

'Nor I,' murmured Edmond.

'The compliment was entirely genuine and is well merited. It is a good production.'

'With what we have.'

'With what you have made, Edmond. With what you have created of them and of me.'

'And of my own performance?'

'*Your* performance? Why, it is excellent. It is! I had not thought to tell you. I have enjoyed it too much.'

There came from Edmond's throat a constricted gargle and then a series of whimpers and sobs. Edmond leaned back in his chair and covered his forehead with his hand. Gay sat down beside him.

'You have done well, Edmond. You have done well,' Gay pleaded. The tears sheened Edmond's skin. He sat quietly, hiding his eyes from view.

'Why – !' he cried suddenly. 'Why, for God's sake, is the world not a better place!'

Gay considered what to do. 'Really I do not know,' he said. 'How, in particular?'

'You cannot understand. It is just that I do not know how I feel.'

Edmond jerked himself angrily out of his chair and glared down into the mirror. 'I do not know what I feel!' He tried to clear his throat. 'It is all in pieces, I cannot reach them, I cannot hold them . . .'

It was a blue dress. But it was also Miss Jarvis – painted lightly, the curls bobbing to her shoulders – a beauty presented. She stood behind his chair. Gay tilted his mirror to see her.

'Will you not say how splendid I look?' she asked him, stealing the words from his mouth.

'Yes, I will. You are splendid. You are arrayed splendidly. There is a splendour about you which is quite forbidding.'

'I am not inviting?'

'I would not presume.'

'You are my friend, John. We are friends.'

'I should hope so.'

'No. I am serious. I want to know that you are my friend. That I do not owe you anything.'

'You do not owe me anything.'

'In case you should suspect such a thing.'

'I do not expect such a thing. I do not think about such a thing.'

'But it is difficult,' she murmured, 'when we are acting and dancing together.'

'You are most accomplished; you owe me nothing.'

He thought that he saw her lips tighten slightly; but she looked around her, and then she asked, 'Has Edmond gone back to Dey Street?'

'No,' Gay replied. 'He is asleep on the chaise in Tom Hamblin's office. He is upset.'

'With us?'

'No, I don't think so. His emotions are stretched in every way. I don't know what exactly is the matter. He worries. He is used. And I am sure that there is a great deal of pain from his back.'

'He said nothing else?'

'He said a little.' Gay bent forward to examine his face. 'At that moment when he stopped the scene in the Flower Garden, he saw how difficult it would be to arrange his life in London. That is what he said. He suddenly could not see a room with Ann and Elisabeth and himself inside it, no matter how hard he searched. I begged the keys off Hamblin. He needs to rest. I hope that he manages to concentrate his mind before Monday. His father – '

'It is his daughter's first Christmas.'

Gay slapped the palm of his hand down on the table. 'Edmond has for ever detested Christmas! He has always accepted the most strenuous Christmas engagements. As have I. How else can one act oneself free of . . . of – '

'You must make sure that he finds some affection,' she murmured.

'We will all greatly amuse each other. I am certain. We have worked too hard and have suffered too much to deny each other a small reward.'

Hamblin's gathering at the Coal-Hole was a noisy and crowded affair in which Edmond and Gay played no great part. They lost each other almost as soon as they had handed over their cloaks and stepped down on to the sawdust. Edmond was snatched away by Lord George Watters.

George Downie asked Gay if he would not mind being introduced to his father and mother, who had come up from Washington, his father being a manufacturer of army tents and only fractionally acquainted with the ideals of the theatre.

Gay knew little about the army and less about tents. Missis Downie was sympathetic, but failed to draw a desired response when she said that she was certain that Gay's father and mother were proud of his achievements upon the stage.

Gay surmised that Mister Downie had abandoned his third son George to the theatre without much concern or approval, and he strove to find some conversation which would cultivate the man's respect for his son's vocation. Missis Downie set to frivolity, but her husband's eyes rose above the family circle and gazed somewhat superciliously over George's left shoulder. The man was an unbending prig.

Such was the hubbub that Gay could rarely hear what was being said, either by George or by his mother; he heard only his own voice, very close to him, agreeing or passing some tepid observation on New York or London. They were a great deal scrimmaged this way and that.

Gay edged his way round towards Mister Downie, who had turned his back on his family and was nervously eyeing a powerful stringy fellow, heavily and quite dirtily lined, who had not bothered to remove his headgear. This was not in itself a sin, as several gentlemen had preferred to retain their hats. But this bazaar oaf, whose build belonged to the common prizefighter, capped his grimy head with a curled hive of dead animal – which more polished fashion was being considerably flaunted by the New York ladies, the temperatures and Mister Astor falling upon them at the same time.

'Well I'm a-tellin you like I told the senator here. Those darned tents rip too easy. If you meet a high brush that'll open a mule's hide then come nightfall those tents ain't nuthin but shreds hanging over his asshole.'

'We'll have to think again,' Mister Downie nodded at the (Gay presumed) Senator.

'Damn right you will. Somewhere along the line someone's foolin someone and we're gettin shorted.'

'The tents are supplied according to government specifications, I believe, sir.'

'Andrew Jackson's government?' the stranger bellowed.

'We have held the contract since before Jackson took office.'

'Well I'd better tail down to Washington and buy that toad-fucker a drink. I've had a dryer night's sleep under a whore's skirts than under one of them tents. No offence, Mister Downie; I understand your family's present. This your boy?'

The Senator looked as keen as did Downie to stray from the subject of tents. Gay held out his hand. 'Mister John Gay, an actor, from London.'

'Glad to meet you. Crockett.'

'*Colonel* David Crockett.' The Senator alongside issued an oily smile.

'And this man is Josh Williams.' Crockett offered a quick mad grin. '*Senator* Josh Williams. From one of our new territories. Seen it once, represented it twice, sold it half a dozen times; ain't you, Josh?' Crockett guffawed. 'Happy Christmas to y'all!'

He slung an arm around Gay's neck and pulled him off through the crowd. His strength was enormous and, Gay reckoned, for the most part latent.

'I am, y'know,' he slurred in Gay's ear, 'the rudest son of a bitch in this town. Maybe that's why none of these people will give me work.' He giggled crazily.

'What type of work do you do?'

'Shit I don't know.'

'What work do you want, Colonel?'

'I should have a job of work, goddam it. No idea of mine to become a Colonel.'

Gay caught sight of Edmond, who was bestowing upon a group of ladies a look of benign indifference. Gay steered this rude and tedious

Crockett into the circle. Edmond rocked back on his heels. He appeared to be as drunk as the new arrival.

'May I introduce you to Mister Edmond Parsloe, *the* Mister Edmond Parsloe,' Gay stressed. 'Colonel Crockett.'

Edmond blinked.

'Cockit?'

The Colonel closed one eye and scanned the ladies, who simpered nervously. 'Which oneufem?' He lurched back, and considered Edmond from head to toe, probably in duplicate. 'Parts slow?'

Edmond smiled and said clearly, 'I have had no complaints, Colonel Crockett.'

Crockett nodded, and yawned comfortably. 'You will, Mister Parsloe. Mind you, if I had your back I'd be play-actin drunk to get out of here the quicker.'

'Would you also be a surgeon, sir?'

'No. But I've seen most every kind of injury more than once. I'll be glad to take a look at it. There's a grogpit right up the stairs there where none of this class of person would gladly poke their assholes.'

'You will accompany us, John?' Edmond suggested uneasily.

'Mister Parsloe, *the* David Crockett may have a number of reputations. But nowhere is he held as a cornholer.'

Van der Hertz leaned forward and knocked out his pipe and opened the worn maroon pouch. Miss Jarvis sat as though for her portrait, although she felt an urgent need to relieve the pressure on her bladder. She was glad of the pungent tobacco smoke for she had once or twice been aware of the distasteful odour arising from her rags.

'I am not boring you perhaps?' Van der Hertz did not look at her, but devoted his attention to scraping the bowl of the pipe with a small silver knife.

'No,' said she, 'you are not boring me. Although I might have told you what would happen with your devices.' She bit her lip, but could not help laughing. Van der Hertz nodded solemnly. At times he was almost a caricature of himself, which made her want to surrender to her laughter. She was a little ashamed of her frivolity, but could in no way control it or want to control it. 'Perhaps you should have cut off your mustaches,' she jibed.

'Do you think that they are devilish?' he enquired of her, and did not understand why she smiled.

On consideration, Miss Jarvis thought that the mustaches might tickle, or perhaps scratch. She had once kissed a boy with mustaches that were like hairs above a baby's ears; she had never been kissed by a tobacco-stained brush.

'But I did not quite resemble the devil,' Van der Hertz decided. 'And perhaps that is why they made a fire only out of my rubber, and not out of me.'

'Were you afraid?'

'Yes. I was grateful for my deliverance; and they were surprised. Such a thick black smoke came off the rubber. Such a bad smell in the snow. I had not expected it.'

Van der Hertz smiled. 'It was very simple, we gave our confidence to the wrong people. To exactly the wrong people.' He laughed. 'And in the wrong city perhaps. I could not possibly have been more wrong.'

'Will you try again?'

Van der Hertz shook his head. 'I have found that I do not know the Americans. Also my morale is not high. I have talked of an idea to Schultz, and we will see. We will make money if the weather is agreeable.'

Miss Jarvis was, if truth be told, by now a little bored. Everything was quite irksome; and Van der Hertz was quite placid. It would not do. She had invited him to the Coal-Hole and he showed no interest in her. For the next how long – perhaps weeks – her evenings would be taken up. He was not the type of man to dance attendance at the stage-door; he would find plenty to occupy his mind and his energies. She stood up, and she was pleased to notice that he was appreciative of her neck and breast.

'Mister Van der Hertz, I fail to see how you can be such a coward, how you can accept this defeat with such a demeaning complacency. You are not the man I took you for; you are so – '

Just then the door opened, and in came the horrible character whom she had caught leering at her downstairs, armed with a bottle and two glasses and followed by Edmond.

At eleven o'clock in the evening the Coal-Hole trickled empty as if by command. Gay had intermittently searched for Edmond, but had several times been called upon by Hamblin to speak with his guests. And when Gay was not extolling the virtues of the pantomime, he was borrowed by Lord George Watters to bolster his reputation as a man well connected to the modern spirit gusting through English society.

As the crowd was first thinned and then sifted into small groups around the alcoves, Gay drank a large glass of whiskey and was not inclined to listen to Lord George Watters any longer. The man was by now tiresomely full of Christmas spirit, referring constantly to 'our' programme of Christmas celebrations, the calls to be made, the entertainments to be attended; one of which would be 'our' amusing evening at the Bowery theatre, as if Gay would perform with a glass in one hand and Lord George in the other.

Gay opened the door to the grogpit and saw immediately that Edmond and Crockett were not, this time, playing at drunkenness. Crockett was balanced on one foot at the highpoint of some eerie screech, Edmond shouting 'From left!', 'From Right!' alternately. Crockett broke off and glowered at Gay.

'Ah!' called Edmond. 'Ah, Watters, we need money. Crockett and I are taking some savages to the London stage. Crockett has a full tribe of savages.'

'Indeed?' beamed Lord George.

'Yes, sir. Yep.' Crockett sat down heavily on a bench. He was gaudy in the lower half of the face, his nose a glowering knob of purple, like an exotic fungus. 'Warriors, medicine men, squaws, chiefs, papooses, a whole damn mess of them. They ain't savages; no, sir, they're primitives. Privileged people. I don't have nothing against geese – I hear you got geese up on the stage – but you ain't seen the spirit of a bear, or a coyote or a fox or a buffalo. You ain't seen how they run the earth, nor how the earth answers back to them. Out there there's only the two damn things, the earth and the sky. One endless sky stretching further than any and every human mind could ever stretch, and one earth running flat to the end of it. That way!' Crockett leaned up and lobbed an empty bottle across the room and it broke against the foot of the door. 'That way.' He grinned. 'The biggest, fullest, emptiness you ever saw. Earth down; sky up. Indians between. Indians and spirits explaining the earth to the sky, and the sky to the earth. Now that, sir, would be what I might call "an actor".'

Watters giggled. Edmond was ill-equipped to raise so much as an eyebrow. Gay had been gazing spellbound at Crockett's pictures, and Crockett stared now at him, holding to his end of a line which might have been made of madness.

Edmond roused himself. 'There are dances the like of which you cannot imagine, young Gay.'

'They're just people,' Crockett grunted. 'And there ain't no cause in them goin west, so they might as well go east as sit still and die.'

'Come, come,' said Edmond. 'They will find a new home in our theatre. The London audience are fond of an entertaining spectacle.'

'There's nothing for nobody in that.' Crockett spat. 'Now why don't we take ourselves off to a decent whorehouse and pay ourselves a Christmas dip, gentlemen?'

'I think,' said Edmond, 'that I will sleep.'

'No you don't, Parsloe. We stick together. If we all stick together one of us'll git our money's worth.'

It being Christmas Eve, they were the only clients at Missis Rutherford's and she had only three girls in the house, the others having gone out of town to visit their families for the holiday period. The girls had gone to bed but were quite willing to be roused, and in the time the men took coffee and light refreshment the girls dressed and shook the curling papers out of their hair and painted themselves decorously and came down to the parlour coiffed and blooming like springtime flowers, for which achievement they were praised.

Jane Robbins had made no festive pilgrimage north and quickly consigned herself to Gay, much to the amusement of the others who were content to lounge in the soft chairs. Crockett had a wicked gift for fantastic tales, Edmond for playing the dry response. Gay realised that Edmond was greatly enjoying himself, and he was glad. It was enough that Edmond was joyful. Gay lay back and day-dreamed, his mind happily composed and skipping excitedly across the weave of Crockett's voice to that distant primitive stage of earth and sky.

In time Missis Rutherford announced that there was hot water and a tub in the back room, should any of the gentlemen desire to wash themselves. The Colonel felt that he might be encouraged to do so, but he would have a horror of being confronted by his filthy clothes at the end of the evening. Missis Rutherford said that the doors were bolted and she was not going to bother herself with seeing any gentlemen out at a later hour. They were in her house until morning, and by that time her maid would have washed the Colonel's clothes and they would have dried over the stove.

'Before our gathering breaks up,' said Edmond, 'and if you will bear with me, I would like to propose a toast. We cannot thank Missis Rutherford enough for her hospitality. Some of us, perhaps all of us, are a long way from home, wherever that might be. I have become a father for the first time this year, and I would appreciate your joining me in my celebration. I have had no opportunity to drink to the health of my daughter.'

There were cries of 'Shame!' and exclamations of disbelief.

'Be that as it may . . .' murmured Edmond.

Gay reached under Jane's arm and stood up with her, lifting his glass. 'To Elisabeth;' he said, 'to Miss Elisabeth Parsloe, a long and happy life, to her and her friends the happiest of Christmases.'

The company stood as one and acclaimed Elisabeth, much to Edmond's pleasure.

'Now, Mister Parsloe,' said the Madame, 'it is quite likely that we shall not go to bed for some time. I am told that your back is troubling you. I have some skill in the art of manipulation and would be quite happy to settle you as far as I am able.'

With great joviality Edmond was piped, pushed and hoisted up the stairs. Once abed he made a feeble play for Missis Rutherford, who despite her ripeness was by no means unattractive, but she scolded him for not taking her seriously. There was then no sound from that bedroom, not that any sound would have penetrated the chatter in the parlour. In due course Missis Rutherford descended, and the girl Sophie crept unnoticed to share Edmond's bed.

Miss Robbins had a prettily decorated room, with blue gingham curtains. In two or three years she hoped that she would have enough money to open a small haberdashery store. She was nineteen. She asked Gay how they did it in London. He said that she should not take off her clothes and that she should refrain from kissing.

From the room further down the corridor they heard Edmond's anguished sobs. Miss Robbins felt the top half of Gay's body tense. She got up from the bed and undressed. When she came back to him she wound her arms round his ribs and held on to his shoulders.

CHAPTER EIGHTEEN

Christmas Day — The Trap Is Oiled — A True New York History of Mother Goose — Mister Edmond Parsloe's Finale as a Cabbage — John Gay Stands Guard before the Underworld

Edmond and Gay arrived back at Dey Street in time to change their clothes and escort Miss Manley to Church at Noon.

Miss Jarvis had called, said Miss Manley, at nine. A gentleman had waited outside in the carriage. If indeed it could properly be called a carriage, mounted as it was like a sleigh on running boards, which were quite appropriate to the ice but which grated horribly on bare ground.

Gay was not anxious to see Miss Jarvis.

Edmond and he dined early with the Hamblin household. On their way back to Miss Manley's they stopped in at the Bowery Theater. Edmond stumbled through the cold darkness with a jar of grease for the hinges on the star-trap.

'I cannot think,' said he, 'that there is anything more we might do.'

'Do you wish it were over?' Gay asked.

'I cannot imagine how it ever started. Can *you*? I have no sense of what I am doing. If I stand aside I observe myself as an object for divine amusement, and that is somehow comforting. But as soon as I pursue any course whatsoever I feel that I am making one mistake after another; and the laughter is sour. I should be more angry, but then I fear that I would be as ridiculous as a small dog chasing its own tail. I realise', Edmond observed, 'that I have lost faith. Worse, that I have never had any faith. That is a waste. I regret it bitterly. I have pig-headedly encouraged this blindness in myself and now I am left to curse such a wastage of my life. You must promise me, John, that you will not sell your soul so short.'

'You are being much too hard on yourself,' said Gay. 'None of it matters. When you are returned home you will have all the time in the world to nurture your faith. You will see her quite soon.'

Edmond laughed. 'Yes. Yes, I will.'

*

On Monday, December twenty-sixth, *Harlequin, Mother Goose* opened to warm applause from a friendly audience. They were fêted, Edmond being called forward several times to receive due appreciation. He was proud and tearful. Gay had never before seen him so ill-governed by these random swings of humour.

On the Tuesday, they had a more difficult time. Edmond fell and was derided by a section of the audience.

Downie took over the role of Clown for the next performance and was cheered lustily for his attempts. It was a bravura display. Gay emerged blustered, bruised and exasperated by Downie's cack-handed gusto.

Ten inches of snow fell during that Wednesday night, and just before dawn part of the theatre roof collapsed. The performances on Thursday and Friday were cancelled. Hamblin recruited a team of labourers who, with the cast and stage-men, dug the auditorium clear of snow, patched up the roof and mended the stage as best they could.

At ten o'clock on New Year's Eve, Edmond – who had previously called on Monsieur Chenevix – donned the Clown's costume and stepped alone on to the stage. He delivered a short and emotional tribute to Joey Grimaldi.

In the sixth scene of the pantomime Gay pursued Edmond from the Old Country Inn, and they met under the stage. Gay lurched forward with his head on one side, his face twisted uncomprehendingly.

'What is the matter?

'Nothing. A head pain.'

'Your head! . . . My back!' Edmond smiled. Schultz positioned him on the platform of the star-trap. 'Hadn't we better head back home?' He raised an eyebrow at Gay, the cue-rope was tugged, and Edmond catapulted upwards. The platform was winched down and Gay took his place. They could hear nothing through the laughter and jeers of the audience.

Above them, Edmond's body lay across the trap. He wondered that he could not move it. The air roared about his face and he caught sight of Rennah Wells in the second row of the audience. Edmond felt like some sluggish caterpillar or, what with the smoke from the stage lamps, like some slothful dragon unable to haul its gross body from its lair. He made several faces, which were highly appreciated by the audience, while he tried to think what to do; he could not hold the audience for very long and John was to follow him through the trap immediately. He stared at Rennah Wells and snarled at him. Downie turned to the audience in large fright, raising a laugh.

Down below, Schultz tugged at the loose cue-rope. Gay's head pounded; he hissed his displeasure and waved Schultz out of the way.

George Downie lumbered towards Edmond, wondering why he did not move. Edmond grasped at his ankle and pulled.

'Go!' Gay shouted.

He came through, and up – a flash of coloured silk, five hundred spangles glittering – and straightway into the turn; head down, back bent, knees coming up; into the foetus.

Up and over; the first somersault.

And keeping tightly folded; in thin air now: over again. Roll. Now loose the legs, now Edmond's blank chequered expression against the boards. Now seeing that he was falling towards Edmond's frightened eyes.

Edmond awoke to find himself in his bed at Miss Manley's.

He remembered being cold and in the lowest of spirits, but at this moment his cheeks glistened and glowed gently. His face seemed swollen; he felt as though he had shed his depression and was rising very fast to the surface. It was as if he was being born; his skin was warm and slimy with the texture of the tender, tight, inner leaves of a cabbage.

Even as he lay in bed the slime evaporated and his skin hardened upon contact with the air. He no longer had any fever; he felt light-hearted, he felt resilient, healed and exultant. He would be well again. He would at last be able to do something for Lizzie.

He got out of bed, took the candle and walked easily into the parlour. He placed the candlestick on the table, next to his writing paper, he sat comfortably in the wing-back chair and died.

Gay saw:

That it was not as it had been with Titou Gouffré. There was nothing that had escaped death, or risen through death. Edmond might still be touched for all that Edmond was. A kind and witty man. Self-effacing. Honest. And dead.

There were many questions to ask him.

Gay felt that he must go out for a walk. He took his cloak, and looked into Miss Manley's parlour. She asked after Edmond. He assured her that Edmond was resting, they were warm enough and Edmond was in good humour.

The snow was quite deep in some parts, but it was a glorious fine sky-blue day, as clear as madness, deep and transparent. Gay's spirits skittered across the planes of blue and white, sliding in fragments away towards the bright yellow sun. The glare tickled his body and furred his eyes. He laughed.

A dray slid up beside him. Gay loved the soft swish of the runners on the snow. The sound was that of a woman's skirts brushing across a marble floor. The horses stopped ahead of him, their breath streaming into the cold air. Or was that yesterday? Gay squinted up but could not see more of the driver than a blurred shadow.

Miss Jarvis's voice came. 'How are you, John?'

'I am fine, thank you. I am fine.' Gay waved.

The driver leapt down and shook his hand. Gay was pleased to see Willibrord. His eyes showed fatigue but they burned alertly in friendship.

'How is Edmond?' Van der Hertz asked.

'Quite well. Quite well indeed.'

'We were on our way to see you both. I have collected Miss Jarvis.'

Gay was suffering from a sensation of vertigo, but he did not perceive this as having anything to do with Miss Jarvis, whom he still could not see. He remembered her cheerfully. For some reason he thought of her as a schoolfriend. He would be quite happy to see her again. He raised his hand to shelter his eyes from the sun and he smiled towards her, at the same time falling backwards against the snow which was piled high against the porch of a house. Van der Hertz helped him up. Gay laughed. 'It is', he said, 'such a glorious day.'

Van der Hertz smiled. 'Shall we disturb Edmond?'

'I think that perhaps you should not. The doctor has called again and Edmond was asleep when I left him.'

'Then we should not disturb him,' Miss Jarvis said firmly. Gay liked her voice. He liked the strength of the decision.

'No, I think not.'

'And the doctor is sure that it is not the cholera?' Miss Jarvis asked.

'That', said Gay, 'is a mischief.' He wagged his finger up at the quaint shadow. 'It is not, and never has been, the cholera. It is a feverous inflammation which has invaded him from his back. Little by little it is being defeated.'

'That is good news,' said Van der Hertz. 'We have a package for you and Edmond. Will you take it? It is quite small.'

Gay methodically accompanied Willibrord to the back of the dray, marvelling at how easy it all seemed. Van der Hertz let down the tailgate and clambered into the wagon, on which was roped a wheeled buggy.

'Are you collecting these chariots?' Gay pointed.

Willibrord leaped down and handed Gay a light wooden box. He laughed: Gay laughed too, without knowing why.

'Yes, I am collecting them, and I am delivering them when Schultz has worked with them. We have a good business.'

Gay nodded his approval, stepped back and was again blinded by the pan of sunbeams which came at him from the surface of the snow.

'So,' came Willibrord's voice, 'you will embrace Edmond for me.'

'I will. Where shall I find you?' Gay thought that he should ask.

'With Schultz.' Willibrord pointed to the side of the wagon and read the letters out for Gay. 'Van der Hertz and Schultz, of Amsterdam Street. Snow Carriages for Hire.'

'But where will I find you', said Gay, 'when the snow melts?'

'At the same address. Where we will be putting back the wheels. There is no need for you to remember, John; you will see it painted on many carriages.'

Gay followed him to the front of the wagon. There was a warm and almost delicious stench of horse urine. Gay caught sight of Miss Jarvis but for a moment, until Van der Hertz sat up beside her and the sun again dazzled him.

'Where will you be, Miss Jarvis?'

'I shall be at the theatre. You will come to the theatre?'

'I will,' Gay called. And he waved, and he watched the dray slither away until it quickly became a mirage flecking the centre of the white street.

Dollars and food. Gay took them out of the box and placed them on the table. He was tired and so went into his bedroom and lay down on the bed. When he felt chilly he pulled the covers up to his shoulders, and soon felt warm, and slept.

Awaking between ten and eleven at night, he lit a candle, and the smell from the brimstone made him nauseous. He carried the candle into the parlour and bent over the table to read Edmond's letter, which said only 'My Dearest Elisabeth'.

Gay fell upon the food. He gorged himself on sausage and bread, pausing only to snuffle around the parlour until he found the wine, with which he washed his mouth and swilled his throat. It took the edge off the cold. He placed a blanket over Edmond's legs and circled him warily, unable to pursue any line of thought, save that he would keep Edmond alive and in good faith. He left the candle burning and escaped to his bedroom. The door closed behind him and he stopped to marvel at the great stillness which seeped up from the city: the atmosphere within his own four walls was flat and airless. There was a twitch from inside his head.

'No!' shouted Gay. 'Leave me alone.'

When Downie called, he was informed that Edmond was out walking. Some days later, Hamblin was sent back to the theatre with the news that Edmond had managed to obtain a passage on a ship to England. Gay did not accept the offer of employment at the Bowery.

Edmond stayed. In the low temperatures he did not rot, but remained sitting in the chair where he died. Gay saw nothing unusual in the arrangement. There were no claims on Edmond. Edmond had stated that he was without faith, and therefore there was no passage of rites to be undertaken. There was no religious office at which Edmond's body might be consigned.

Edmond had very fine and elegant fingers. And in daylight a most beautiful face.

Gay considered Edmond sternly, but could find nothing of Edmond that was missing. The eyes were quite still. Without admitting it, Gay began to talk to Edmond. He let his mind run on, his lips did not need to move. A fly settled on the fine lash beneath Edmond's left eye and Gay shuddered at the interruption.

One morning, Miss Jane Robbins called at The American Theater in the Bowery and learned that the English actors had departed. She was escorted by Colonel Crockett, who was most angry and disappointed at the actors' absence, having no desire whatsoever to trail his posterior over to London without their having first ascertained an English interest in his spectacle of the savages.

Crockett happened to recognise Miss Jarvis, and she believed that Mister Gay had not returned home. Crockett and Miss Robbins went directly to Dey Street.

Miss Manley did not know if Mister Gay was in, but she assured them that he did not like to receive any visitors. Such was Mister Gay's nature, and as long as he paid his rent she saw no reason to disturb him. She had been obliged to turn away several of his friends, and at her age she did not enjoy climbing to the top of the house on yet another fruitless errand.

She made quite an issue out of their arrival, excusing herself and elaborating on her terms of duty to a repetitious extent. Jane saw that the old lady was quite worried about the silence from the top floor of her house. Her fluster was calmed by Jane's graceful demeanour – a mention of Boston did no damage – and Jane was given permission to knock on Mister Gay's door to see if he was home.

At first, Jane thought that Gay was dead. The windows were curtained and a stubby barrier of four candles burned on the table amidst the large pool of tallow, which had hardened about the remnants of food and had formed a shoreline around a sheet of greasy paper. Behind this pool Gay's face rested on his hands, its expression fixed and serene, the eyes glassy with a dull glow of candlelight. His cheeks were pinpointed with dried blood; otherwise his face was white-yellow, standing out against the dark loom of his shoulders.

Having buried her father and a brother, Jane was not frightened in the presence of death. Gently she walked across the room and opened the curtains. The sky was overcast and there was no great rush of light into the room.

When she turned she saw Mister Parsloe, and he was quite obviously dead; which made her think that Gay might not be so. She bowed her head. The light from the candles was sickly now, the grey and the yellow tangling feebly in an ugly smear. There was a hatpin by Gay's forearm, reddened at its point. A smell of urine seeped through the fug.

In the middle of prayer Jane was able to think quite quickly and clearly. She made her decision. She turned back, drew the curtains together and quietly left the room. She informed Miss Manley that Mister Gay was taken sick, and that she would return with a doctor.

Jane was nothing if not capable. She saw immediately that Miss Jarvis was not of a practical nature; but she took off her the name and address of her husband, who was acquainted with both John Gay and Edmond Parsloe. Mister Van der Hertz and Mister Philip Schultz were concerned to be of assistance.

They managed to sit Gay upright. His eyelids closed and his head began to totter uncontrollably from side to side. His jaw was so clenched that Jane was unable to force any food between his teeth. They laid him in the bedroom.

By the late afternoon, Gay's possessions were boxed and removed. The doctor had found no signs of the cholera. But when Mister Schultz's men brought up a box for Edmond they found it impossible to separate him from his chair, other than by breaking him in half; for the insects had so eaten away his anus and the lower part of his back that the flesh was part and parcel of the upholstery.

CHAPTER NINETEEN

Resurrection and Flight: the Rude Mechanicks

'O my soul, thou hast said unto the Lord, Thou art my Lord: My goodness extendeth not to Thee; but to the saints that are in the earth, and to the excellent, in whom is all my delight. I have set the Lord always before me: because He is at my right hand, I shall not be moved. Therefore my heart is glad, and my glory rejoiceth; my flesh also shall rest in hope: For Thou wilt not leave my soul in Hell; neither wilt Thou suffer thine Holy One to see corruption. Thou wilt shew me the path of life; in Thy presence is fullness of joy; at thy Right hand there are pleasures for evermore.'

The air had him now. Not for a moment could he sit or lie down or walk without the air relentlessly disturbing him. If Gay lifted a finger in his defence he was perturbed by the suddenness of the movement and horrified at his defiance.

Wherever the air takes me, there will I go. The air has sucked Titou to his death and has swept across Edmond's eyelids. The air is the authority in all this and the air is victorious.

'Amen,' said Missis Rutherford.

'Amen,' said Jane, Topsy, Alice, Charity, Kitty, Maria; together but not in unison.

'Thank you, John,' said Missis Rutherford. 'You do have such a fine strong voice for the scriptures.'

Jane in a flannel nightgown reminded him of something in his childhood. It was perhaps the thickness of the material. He slept in Jane's bed each Sunday night, when Jane was not entertaining. He didn't like to sleep with her, he preferred to sleep in the room behind the kitchen which was offered to him while he made his recovery; during which time Edmond was buried and Willibrord Van der Hertz and Schultz came sharply and then faded, leaving him to Jane. No, he did not like to be in her bed, but he recognised something of a contract in this arrangement.

There was no duplicity in Jane. Her manoeuvres were conducted quite out in the open. She had saved her money and wished to leave Missis Rutherford's on the first of May. She wanted to rent premises and to open a small haberdashery. 'It will be hard at first,' she allowed, 'but we shall make a go of it. Will you please see Mister Wells, John?'

When the Exchange had burned down at the beginning of the year, the brokers had arrived and had crowded on to the sidewalks and had attempted to conduct their morning business in the middle of Wall Street itself, up to their shins in mud and fire-blacked slush. Rennah Wells, who had watched the blaze with interest – and with gratitude for his first warm night in New York – found himself, as the tallest person in the best vantage point, being seized upon as a centre of communication and reference. In the general insecurity and fevered assertion his dispassionate manner – and above all the simple fact that he did not move – made him indispensable to the brokerage firm of Heath and Co. A number of shrewd or fortuitous comments on the godliness of certain hawkers found favour with a group of senior men who descended from their Hertz carriage at a later hour in the morning. The razing of the Exchange was not for them a disaster, but the destruction of the civilised veneer gave the maximum possibility for venting spite and personal dislike. Such would undoubtedly fall on certain heads – Rennah suggested – because of their shape and the dearth of moral qualities evidenced by the structure of the skull.

Such opinions might not naturally have influenced the American economy on any other day, but Rennah found himself carried along as a convenient pound-post to the empty warehouse of the bankrupted North Eastern Cement Company, where the Exchange found a temporary home. Thereafter he operated as a free-lancing adviser, deciphering not propositions but the character of the bearers of propositions; which surveillance at a later date scuppered an ingenious ruse fronted by Lord George Watters; who took his apoplexy to Missis Rutherford's, where Jane learned of Gay's connection.

Gay sat quietly in the corner of Rennah's room. He said nothing that would help Jane's cause. He gazed at Rennah. He picked at an untidy shank of hair which fell over his right ear. He sometimes appeared to take an acute interest in the proceedings, sitting bolt upright, and he twice held a single finger up on a level with his nose as though focusing on the pulse of a mutual interest. But Jane, whenever she glanced at him, could not see any sign that he was either willing, or able, to become involved.

The atmosphere was unhealthy. No matter how modestly she lowered her eyes, no matter how earnestly she presented her schemes, Rennah Wells would not concern himself with her. He hung away from her, his long body drooping down from his shoulders, like a folded bat. He spasmodically unwound and flapped around the room, in a high-spun voice bleating clips of gospel talk and abstruse reasoning. She was at first befuddled; then she was alarmed and angry that such a creature should presume to declaim on her prospects. It was evident that Rennah Wells knew nothing whatsoever about the establishment of haberdashery in New York; nevertheless he had the gall to assure her that the Lord would be willing to assist a lady of such industrious and graceful character.

Jane thanked him and hurried John out of the room.

Once outside in the street, Jane gathered back into her bosom those scatterings of calculation and ambition which she had laid before Mister Wells. She was hopeful. She was determined. Beside her, John hemmed and hawed, trivial with sapless agreement, until she could no longer contain herself.

'And *he* was the passenger on the Moravagine? That man is Rennah Wells?'

'Certainly.'

'And is that how they conduct business in London?'

'Possibly.'

'Oh come come, John!'

'Well, I know nothing of business,' Gay hastened. 'And Mister Wells is from your country, not mine. As I remember, his family is from Boston; you might be more familiar with the name than I. I am only familiar with the shape.'

'The shape?'

'His shape.'

'But surely you must know something of his qualities?' Jane complained. 'How may you judge a man by his shape?'

'That is what *he* does. It is a science. There is much to science which does not meet the eye. For instance, it is possible that an exact formulation of movement may unlock the greatest secrets – '

'Of what, for instance?'

'Of Beauty. I am certain that there is a key. And then surely there must be a key to Death, to the understanding of Death.'

But Jane understood only that Gay held no key which might fit her ambitions. Furthermore, as she instructed him, she was sufficiently commonsensical not to be further insulted by the crass pretensions of Rennah Wells.

Gay again visited Wells, this time on his own. He was not acting on Jane's behalf and Rennah never mentioned her name. The nature of the affair demanded confidentiality and Rennah delighted in such loftiness. Their contract was straightforward. Gone was the pretence at innocence which had so disgusted Edmond on board the *Moravagine*, gone was Rennah's feeble attempt at dissimulation. Together they went out through the night and dug up Edmond's body. They severed the head; which Rennah carried back to his room.

'You going home?' Rennah asked. And he spat. And Gay had never before seen him spit; it seemed an unusual thing for Rennah to do, out of character for the precise mechanic. Gay saw no reason to discuss his ill-formed plans but Rennah leered a persistent interest.

'You may wonder why I asked you to do this for Edmond – '

'I don't wonder.'

'I beg your pardon?'

'I said that I don't wonder.'

'But *I* do. And I will not leave him. He knows that he does not belong here, and I know that he must be buried where he belongs. *I* must go on, I want to go on. I am untried.' Gay stopped himself short. 'And I have no choice in the matter, Mister Wells. I am driven, often most painfully.' Gay felt for the side of his head.

'How do you mean "go on"? You mean west?'

'I mean only that I cannot go back. I cannot *look* back.'

Rennah perked up. 'I've been out that way before. I've been west and made a living.'

'A living?' Gay laughed. 'I don't think so.'

When Edmond's skull was plucked and peeled, and scraped and picked clean, and boiled pure, Gay returned and paid Rennah a further instalment of his fee.

Rennah sulked. Gay didn't understand his reasons for sulking but he worried that Edmond would no longer be safe. So he got Rennah talking. He got Rennah's advice. He got Rennah's palms resting on the crown of his head, the long fingers hanging down like spider's legs, probing and tip-tapping against the swelling at his temple. He got Rennah's judgement, Rennah's spite, the tip of Rennah's tongue avid over dry lips. 'I doubt whether you'll last a month,' Rennah delivered. 'Maybe. And that's if the fluid don't come any faster. Sometime it'll burst, and you'll end quick, Mister Gay.'

'Thank you,' said Gay – standing up quick – feeling still the clammy drape of Rennah's interest. There were moments, as now, when he felt as though part of his mind were trying to turn itself in a slow somersault, scraping raw against the bone of his temple.

Rennah stalked round in front of him, the eyes were a weak blue-grey and they did not hold overmuch concern. 'What'll you do?' he demanded.

It was not that she made him wash. Rather it was that Gay could not bear the sound of Jane's voice. It was unfortunate, but he writhed in exasperation every time she opened her mouth. That peculiarly eroding tone of concern, that ponderous indication of her excessive sensibilities, as practised as was her coyness before any gentlemen. He liked her well enough in every other way, but he could not bear the sound of her voice. He could not even concentrate on the banality of what she said. It was, however, quite clear that Jane's sense of hospitality would not extend to the arrival of Edmond's head.

'What'll you do?' Rennah insisted.

'I don't know. I have no money and I cannot get home.'

'Well.' Rennah grinned. 'I have family in Boston, and they owe me a favour for delivering up that Church man. Where there's Church, there's money behind.'

At the end of May, Miss Jarvis – at the request of her husband Mister

Van der Hertz — went into a haberdashery on Tenth Street, where she learned from that Robbins whore that Mister Gay had been gone some while since. He had taken one or two belongings and had disappeared.

CHAPTER TWENTY

Maggot as Pilgrim

Gay was much of an invalid in the middle of that coldest of winters which lingered on and on, stubbornly refusing any accession to spring. His head pained him more frequently and more deeply, the Maggot turning away from Rennah's fingers and burrowing for safety. It left a pulpy cushion beneath the skin at Gay's temple. It whispered to him – take me to the wilderness – and Edmond's voice whispered to him – take me home – and what with the two of them there was no peace; and there was no money.

Rennah Wells took him from Jane and lured him to Boston, although Rennah was in two minds about falling upon his family, not knowing how he might be greeted. To Rennah's surprise he had served them better than he had intended. His step-father Henry Marten was grateful. The best had been sedimented out of the Reverend Venn. A slim volume of the *Spiritual Exercises* would shortly be published, and the Reverend himself had been happily depressed into a slow and cloisterish regurgitation of his *oeuvre*. Marten foresaw a steady profit, with but a little curt encouragement being the sole expenditure. He had his author where he wanted him; so much so, indeed, that he was able to lodge John Gay with the Venns.

The Reverend had neither the time nor the depth of soul to communicate with John Gay. Out of print, Edward Venn carried no powers which might reconcile ghosts or settle sundered souls. But Missis Venn ensured that Gay did not starve nor freeze to death. Nothing could endear a human being to the Reverend, but his long-suffering wife had so delighted in the snippets of entertainment provided by Gay's legs aboard the *Moravagine* that she soon set about obtaining him a half term of employment as a teacher of dance at Miss Amelia Whitley's Academy for Young Ladies.

Gay thrived, his spirit succoured by the innocence of his pupils; the Maggot turned on its tracks and rose gently towards the surface.

Meantimes Rennah stuck in his family's gullet.

Come Spring, the good citizens of Boston emerged from their Temperance Societies to take up the cause of the Mississippi Indian tribes, lambasting President Jackson for his expropriation of their land. A Society of Friendship – in conjunction with the leather manufactory of Crocker – put up a team of mules and provided a wagon filled with cases of hymnals, shoes, copies of the Constitutional Declaration and an especially printed edition of *Spiritual Exercises*. Edward Venn came to a service of hymns at Miss Whitley's, and he spoke of a Mission to the Mississippi tribes.

One week later Gay was dismissed from Miss Whitley's for the improper habit of 'adonising', his strange attitudes being but a desperate response to the sharp and lurid visions which beat across his mind. He offered his services to the Mission. Edward Venn was only too happy to vouch for his character. Rennah's family were only too happy to put forward their own champion.

'Home?' Rennah spat, as they set out together. 'There ain't never no point in going home. Bring your friend, Mister Gay, and we'll have pretty much all we need for a whole damn church.'

'You preach?' Rennah asked. 'That kind of thing comes in useful. Most all actors preach.'

'No,' said Gay, and offered no further comment, for indeed he was hardly the master of his own words. Within his head the conversations raged, quite out of his control. His eyes played the part of a lugubrious coachman, behind whom his spirited passengers disputed uproariously. He let them get on with it.

Rennah sneaked a look at Gay's head – the smooth, full protrusion above the temple. There it was; yep, there it was, alright. Rennah knew better than to make a play. Praise be to God for the shape of John Gay. He sat back easily and grinned. Praise be to God for the Reverend Venn and London. Well, London. He had never before tasted such iniquity, and, bless me, if he didn't have something of an appetite for it. In London, bodies were cheap. Heads, praise be, were at a premium.

Rennah sat back and grinned. He saw no end of Good Business coming from this affair.

Out of the mist edged the stillness of long-stemmed pines, anchored in the dark forest floor. Their branches were lost to view, their feet were swaddled in rotting needles; through their utter silence the shriek of a bird resonated like a fiery ribbon. Amongst these trees there was no sense of distance, but of vast dark space. The gloom corridored in every direction, the corridors altered at every moment. The mules and the wagon might have been on a treadmill, for hours at a time remaining in the same place while slim trees in the blinking of an eye hopped backwards.

A flash of light-blue sky opened like a fan. The sheer cliff of rock gawped; the river flew hundreds of feet, smoothly, a brilliant white leap out into the sun like a shout of joy. Mountain ranges, glades, huge monuments of rock, starkness and gentleness. Splintered trees leaning across ravines, streams solemnly curtseying around massive boulders. Savagery, generosity, infinite age and a vast sweep of sky curtailed only by the presence of Rennah Wells: white-yellowish skin like stucco, a scrubland of wiry black hairs glued to his pockmarked cheek and, no matter what he ate, his smell.

Rennah assumed that there had to be some hard money put aside somewhere. He assumed that Gay, sponsored by the Reverend Venn, could be presumed to have the authority to call upon that money. Wells assumed so, hauling back on the brake-stick down before Amherst.

'No sir,' he told Gay, 'it wasn't like this in the beginning. Why, ten years since, a man went on alone with his faith. One or two weeks between seeing another human being, living off the Lord's mercy and whatsoever the land provided. A man was hard put to keep himself alive.'

'You've been there, to where we're going?'

'Maybe. Maybe. Saukenuk.'

'Indeed.' Gay nodded, and wondered.

He tucked his heels up on to the seat and sat with his knees as high as his chin, his right forefinger resting on the pulsation at his temple.

Rennah saw the pothole in the road. They probably wouldn't have avoided it anyway, but he made no demands on the team. The front of the wagon tipped, Gay rolled outwards; and then rolled back, and smiled peaceably, irritating the hell out of Rennah.

There was a very light green, stretching away from the Erie canal. It was the flimsiest green wash of Spring, balanced over a grey mat of dead and sodden stalks. Water slushed against the mules' feet and the wheels of the wagon. To Gay, who had not cacked solid in a week, it seemed as though the earth itself was trickling into this endless canal. Beside him Rennah Wells belched out a litany of vapid braggadocio, the collar of his shirt chafing raw the eruptions at his neck. Gay was cold. His bones were sore and pulpy. Why was he here?

'The Lord guided me to the river. I stood on that bank across from the Saukie village and I took that first step into the waters. It truly came on me alone to take the Lord upon my back and carry him across the Rock River into the midst of the heathen, protecting Him from their arrows and their ignorance.'

'No slings?' murmured Gay. He cleared his throat. 'The redskins had no slings?'

'Slings? No they don't have no slings. They don't have no wheels neither, what with not believing in their usefulness. They're a different people.'

They lost the Erie canal in the swampy, overladen town of Buffalo; and as they headed south the lakewind came between them, whistling such pitterpatter back up into the Alleghenies. Gay felt not that he was going backwards through time, but that, with the changing personage of Rennah Wells, he was travelling backwards through a species.

Gone were the fine Albany farmsteads and the ladies with strips of lace or silver cord adorning their heads. Now there were patches of ill-cleared ground hacked out of the forest. The cabins were rough and grimed from winter fires, the settlers drab and make-do in their dress; women bitter and sturdy, men furtive.

Cold and clear and firm came the days. Great flocks of birds slanted in from the weak sun down south. Something fell out of the sky without Rennah hardly bothering to aim the rifle. Within the space of two days the wagon was hung about with feathered meat; smeared eyes, heads lolling on twisted necks, bodies swaying to the jolts of the wagon like a thick, down petticoat. Gay questioned the reasons for such slaughter.

'Trade,' said Rennah. 'I don't see no reason to use up the Church's money on vittals when the Lord provides.'

The Lord provided. The skies were streaked and blackened. The edge of the lake was thick with strident hollering. But there was no trade. Every man in every homestead they came across had himself a morgue full of birds, with no spare cornbread to wipe the grease from his lips. There wasn't even hay to be had without paying. Wells dug into his pocket; he cut down the rotting carcasses and left them on the side of the trail.

Wells took to preaching of an evening. Bread appeared on the tables. At first he offered a tentative and milky consolation, which merely added to the gloom inside the cabins.

But the more Wells preached, the more preposterous became his threats and assertions. Gay saw that they were inspired by his unease in human company; he had a great need to be taken for a man of spiritual wealth. As if diseased the preacher was unable to restrain his spite, his tongue beat upwards like an entangled bird. Gay stared into the firesides, listening to the shrill hiss of damp wood, wondering which of the many Rennahs he detested the most.

'How come you don't preach?' Rennah insisted.

'I am an entertainer.'

'That might be a fine conceit for a man to hold out in these parts.'

'Any conceit is better than none at all, especially if it might make some money.'

'You ain't popish!' Rennah's eyes swung wide.

'No, but I take it that neither of us has any money.'

'Leaving aside the Church Fund.'

'Oh, Mister Wells, I wouldn't have you spending that. You must have dug into it already.'

'What I spent was give me by my mother.'

'Then I am personally in debt to you,' Gay hastened to reassure him. 'And you have your career as an artist. Which will take time, and some confidence on your part, until you are rewarded . . .'

'Until you get the Church Fund up from Saint Louis,' Rennah pointed out. His eyes flicked nervously from side to side of the track.

'What Church Fund is that?' said Gay. 'And what would such a fund have to do with me?'

The mules' feet slapped on through the ochre slush. Gay saw the genuine greed and credulity in Rennah, and laughed.

The next thing he knew Wells had stood up and was taking a swing at the side of his face. A murk shot through behind Gay's eyes and then he fell down against mud, cold, with mud clogging his nostrils and a pool of dirty water swirling through his mouth. When he turned his face up and spat, he saw Rennah's face like rotting bread way above him.

Wells fell with his knee on Gay's stomach, his hand took hold of a tuft of Gay's hair and pulled it back. Gay couldn't decipher what the man wanted to do. Wells himself seemed uncertain, his eyes hot and reddened, he didn't seem able to concentrate. The ball of his hand leaned on Gay's forehead, then his nose, then his chin. His fingers dug into Gay's neck like wedges, levering the head to and fro, like he was trying to prise open a jar.

The mud came up around Gay's nose. There was a time when he thought that he was dead. Struggle did him no good. His body was muscular but Wells was long and curled and winding and flexible as a snake, the fingers digging into his neck like teeth, darkness coming like the inside of a closed mouth. Gay was overwhelmed by a feeling of perplexity. He lost the feel of Rennah's body, he could not understand why Rennah chose to tinker with his mind, what it was that Rennah was after. But the answer to this came easy, and suddenly, and it was far too much for Wells. Gay didn't understand it either, for he was suddenly splashing back to the wagon for the gun and Wells was curled slithering and screaming and holding on to his belly in the mud.

Rennah gathered himself into a bag of gloom. Whenever they pulled up to a homestead or settlement he cried out to the settlers as though he had a nest of wasps under his shirt. Gone were the words of consolation, exhausted were the storms of retribution against the ungodly. Wells stank of defeat.

Gay wondered how they might progress. Wells chose to discard his boots and most often stood barefoot among the settlers, his hair matted with mud. The greater number of the settlers were in no position to respond to such a bald-faced demand for charity, and they were generous enough in hiding their disgust. On one fine day of Spring madness the mission was pelted with abuse and Rennah was laid low by a large rock.

The preacher was groggy for several days. Gay whipped on the mules. He was not in the mood for accepting nonsense. He sold *Spiritual Exercises*, bartered soul for belly food. He parted with two locks of the Blessed Virgin's hair and pushed gruel down between Rennah's clenched teeth. He once nearly got Rennah some staying under a roof, and with a fireside to dry him out, the woman's husband being broken-legged. She came to the back of the wagon looking for shoes; she fitted herself out then showed Gay a massive lunar rump and said that he could do it how he pleased, only to do it without delaying and be sure not to mark her about the neck.

'Take the shoes,' said Gay. 'They are gifted by our Society in Boston.'

'He ain't no preacher,' said the woman. 'I don't want none of your Lord's business, nor to be beholden for nuthin. If the Devil gives you a pair of shoes you follow him down into Hell. I don't want no givin, Mister. Git started.'

Gay understood perfectly the turn of her logic. However, frightened either by her wants or by his lack of them, the woman ran off without the shoes and bolted the door.

Wells took for the better, snarling at Gay occasionally and othertimes staring ahead and gossing a thin stream of brown juice down between his feet. When they ran out of daylight, and if they had come across no-one else, Gay put the mules on a hitching line and collected wood while Rennah lit up the fire from the pot which hung off the back of the wagon, swinging it whistling around his head until the pot glowed and sparks flew off like demons. Then, as they were seated comfortably enough with strips of venison browning in the skillet, Rennah would give out his Grace.

'You ain't goin to survive. The Lord will strike you down.'

'Amen,' said Gay. 'Tell me about it sometime.'

Rennah picked up the reins. They started to see Indians, most often a woman with a settler, and several times a pack of five or six men, once a file of twenty or so warriors with women and children; but Rennah wanted nothing to do with them besides nodding and grunting and driving on. He laid his rifle across his knees as though he had seen someone else do the same thing, and Gay couldn't imagine but that Rennah Wells survived on gesture alone, his Good Lord wincing as Rennah flummoxed his way from pit to post.

Fifty miles west of Cleveland. Out on the edge of nowhere, a high grey day of windblown havoc. The lead mules were sullen and refractory, one of them pissing a white fluid. The trail was poor, the whip was out to no useful consequence. Gay saw a large hare stand up on its hindlegs, the wind gusting its fur. Rennah was too slow with the rifle. They hadn't eaten well in two days. Gay said, 'I will preach tonight, Mister Wells, if you aren't especially minded to do so. And if we should find some few souls to comfort.'

Lord knows whether souls were comforted, but they surely were entertained. There never was such an amount of movement in a preacher, nor so many pictures to what he said.

Rennah couldn't make head nor tail of Gay's theme so cut about it was with fire and fishing and the great white bird of the soul, and gold and cold earth and storm, one time the ark of Noah and next the live crawling mask of Satan, all rolled like coloured artillery shot round a cabin; folk ducking, the preacher waving and flicking his hands at each delivery, spirits arising and descending like spiders on a line, the Saviour wrestling the demons into tranquillity, the head of Job a-perking up like a prairie dog.

If Rennah in his heyday had made the world tilt into the west, then Gay cavorted east and west and back again, balancing the ends of Creation like a man spinning plates on sticks, only to snatch them up at the end and lay them in a regular pile on the table.

At this point, Gay looked to Rennah to take his audience on to prayer, but Rennah hid away.

'Well then; look into your hearts!' commanded Gay. 'With the open eyes of little children, and find there the message of the Lord!'

While they searched, Gay slipped from the room and fetched in Venn's works, setting them on the table. He accepted forty cents and a package of venison, and a jug of whiskey was placed before him.

Gay sipped but little of the spirit for it tasted filthy, as though his gullet had been shaved with a blunt razor. Of the women all but the lady of the cabin gathered their shawls and children and returned to their firesides. The men brought stools up to the table and questioned Rennah as to his route and what he hoped to find at the end of it.

On every private occasion Rennah had represented Saukenuk as something of a stately garden whose ornaments and follies merely needed re-siting by the Lord in order to give the full reflection of a divine harmony. Much to Gay's surprise, Rennah now presented a most damning picture of this paradise. Menace seeped from every Indian house. Infernal chants gathered savages from the west to swarm along the banks of the Mississippi. Rennah conjured up blood, fire, dead families, burned crops, violated women.

Several of the settlers had heard tell of violated women. Their host ordered his wife to a neighbouring fireside. There was indeed a white girl of good family, not a hundred miles to the west, who had been taken off by six Indians, all of whom had their way with her. Damn near every kind of way that could come to a savage mind, treating her like a crittur, carrying her around half naked. Rumour had it she was a fine-looking girl, one of them Sweedies with light gold hair, firm and young, not like to be dragged naked through mud, the skin scraped from her knees and belly.

The fable unwound and the whiskey got drunk and the body of the Sweedie got more light golden. The men stayed long and ended unconscious drunk, burying their imaginings on their arms against the table. Rennah snuffled and snorted noisily. Gay lay on his back, staring at the slanting plaque of smoke above his head.

Rennah shook him awake in the early morning, a grey dawn hanging off the trees. There was nothing but one single woman about and she served them with a cup of hot water.

'Why is it,' asked Gay as he climbed back on the wagon, 'that you just look for the fear and lust in people?'

'You seen them. That's how they are.'

'It's not how the women are.'

'Women? Them women ain't no better than dogs.'

'Do the Indians keep dogs? Sweedie dogs?'

'She ain't no Sweedie. And no-one kept her, not long enough.'

Wells and Gay had themselves a competent double act for a while. Maybe Gay stole a deal of Rennah's thunder, or maybe Rennah couldn't hold to his dull side of the coin. One night Gay heard a gagging coming from the back of the wagon, and there was Rennah's seed fallen deep down upon childish burrow in the course of God knows what parable. Rennah blubbered, but that was no singsong to compare with the descant he gave out when Gay wrapped his cock in the mule whip.

Rennah took his punishment like a man. He walked behind the wagon. Ostensibly for his own benefit he thrashed at his back with a willow switch. Such a regular noise revolted Gay, but it both perplexed and inspired the team of mules to some consistent effort.

This hollering, bloodstained reed drew a sizeable congregation from the ague-stricken settlement of Detroit. But when at sunset the Lord reclaimed his throne in Rennah's head and thence urged him to ford the shallows of the Saint Clair river, he was met on the far bank by Captain James Pilkington of His Majesty's Seventh Hussars, who promptly consigned him to the Fort Malden guardhouse.

CHAPTER TWENTY-ONE

Evenings with the British Empire — Captain James Pilkington — Versions of Lady Catherine

Gay had no idea why Rennah should have led him to Fort Malden, unless it was that Rennah had decided to rid himself of any fellow traveller. Such a cavalier quittance was not convenient, for Gay had little wish to attach himself to an English outpost.

In Captain Pilkington's opinion, however, regular doses of rum and laudanum served to disinfect a body of unguarded petulance, captious folly, spiritual ambition or democratic fancy. He chose not to offer a single drop of this prescription to Rennah, but he ensured Gay's good health. Rennah was dumped into the guardhouse; Gay was offered lodgings within the officer's quarters.

The prescription was most effective. Pains which Gay had carried four thousand miles in his head diminished as to be almost imperceptible. Voices settled.

As to Rennah, Gay was hard pressed to imagine how they might go on together, for Rennah had reduced himself to a morbid pretension, and there seemed to be no further arrangement within which they might support each other's company. Qualmed by conscience, Gay feared that Rennah might even take his own life, and he set out to ascertain the preacher's condition.

The garrison must have been undermanned, for he was not accosted as he crossed the compound and there was nobody guarding his caged companion. He saw immediately that there were no materials with which Rennah might contrive to crucify himself, and the ceiling was so low that Rennah would have found it impossible to hang his length to its satisfaction.

'I have brought you some food,' said Gay, and was at once invited to prostrate himself, to search through his heart for the ways of righteousness, to seek out false pride and so on. Rennah seemed to have recovered something of his normal unbalance. With no little sense of irritation Gay confessed to his lack of worthiness and suggested to Rennah that they should settle upon going their different ways.

'I am used to tribulation,' Rennah moaned.

'Then I leave you to revel in it.'

'Satan! Satan!' And Rennah then came out with a somewhat peculiar summary of the credentials pre-requisite to a descent into Perdition. 'Lawyer!' he hissed.

As Gay stepped back across the compound, he felt hugely relieved. The clearest, deepest night lay off the earth in playful benignity, stars winking down the channels of darkness. He inhaled pleasurably, several times, and walked to the wagon, where he took down his bag and the box containing Edmond, and carried them back to the Captain's quarters.

Gay stood with his bag and box, halfway down the room, and it seemed as though the Captain had quite forgotten about him; but he observed that along the interior wall of the room a door had been left ajar, to which thin slit clung a feeble light.

It was without doubt a woman's boudoir. The lamp glass was a rosy pink. There were bottles of perfumes and eaux. Other items suggesting intimacy were neatly arranged around a small mahogany dresser which stood beneath the curtained window. The bed was ornate and set with fine linen. There was a large armoire; which held an army of wispy materials and rich colours. Gay returned to the salon.

'Does not Missis Pilkington usually sleep in that room?'

To which query the Captain, from a strange state of remote priestliness, wove the following fantastic story:

That there was no Missis Pilkington. That the room was at one time inhabited by a very great beauty, a Lady Catherine Jenkin.

She had become quite savage by imitating a redskin way of life. Her husband had imported every new frippery and contrivance in an effort to regularise her tastes, but she would have none of it. Not a season passed without a new cargo of brocade and taffeta arriving by boat or wagon from Paris. Silks and satins, every species of shoe and ruffle and undergarment.

Her husband had behaved with the utmost dignity, standing by her and seeking to comfort her. But her mind was taken, and one day her body, too, left him. He searched for her, and prayed for her; until the Indians brought her back, having no use for her. She was now quite in her own world, quite beyond reach even of her own husband; though her person was returned by him to England where he hoped that the customs of civilisation would restore her mind. She had left behind all her possessions, claiming to have no need of them.

Gay was not quite convinced by what the Captain said, but he had no wish to offend him by setting snares. He briefly explained who he was and the absurd nature of the mission he had undertaken but temporarily with his unhinged companion. As Gay spoke, his words seemed no less fantastic than the Captain's own offering; so that at the end of the evening they sat in a harmony of bemused silence, each man twiddling his history around his mind and staring emptily heaven-wards.

In the late morning Gay drew aside the curtains to observe a creamy grey mist. Light rain beaded the windows. He crossed the room, untied the wooden box, pushed his hands down inside, and lifted out Edmond's skull, to which the sawdust had stuck like stiffened mash.

Edmond's bone had yellowed slightly, save for where the sawdust had stuck fast. Gay took a hatpin from Lady Catherine's dresser and picked the head clean; so it now seemed that Edmond, in his mottling, was suffering from a subdued skin disease. Gay set the skull atop the dresser, took his place on the end of the bed, and consulted the globe of bone.

Much later, his head beating against a band of pain, he stood up and walked to the window, where a pale disc of sun swayed through the flimsy sky. Gay opened his bag and took out the mask and cap, the ruffed shirt, the blouse and pantaloons; for it had occurred to him that he was without any money whatsoever and would have to ply his trade. He hung the Harlequin costume from the door of the armoire. Since leaving New York he had only rummaged through the bag, refusing to acknowledge the startling reds and greens and blues and the silvered spangles. Boston had been uniformly drab and, heading west, such diversification as there was tended only to explore the further possibilities of drabness.

Within this armoire there was at least colour; and expensive colour, as Gay saw, and in an astonishing variety of size, as though the wearer swung between gluttony and abstinence. Furthermore, all the clothes might be said to be for evening wear, as if this occasionally large and tall person had nothing to do all day but to lie a-bed, her mind swayed into reverie by the rich musks at her side, with her sole obligation being but to arise and carry herself gracefully towards the dusk.

That evening, the Captain's rum again eased the pressure within Gay's head. He raised his glass. 'To Lady Catherine Jenkin, wherever she may be!'

'By God, you take too much liberty, Mister Gay!' the Captain complained. 'You may do what you will with your acting, for that is within your tradition; but outside those confines you have no licence to offer insult, sir. It is my belief that a lady should be respected. Lady Catherine is a remarkable creature, perhaps the most estimable representative of her sex.'

Gay did not offer an apology, for his own pride had been somewhat damaged by the Captain's brusque refusal to sit through any Harlequin entertainment. He had, in his time, seen quite a sufficiency of Harlequins. He had recently been singularly unimpressed by the spectacle of a dozen Harlequins skulking through Philadelphia in the way of announcing the arrival of a circus.

The Captain gazed out through the lamplight, past Gay. He put down his cigar. He raised his eyebrows and expelled a good deal of smoke, some of which infiltrated his beard, other of which caused him to shut his eyes until the offending cloud took its place elsewhere.

He began his second story:

'There was a Lady Catherine *Pilkington*,' he announced, much in the way of a casual observation, which Gay perceived as a light overture to what was edging out of the wings of his mind. Gay responded politely.

'Indeed.'

'Still is, I shouldn't wonder. I thought the world of her. Not a great beauty, but a beauty. A beauty of character, Mister Gay.'

'Indeed.'

'To which a man would offer whatever portion of the world he might hold dear. Without demanding anything in return. Would that not be correct? I think that it is correct. And I also believe that it is natural for such an attitude not necessarily to impress a woman. Would you not agree? A woman's love is simply there, in a quiet existence of its own. It is not noticed. A woman's love is falsely coloured by our expectation.

'Mister Gay, I am here, at more or less the end of the world, because I could not restrain my expectations of my wife. In all innocence she unleashed the most frightful passions within me, Mister Gay, a most piercing sentiment of love and yet an exasperation at her own indisturbance. My God, she was so composed. She exerted the most absolute self-possession in the face of my feelings. I was taken by the wildest hatreds towards her, I could at times hardly restrain myself from violence against her person. "You have my love," she would comfort me. "I do not know what else you want of me. What do you want of me?" And I had no answer. It was as if our passions were confined within the smallest space and she, conserving the supply of air, breathed slowly and calmly while I fought in a frenzy of suffocation. My behaviour was that of a child, Mister Gay, whose bitterness knew no limit. I was obliged to remove myself entirely from her, so loathsomely anguished were my feelings. Indeed, at the end, I could hardly bear to set eyes on her. In all honesty I feared that I might assuage my hatred for myself in some form of vengeance against her.

'I saw no way other than to accept this posting. I believed that I would at least preserve her from harm. And yet I hear that her heart is broken, as is my own.' The Captain stroked his beard. 'In short, Mister Gay, I doubt very much whether we men have the capacity to understand a woman, and still less do we have the capacity to understand ourselves.'

The Captain showed no interest whatsoever in entering upon a conversation, apparently wishing to indulge himself in a presentation of his own shortcomings. Gay appraised him as an unfortunate man, encumbered by a sense of his own solitude, above which he could not rise and which he chose to exacerbate. He perhaps found some recompense amongst the cloisters of a military career, or did he forever take refuge in such embroidered yarning?

All at once the Captain accosted him, possibly detecting Gay's mistrust. 'But why are you here, sir?' he demanded. 'For what reason have you arrived here, at the edge of the known world, with your hotchpotch of theatrics and your Yorick?'

'For what reason,' Gay sprang, 'do you place lavender amongst a woman's clothes?'

There was a sudden antagonism in the room. Each accused the other of infringing the laws of privacy. The Captain persisted in questioning Gay's motives. Gay did not wish to be taken seriously for he had no reasonable answer. 'I care not for myself,' he declared with a flourish. 'I am an actor! I am nothing more than that which I create.'

At which the Captain promptly wagered him a hundred dollars that he could not create a woman.

'Done!' said Gay, who needed the money.

On the third night, as Gay sat before the glass to apply the last of his colouring, his strongest feeling was one of joy. He recalled Edmond's angry exhortation in New York before they were to entertain the Hamblins – that he should give of his utmost if he would survive – and he felt that he was in some way living up to Edmond's expectations; and he was joyful.

Beneath his joy lay pride; a confident, marvellous pride – for he was, as he saw in the glass, extraordinarily beautiful.

He wiped his hands. He lifted the wig and dabbed perfume behind his ears, and he then buttoned up the white kid gloves. He sat quite still, as if to impress this portrait upon the surface of the glass.

He welcomed the anticipation to his belly. It was common to the moments preceding any entry upon a stage; and, as was common to all his entries, the precision of his gracefulness quieted his anxiety.

He was initially reassured by a startling evidence of his success. The Captain stiffened to attention. His eyes lingered between Gay's face and costume. Gay felt sufficiently confident to raise his own eyes which, to his horror, travelled up the thin lank length of Rennah Wells, who was furtively scrutinising the lady's ankles.

Silence teemed. Gay strove to master his hatred. He did not know what to do, until he realised that he had quite quelled the two men into a pathetic docility. He allowed himself to float passive, swaying with the veils of scent around his body. And then he was a little alarmed, for having thus presented himself he could not now think what to do with these stupefied creatures.

'My dear . . .'

The Captain came across to him and held out his arm for Gay, who maintained a proper distance from his escort. The walking was not difficult, for the Captain made every allowance for the shortness of the female step. The skirts were not constrictive, but they brushed and rasped from side to side, an exquisite disturbance to his groin. Gay blushed.

'May I introduce the Reverend Edward Venn. Lady . . . Catherine.'

'Reverend Venn.' Gay scarcely bothered to conceal his repulsion for Rennah, such *froideur* being most lady-like in the circumstances.

Rennah jerked forward and bowed. They exchanged rather less than what might be called a glance, and Rennah did not seem to recognise Gay. He made lumbering pretences at eloquence but appeared exceedingly top-heavy and grotesquely mannered, being no doubt convinced that such elaboration was the cornerstone of Boston religious authority. Gay struck quickly.

'Forgive me, sir.' He smiled coyly. 'But do I not recall your name being printed beneath many uplifting interpretations of the scriptures?'

Rennah wavered. Fright and avarice scudded across his eyes as he strove to understand what risks and what rewards he might expect. A painted smile tipped him into audacity. He mumbled a modest acceptance of the compliment.

There was a decanter of port wine on the table but the Captain made no move to encourage Rennah's stay. Instead he escorted Gay across the room to a chair and went back to take up the coat-tails of a conversation which Gay had only heard as a low murmur before making his entrance.

'The point, sir,' he announced to Rennah, 'the point is that His Majesty's armies have no right and no reason to enter those territories, or States as they now are. There is no military alliance between His Majesty and any tribe residing within the States. The movement of any such tribe is a matter of domestic policy for your Washington government. It is no secret that Chief Black Hawk visits Fort Malden each year. He is accorded the position of ambassador and is given all respect due to that position. He is, sir, a gentleman, and a military gentleman. Fort Malden has always recognised him as such and will continue to do so. That is His Majesty's policy. And I will obey my orders, sir, despite a deep personal revulsion for the shameless conduct of the politicians. May I take it that you have understood me, Mister Venn?'

Such a feat hung in the balance, as did Rennah's gawping jaw which Rennah promptly slammed shut like a barnacle-encrusted clam, smacking his mind into its half-life. He jutted out his chin.

'You mean, you ain't goin to move.'

'No, sir, I am not going to move. I am not even going to offer you dinner. What reason, Mister Venn, do you have for your concern?'

'The lie of the land,' said Rennah. 'I was just seeing the lie of the land.'

There was a knock at the door. The Captain stared at Rennah and walked out of the room.

Gay heard nothing. The stove made no sound save for the soft brushing of hot smoke as it travelled up the flue. He heard nothing, and he felt nothing until he felt Rennah's fingers, hot and damp, sliding down over the wig towards his temples.

'Well, shit . . .' Rennah murmured appreciatively, his fingers caressing Gay's skin. 'You whore of Babylon. The Lord have mercy. You think you could rid yourself of me?'

'No.'

Rennah cackled nervously.

Gay explained himself.

'Captain Pilkington will get rid of you. You are as mad as each other, and he will do what I tell him even if you won't.' Gay rose from his chair.

Rennah grinned sheepishly. The smell of fart eddied upwards past Gay towards the stove. When the Captain returned he found Gay, *en hauteur*, fluttering his fan. He apologised for his absence. He ordered Rennah to find his military escort outside in the courtyard and Rennah departed to the cells.

Once again the Captain apologised. He suggested that the warmth of the evening might be enhanced by the partaking of a glass or two of port wine before dinner was served.

The Captain poured himself a dose and sat upright. He took refuge in

his cigar, his head slightly tilted back, his ██████████████
vacant space above the window, as if he hope██████
musical note. Though there was no effect of supercilo██
posture seemed to indicate Gay's dismissal. As if to confirm ▪
Captain said, 'You have made a great success. I thank you.'

Gay stood and dropped a half-curtsey. Raising his head, he interrupted a quick appraisal of his neck. The atmosphere within the salon was strikingly forlorn, anchored around the Captain's flask and spreading a circumjacent defeat throughout the room.

'I am no Lady Catherine,' murmured Gay.

Had he not heard Pilkington's speech to Rennah, and witnessed the firm principles of his honour, Gay might well have rustled quietly back to his bedroom, insisting on his contract despite the desolation in the salon. His Lady had taken much work, and he had a right to payment. But the Captain was neither a merchant nor whoremonger; and Gay, without obligation, found within himself a respect for the man and a dismay for his feelings. He was touched to see the hundred dollars being placed discreetly beside his setting at the dining table.

He accepted a dose of rum and the steady, grateful gaze.

'Shall we not dance?' he suggested.

'Madam,' the Captain stated solemnly, 'you cannot imagine what pleasure that would give me.'

They began considerately, Pilkington not knowing of Gay's talents as a dancer. He himself was remarkably adroit for so stoutly proportioned a man. He handled his partner expertly, removing from Gay every responsibility and initiative, taking great pleasure in thus exercising his authority. Gay succumbed to such mastery. It was a strange and acute sensation to be thus manipulated, to surrender with the certainty of being claimed. There was a firm pressure about his waist and back. His slippers scratched lightly across the floor, the skirts flung out like fishermen's nets, arcing away through the air, swivelling and foaming in around his calfs with a dizzying rush. Pilkington hummed the first tune and thereafter gave moderate voice to a string of linked melodies, pressing his finger against Gay's shoulder to give warning of the change in rhythm. His rich brown eyes were courteous and attentive, bestowing his pleasure upon Gay in a generous and reverential manner.

. . . not hear the knock at the door. The Captain did not break step, but he called, 'I have no need of you, Subbie. You may retire.' And he took up the serenade without further interval.

There was no other interruption. They danced for the best part of an hour. Eventually Pilkington weakened and rested his arm about Gay's waist. He led Gay to the window. Gay breathed pure moonlight and was dazed by the sudden stillness of his gown: he looked down at his hands, slender within the white leather gloves, and at the thicker, stronger fingers which covered them; until he could do none other than meet the Captain's doting surveillance.

'I do not like to be kissed,' Gay whispered.

Pilkington raised Gay's hands and pressed his lips to them in turn, upon the knuckle.

'My dear boy, I bid you what remains of a splendid night,' he said; and he bowed, and he left the room.

That was the last Gay saw of the Captain's moral fibre: for when he awoke, disturbed by the echoes of some strange, destructive sound, he wandered into the salon and saw that Pilkington had hanged himself from a beam above the upturned dining table.

He removed a long and ugly dirk from the Captain's belt, he packed one or two accoutrements. There was a single sentry, high up on the stockade, but this man paid no attention as Gay plus mule stole into the night.

CHAPTER TWENTY-TWO

The Shaman Waboshiek Befogged – He Smells the Maggot – He Visits Gay in Chicago, Dressed as a Dog – He Visits Edmond in the Forest, Dressed as a Bird – And He Takes a Specimen from Gay – He Visits Gay in the Wilderness, Dressed as a Mouse – He Leaves Gay in the Company of Death – He Being the Shaman Waboshiek

A breeze swayed the blue-stem. The rays of the sun touched the hilltop grass and then, blade by blade, came down to warm the valley. Waboshiek felt the imminence of the coloured man, the dancer.

Waboshiek rode the drum. He climbed, and with his spirits he went to search out this dancer. He would not normally have bothered, for from the east came many ripples of sightless death following the pulse of fog. The pulse had come, and had swept through Saukenuk, and had gone. But there was no foretelling of this new manifestation which he did not recognise and which would not offer recognition.

Each time Waboshiek smoked he saw the twists of the wind which devoured itself. Trees, rivers and earth were sucked up past him into the wide gyrating funnel of the wind.

He considered carefully as to who might be sending him such a spirit, but he could trace no source. It was not strong enough to threaten him. It surely referred to the dislocation which had taken place at Saukenuk.

Waboshiek became irritable. He withdrew. He rode the drum. Amongst everything else he saw the miserable Dungbeetle preacher, who had crawled back into the fog in the east, feeding on his crossed bits of deadwood. But ahead of him was the coloured man. The coloured man was a bright little shell, fizzing with gesture. Waboshiek understood such gesture – in a way remarkable, coming as it did from a man whose race never communicated with anything other than deadwood. It amused Waboshiek that the coloured man seemed to have a soul. The coloured man was transparent and should be dead, save for the Maggot in his head.

Waboshiek waited. To pass the time he entertained himself with the coloured man and grew his hair and got on Catherine's nerves.

The few hundred habitants of Chicago, their numbers swelled by squatters, drew their boats in from the lakeside for their celebration of deliverance from the Indians. Oven-pits were dug in the street. Spits were greased and guns sounded off.

They ate: Broiled Trout, Baked Black Bass, Venison and Buffalo Tongue, Mountain Sheep, Wild Goose, Quail, Redhead Duck, Jack Rabbit, Blacktail Deer, Coon, Canvasback Duck, Blue-wing Teal, Partridge, Widgeon, Brant, Pheasant, Mallard Duck, Prairie Chicken, Wild Turkey, Spotted Grouse, Black Bear, Opossum, Leg of Elk, Sandhill Crane, Ruffed Grouse, Cinnamon Bear, Butterball, English Snipe, Plover, Red-wing Starling, Grey Squirrel, Antelope Steak, Oyster Pie, Pyramid of Wild-Goose Liver in Jelly, Boned Quail in Plumage, Prairie Chicken en Socle.

Gay came upon them at night, drawn by the smell from far up the shoreline. He did not travel late in the day, when the sun blazed down from the west, for the sun scraped at the sockets of his eyes and he could only advance into a glaring mist, nudged forward by the snapping teeth of the mule.

The town stank of roasting flesh. A greasy smoke collected in the main street, where half-dismembered animals were thrown up beside the glowing pits and lines of huddled, charred birds were strung across between shacks and tents. Dogs sped maddened through this gallery of corpses. They fought viciously and shortsighted amongst each other. They ran as if wind-crazed, with banners of intestine flapping and bouncing behind them. There was free liquor in appreciation of the Post's deliverance.

Gay missed the point of it; or perhaps missed the centre of it, there being no centre. He gladly offered the mule to the hellish gorge, but mules were held sacred. He reached the end of the street and sold off that malevolent creature to the one sober man in the Post. The mule fetched good money for the trading was fur-rich come early summer. Gay ate bread and warm meat of quibbled origin. He drank a glass of penetrating filth, took one look back downtown and then crawled on to the dry sand beneath a shed, where he slept to the lap of the lake.

Next day he scavenged and slept, his head thick with pain. Mid-afternoon he threw himself into the cold lakewater. The shock of the cold and the perturbing stillness of the water took him from himself. He stood on the shore, shivering with hatred, and then he wheeled and ran, along the hard damp strand, past the canoes where a man in a waterlogged bearskin coat floated face down. He ran two thousand paces north and returned, quite dry, as the lake greyed over with dusk decline. He purchased another glass of penetrating filth and wandered amongst the carcasses in the street, picking at a loaf of warm bread. The bones did not interest him although he collected a dozen different beaks, beautifully lacquered by the heat of the ovens.

Festivity crammed into the cabins, away from the wreckage. Gay knew better than to present himself for sport. In the eighteen days since he had left Rennah there had been no-one to avoid. He went back to his lair. In the shed above him the trade was in hamfist vociferation, gruesome puling, snore and puke-ballad. Gay bedded as near as he could to the lake without losing the cover of the platform on which the shed rested.

At dawn the shed stank. Shiny vomit lay about, strenuous in a reek of pine sap and corn whiskey. Straight in under the shed came the sun sliding pell-mell across the glass lake. Hurling a wall of light up against his eyes – at first a scarlet screen then a white magnified brilliance – firing the pain in his head. He twitched, and flinched, and burrowed into the loamy sand but the pain was awakened and rampant.

A dog ran in, weaving between the piles, and sniffed at his head. It gaped a rancid, bilious alcoholic breath over the side of his face. He covered his head with his hands. The dog ferreted and pilfered at his groin. It slobbered and straddled and snuffled at his crotch, its hard thin penis switching madly at his thigh. It had its way, yelped and ran off a few paces, slouched and licked itself.

The dog did not again molest Gay but remained overbearingly attentive, bringing him a selection of decaying meat and whingeing at him. Gay crawled away from the sun. The dog became agitated. It did not have the cheerful stupidity of a puppy, nor the unpredictable temper of a wild dog, but it was unable to settle and was perpetually aggravated by its ears, its paws and its tail; and it was exasperated with him. At some point in the midmorning a pack of dogs skirted the shed and showed some interest in making mischief. Gay seized his stick and knife; but his own dog's lips pulled back in a racked snarl and its fur splayed upwards and outwards to a remarkable extent. It stood up on its hindlegs and so transformed itself into a bear-like, warring apparition that the pack could only group quickly in protest before swapping defence for flight. Gay was startled; but in the twinkling of an eye the dog subsided and became abashed, almost frightened by its feat, as though it had for a moment lost all sense of its own identity.

The pains left his head. As had happened before, his surroundings were presented to Gay in an unnatural clarity; as if a dry, wintery sun chose to pick amongst a denuded atmosphere. Buildings, trees, fenceposts, rocks; all were isolated within their individual outline. He bathed once more and ran up the lakeshore. The drowned man was being pulled from the water like a hirsute bat. The dog did not run with Gay but sat on a bank staring out at the lake. When Gay returned he noticed the dog standing on a rock, some fifty yards out into the water. It lunged sporadically a front paw down into the lake, and Gay saw that it was fishing.

From the trading post he purchased a compass, strips of dried meat, a burlap bag which might be strapped across the shoulders, and a comet tin such as Rennah had hung from the tailgate of the wagon.

His mule was one of two dragging an unfinished beam crossways down the main street, playing Charon with the carcasses which snapped and splintered as they were caught up in the wave of carrion. As he passed the mule, Gay spat cleanly at its nose. With the sun's height he quit Chicago and followed a light green trail into the shade of the forest.

The dog caught him and snapped at his heels, pushing him forward. Gay whacked it with his stick. The dog followed him happily enough for a mile or more, than it ran ahead and ate grass and vomited violently, back arched like a concertina. It walked on until its back went soft, and it couldn't drag its hindlegs. Syrup came out of its eyes. It dragged itself away from Gay and the lid slapped shut on its life; yet the day was warm and sunlight purled through the trees like a sonata.

The night rained. Gay was not wary and lost his fire, the tin being cold and blistered with damp come dawn. There was nothing to do but to run on, birds halting their arias, wet grass bowing despondently. His feet slipped on the Boston soles. The chill sank hard about his neck and thighs. Every now and then the trees stirred and as from a sower's arm let loose a beaded shawl of water, which pounced across his shoulders. On he ran. In his black clothes he looked like nothing so much as a shadow which nobody wanted to chase.

The rainbow came one noon and with it came the end of the track, which curled round upon itself to disappear down towards a stream. Gay had passed above two cabins, neither of them showing any signs of life although being in good repair. As was the cabin in front of him.

Gay hallooed but the sound was drawn away amongst the trees. There was a child's barrow outside the cabin and a strong goodness about the place. Inside was tidy, in the way a woman would leave it in order to assure herself of the pleasure of returning home. He washed his mudded clothes in the stream and laid them out on the roof to dry. Having nothing else to wear he put on the Harlequin costume. In the corner of the cabin there hung a haunch of venison, wrapped up in muslin, a scent of burned juniper weaving through the room. Gay left money for two slices on the table.

He sat on the porch steps to eat and when he had finished he swept the steps clean and replaced the twig broom against the doorframe. The family must have gone partying to Chicago. There was no breath of wind to the forest. The sky had cleared with a lazy powder of blue, the sun held off by light green foliage. Birds criss-crossed the forest roof with a tracery of echoing song. Gay fetched out Edmond's head and set it on the top porch step.

He begrudged Edmond nothing but after several moments he felt alone, even lonely. There wasn't much life in the skull. He walked several times around the cabin, each time coming back across Edmond's head which rested inert on the step.

At the back of the cabin a path rose towards the edge of the forest. Gay covered half the distance before considering that he should not leave Edmond untended. The consideration was not for Edmond but for the family should they suddenly return home, especially for the children who would be frightened. Indeed Gay thought that the family *had* arrived home, for leaning against the porch was a slender man, elegant in black britches and fitted coat, who showed a keen interest in his domain. It was only a bird of prey, black and bigger than a raven, perched on Gay's trousers which had slipped from the edge of the roof and lay hanging from the porch rail. Apparently dead and stuffed, it ignored Gay as he reached two hands around its body. It shuffled sideways. Staring at Gay with spite, it dug its beak into his head above the temple. Gay let go of the bird but it managed to take a tuft of his hair before launching itself off in a low sweep between the trees.

The path rose to the edge of the forest, and beyond that the Spring-flowered prairie rolled and dipped and rose far away to the heavy red sun. Gay stood with Edmond's head under his arm. His warm spangles shivered. He held his friend's rosy skull aloft and showed Edmond how he might dance if he were still at an age to be nimble.

The sleep that night was undisturbed. On awakening, Gay's first thought was that he had slept remarkably well, a luxury for which he was grateful. His one dream had been of that same view across the open prairie, only the prairie had been closely cropped, like a lawn. Not fifty yards in front of him the back of a great serpent had pushed its way out of the ground, scattering clods of earth. It rose to a height of some fifteen feet and there was still no daylight beneath it. Appendages, like roots, grew off the back of the serpent, making it even more monstrous. It did not have a head or perhaps the head had surfaced many miles away. As Gay advanced the body sank back into the ground, the earth followed it and the surface of the land was as before. There was but one narrow join through which a small part of the body could be seen. He scraped away at the earth and with his knife cut out a sliver of the body. The morsel was not of flesh but of white succulent root, like ginger or thistle but sweet-juiced and delicious. Gay awoke with the taste on his tongue.

He tidied the cabin, shouldered his affairs, and took the path up towards the prairie.

For five days he and Edmond wandered knee-high in colours, talcum-scented and lispy with bee-song. Pale, eternal blue laced with fragile white. Tangled purple. There were times when he could hardly bear to raise his head against the million million pinpoints of colour which swayed and frothed for many miles on every side of him. He was dazed by the rich swathes of light, and by the numbers: twenty, two hundred flowers at each knee, a thousand as he raised his eyes, with hundreds of thousands pressing in from the sides. Sometimes there was a limitless fundament of blue.

He waded on. He took comfort from the colours which he himself wore; his own colours, red and green and dark blue stretched across his thighs and forearms in secured diamonds, patterns of colour within an exact stitching, guaranteeing him against the insolent recklessness which massed away from him on every side.

Unless he made an especial effort he did not see his feet for hours at a time. From mid-thigh he floated on a rippling pond of colour, and might at any moment be washed across the surface of the prairie. Sometimes he fell headlong, or sideways, for no reason, finding himself in a green shade, convinced that he was still walking even though he was paralysed. His feet lived in a dream world, neglecting the needs of his body.

He once in a frenzy jumped and trampled flat a circle of sufficient diameter that he might lie down and see all of his body, and he saw that his ankles were bloodied red. His feet were not sensitive to touch. At the perimeter of his circle there were any number of insects, crawlies, hoppers, inquisitive antennae, which lived beneath the fluid crust of colour. When he walked he trod upon a mat of tangled dead growth. There was no earth. The vegetation fell into smaller and smaller pieces – rotted, compressed – until it was seized upon by a root. The surface of the prairie was nothing but a writhing web.

In the damp mornings he slipped amongst dew-misty shallows. By midday the stalks were toughened and the flowers brilliant. His thighs drudged against a weighty curtain. The prairie was still unmarked, subsiding gently and rising again, the sheets of colour ruffling at the slightest breeze. The sky was cloudless, his progress being occasionally darkened by vast floods of birds winging noisily to the north. Hawks and larger birds of prey sometimes appeared from nowhere to wheel overhead but there was no sense of journey to their whimsical and silky flight. Gay had a compass and he had the sun, but he still was not convinced that he was heading in any particular direction. When plumes of black cloud came up ahead of him and reached shiny-rimmed to blot out the sun – dark unease coming over the land – Gay turned to his right and forced onwards, his soul imploring the last of the wind-whipped birds for guidance.

The prairie became still and thick with congested light. Cloud loomed over him like the gigantic black body of a slug. Thin feelers probed the land – flickering, stabbing – to see where the rumbling beast might collapse. The storm droned across his head, the weepy tentacles of lightning draped venomously. They searched for a tree, a shrub, any creature on which they might alight. Gay weaved and ran and fell. The lightning danced. The grasses shuddered and a great crash started from behind him as if the heavens had hit the earth head-on, and stopped. The shock grumbled back through the dense body of the storm.

There was silence, and then the grasses around Gay rustled as though giving way to the crazed thrashing of wounded animals. Something – hoofs? – kicked down on Gay's back. All around him the hoofs thumped. He drew his legs up to his chin and covered his head with his hands, warding off the blows. A minute later they were gone.

It was cold. Gay could not stop himself from shaking. The sky was a deep felted grey, the lightning no longer danced. He stood up. Scattered around him in the flattened grass were white rocks of ice, cold, thick as his fist. Above the prairie, to the west, there was a long slit of blithe blue sky.

The flowers were beaten down. For perhaps two hours Gay walked amongst the ice cobbles, slitting open the bodies of rabbits and sucking on their sticky warm flesh.

The grasses became coarser and more dense. Despite its tricksy undulations the mean level of the land had been rising steadily. The flowers were patchier and already withering, the grasses stern and thicker stemmed.

He came out upon the flat lid of the prairie, a knee-high stubble bland and close-ranked to take on the summer. He was freed from colour. He saw, heard, and smelt acutely. But the sun harassed him without pity. He suffered again from the head pains and was obliged to limit his progress, travelling only along the extremities of the day.

Quite suddenly he was accompanied through the light grey hours by a mouse. The mouse jumped! It jumped six or so feet into the air and covered double that distance before arcing back into the grass. It scared the dying daylights out of Gay when it first rocketed past him. The third, fourth, fifth, sixth and seventh times he went to bat it into the distance, but the mouse sailed past his flails, quite joyous in its varied trajectories. He grew fond of the mouse, and as he grew weaker he envied the creature its vivacious frolic.

He prayed that the mouse might guide him to water, for since leaving the flowers he had not been able to refill his flask. The mouse remained tirelessly oblivious to his needs. Gay grew exasperated and might have killed it, had he possessed sufficient vigour.

It was an hour after the sun had risen. Its gold leaned heavily against his back.

His own shadow teased him. Dismembered, it flitted in particles over the stems in front of him. Light-headed, heavy-spirited, his tongue rasping dryly against his gums, Gay surveyed the monotony of the prairie. He had been struggling for three hours. Behind him his trail showed clearly for a hundred paces or so and then the grasses closed up and the prairie was unmarked.

Shielding his eyes against the sun he walked back seventy paces. He had, some moments before, started counting. The mouse had not risen according to wont and he thought that it might be injured. Gay waited, but the little body did not hurtle through the air. He searched. He half-heartedly flattened the prairie, until it occurred to him that he might have flattened the mouse. He lifted some of the grasses but they were sharp and opened scratches on his hands. Desolate and devoid of confidence he lay curled and waited for the day to pass.

Thereafter he travelled only by night, the darkness itself offering him some alternative form of companionship. The moonlight and the smells encouraged him to believe that he knew where he was going, the infinity of the prairie no longer being so apparent.

An instinct toyed with him in the pitch blackness. A path-smell came. Something decayed and barely alive; but not yet dead nor as indifferently animated as the wilderness. A narrow confining smell for which he eagerly ignored his compass.

For five hours he followed this trail until it got fresh and he came back upon himself and his senses. His was the only trail on the prairie.

The circular nature of things banal and great seized him and spun him in fury. He shed his baggage and he shed Edmond. He croaked at the sky, imagining that the raw noise would open a trail and even reach London. But the reedy little plea reached nothing. It bounded back and prodded upwards inside his head. It fired his temples and the pain punished him for his temerity.

The day rode in to look for him, no less spiteful for being softly cloaked. Gay left his worldly affairs and stumbled away from the first putrid vinegar of sunrise. The ground rose and saved him from falling with the weight of his head. The ground rose so far and then burst into flame. It blistered green, and those same sunbeams pinned Gay's colours to the side of the slope. He climbed higher, not knowing what he was doing. The ground levelled off.

The coloured man ran wildly over the scrub, clutching his head.

Waboshiek laughed. On the riverbank the dwarf D'ane Rappape fell down dead of a broken heart. This timing was coincidental; for D'ane Rappape was longer in years than in inches and could not in his wildest dreams have hoped for any extension. His brevity had served him well, Waboshiek considered, the Americans having spared him for their sport. So.

So amidst the ashes of Saukenuk there were but the settled and unsettled dead, and himself and Catherine left to live amongst them for their protection. Relief sighed through the trees. Waboshiek flicked the coloured man off the face of the earth.

CHAPTER TWENTY-THREE

The Comfort of Death – Death in the Flesh – Death as Trickster – Titou Gouffré Appears as an Indian Runner – Gay's Life Is Saved

Gay fell upon the sluggish water, which stood in the hollow beneath the mound. He gorged himself before climbing back up the slope to hide from the sun. The rotted shack teetered towards collapse when he entered, the base of the south-facing wall being but a brittle pulp of desiccated termite larvae. Gay lay down on the crumbling floor. His head was buffeted by pain. He vomited but once and cleanly, thereafter he retched up a thick stinking gloy; from which he pushed himself away across the papery boards, scraping fine dust, which smelt like flour, up into the air.

The owl bitterly resented Gay's arrival and tried to put the fear of God up him. Day lapsed and the owl hallooed.

Gay was ransacked by visions. There was no continuity to the visions. Growing too swiftly within his head they fled half-formed. Death danced in amongst the procession, weaving and curtseying and beaming curtly, a most alluring hostess. He wondered how it was, what with Death shadowing him at every turn, that his own life clung to him. Death it seemed was not naked, but had laboriously attired herself, and his own costume teased from her only a sour smile. She had no wish to dance with him. Yet she presented herself to him like a whore and he was too weary to respond, so jaded that he made no move to avoid her.

> 'For she came over the hill that day
> And took Poor Tom away away
> So where he was they dared not say
> For he was down below – oh!
> Down in the cave where the fires were hot
> She left Poor Tom to rot to rot
> But he didn't care a jot a jot

For he was down below – oh!
The Devil asked me on Midsummer's Day
If I would journey that very same way
My mistress took me then to play
And I went down below – oh!'

Edmond's voice faded.

There was so much deadness in the shack. Nothing stirred across the bleached, bone-coloured boards.

At dawn, thirty antelopes gathered beneath the mound to drink. The air itself hung cold. Gay awoke and reached for his knife, he shed his suit and slithered down the slope.

The antelopes were frightened away, but they were inquisitive as he bathed. They came back and stood innocently, grouped like sycophantic priests, bringing flies to pester and feed off his skin. One of them came closer, little more than an arm's length away, then its nose touched Gay's shoulder affectionately, the touch like a warm feather. It nibbled at his hair with a sharp, upwards tug. Gay rose forwards out of the water. He got a hold on the creature's leg and snapped it with his knee. Two horns grazed down Gay's chest. He seized one of them and stabbed his knife into the top of the neck. The creature tried to shake free. Gay stabbed it in the cheek, again under the ear – and as it rolled to see what was the matter Gay broke the other front leg and stabbed several times at the base of the neck until it didn't move.

He dragged the body out of the water. The rest of the herd were nowhere to be seen. He crouched. He slit the creature open in several places but in truth he had no idea what he should eat. His appetite left him. He picked at bits of flesh. He could do nothing with the creature, but he knew that he must apply himself to eating. Even if the flesh was regurgitated he must try again, chewing patiently until it fragmented, sucking yellowy fat away from the hair, licking the bulge of red flesh at the top of the leg. For the flesh was beneficial. He had not to mind the light musty smell at the creature's crotch, rich in trepidation, nor the glossy stupor of the eyes. He tried again. He sucked on the red-stained transparent skin between the ribs, and the thin white pipe going to the heart, and he sucked on the heart itself, still heated, compressed and dense.

He pulled his head out from inside the rib cage. His mouth filled with vomit but he swallowed; he stood up so that the vomit would have further to rise. Some of it persisted and he spat. Some hung suspended in his stomach. The gore began to skin over his cheeks and forehead. But he strove to keep the creature down, and walked to ignore his stomach. He walked to collect his comet-tin and compass and shirt and Edmond, all of which he had abandoned the previous day, and he walked faster to keep the flies from settling on his face.

He moved around the mound, tracing the folly of his earlier self-pursuit.

He never lost sight of the shack. There was a dull sadness about the place. The sadness did not extend, but was enclosed within the perimeter of the mound; as though the mound lay in shadow, although it was most exposed to the sun. There was nothing up there, there was no form of life. When Gay climbed upwards, having rescued his sundries and his Edmond, even the horseflies ceased to torment him.

He placed Edmond with a fine view across the grasses to the north, not inferior to the view which Edmond had appreciated from the hotel window on the island.

When the sun fell, the antelopes returned. As soon as Gay moved they ran off, not in a gallop but in leaps tensed against the surface of the prairie. Strange half-creatures of the air they filtered quickly into the dusk.

The air became chill. Gay went back to the shack and put on his costume. When the moon came up he saw slow, plump rabbits grooming themselves on the grass. The prairie shone silver. Gay looked across at the rabbits and they looked across at him. There came a deathly screech and there was not a rabbit to be seen.

A moment later the same screech shuddered across the prairie. Gay looked back to the shack for safety and there was the owl, atop Edmond's skull atop the tilted roof of the shack.

Almost as if yawning in mockery, the owl spread its wings and at its leisure glided down towards him. Gay prepared to defend himself, but at the last moment the bird swung away from him and alighted on the bank on the other side of the waterhole, at the edge of its territory. It gazed at Gay, its eyes pinpoints in miniature pools of blank white gold. It preened its socks. It shook itself out and settled itself down: and it gazed at Gay, crest rising slightly as if in all politeness to question him as to what he thought that he might do now.

There was nothing to do. The waterhole lay deserted under the moon, a silvery silk which nothing would disturb.

The owl hallooed gently. Eyes rolling, it shrieked suddenly and violently, shivering the prairie and raising Gay's hackles. It stayed for a moment on the bank, shuffling away, then hauled itself into the air and flew off.

He lost sight of the bird and lay with his cheek against the ground, his heartbeat taking some while to settle. The owl's hooting grew fainter and fainter, and when he looked up again the rabbits were out, bathing themselves in the moonlight.

Surely and slowly one of the rabbits neared. But at Gay's shoulder there was a flapping of wings; feathers beat past his head and the owl pounced on the rabbit. Seizing it by the shoulders, wings buffeting the air.

The rabbit was dead in a trice. Companions fled. But the body was heavy and the owl strove furiously to lift the weight off the ground. When Gay advanced, the bird dropped its kill and flew away.

He slept deeply. He did not hear the owl go out again, nor the prairie dogs niggling at each other over the antelope's bones. He did not see the antelopes at dawn, nor did he watch the prairie dogs' unsustained attempts to chase after them.

The sun trekked round the sky. He awoke in the afternoon and the sleep still would not leave him, clasping him like a leaden lover. Thus encumbered he trod heavily down the slope and sat facing the water, wetting his lips and taking two swallows and that was enough. The day was pleasantly warm and not oppressive. He fancied that he might nap. He returned and lay down on his pallet of dry grass, thinking comfortably that he might also lay Edmond to rest, that he might entrust the much-travelled head to a small grave beside the south wall of the cabin.

Gay was just as tired when the same shriek of death penetrated his sleep. This time, it did not frighten him. He crawled lazily to the doorway and looked out. The prairie was again that silver-lit stage, beautiful and empty. His owl called softly across the cabin from behind him, lulling him into contentment.

The owl hooted loudly; from somewhere down by the pond, Gay thought, although this could not be so for his own owl purred monotonously close by. Perhaps it was the owl's mate, for the bird below hooted again and then hooted from the sky – although Gay could see nothing in flight – and the call circled overhead and departed across the flat plain, tenuously reaching back to the waterhole before falling silent. Gay's eyelids sank. He propped his chin on his hands.

Beneath him the rabbits lolloped from their burrows. A shadow moved. A hairless orange creature jumped up and seized one of the rabbits. Now obviously a man, it stood and held the rabbit by its ears up to the moon. The rabbit kicked once and then did not move. The man brought it down and chopped at its neck with the side of his hand.

So, thought Gay, that is how it is done, this luring. Only the voice flies, like a spirit, but that is not what the rabbits believe. It is a ventriloquist's trick, by the owl and by the savage.

This savage, this Indian, was a strong and beautiful creature, moving gracefully amongst the moonlight. Gay was pleased to watch him. His comet-tin twirled in the air, glowing red and sending up a shower of sparks which withered against the sky. It was quite splendid, quite peaceful. Gay yearned for such dissipation. He sank into a daze, his owl moaning in serenade.

A thin seasoned smoke drifted up the hill, arousing Grey to the smell of cooked meat. He stood and walked to the edge of the slope. The Indian looked up at him and Gay hallooed.

The Indian considered Gay and was not frightened, but he had no wish for Gay's company. He collected his belongings. He tied the comet-tin to one end of a staff, and he tied what looked like a full animal bladder to the other end, which was decorated with a deer's tail. He balanced the staff in his right hand and began to run, naturally at first and then in long lopes, not giving the impression of great speed but nevertheless covering a stupendous distance with each stride.

Gay stared in disbelief as the Indian followed the perimeter of the mound. Walking swiftly above him Gay could hardly keep level with the runner, who must have covered ten to a dozen paces for each one of his own, and that through, or over, the higher grass of the prairie flatland. The antelopes themselves could not have advanced at a much greater rate, nor were they any more graceful. This creature, this man, skimmed over the grasses like a flat stone across water. Gay could not comprehend what he was seeing.

He reckoned it as some madness, or wild fit, such as a dog might suffer. The runner would surely fall headlong at any moment, or hit some obstacle which his senses could not possibly anticipate. But the runner completed his semi-circle of the mound. He did not for a moment consider reviving Gay's trail – which might have been easier – but ran off at a slight angle, with the same sublime fluency. The feather on his topknot of hair waving behind him and his staff keeping at a perfect parallel to the ground, he trailed but a thin tentacle of smoke from the glowing comet-tin. Gay gathered himself from his torpor and paid his respects to the departed figure.

'Ho! Titou! Tee-too! Ho!'

Gay returned to the pond and ate what was left of the rabbit. He layered his comet-tin with embers, plucked moss and cress and filled the tin and whirled it round his head, scattering red into the silver night. He fetched Edmond and was inspired to dance before the dark sockets of his eyes, ignoring the pleas of the owl.

Although some of the grasses flared briefly, his fire would not take hold of the shack. With Edmond hanging from the front of his stick, with a small bag of theatrical make-up, two legs of rabbit and the comet-tin hitched up behind, Gay left the mound.

He blundered into the Trembling Lands, a stagnant expanse of suppurant marsh and tussock. The fury of the insects kept him from sleeping, the flesh around his eyes swelled and barricaded his vision. Jolting onwards like some pathetic machine, coughing up the flies which blocked his throat, he constantly disturbed birds which rose outraged about him. When the sun fell he shuffled his feet from side to side so that he would not sink into the mattress of dead reeds, and he simply stood still for hours at a time, not daring to attract any further hatred.

One afternoon with no sky, when a thick sun poured down like scalding blood, he picked his way through a screen of bulbous-headed sedge and saw the Rock River, some two hundred yards away. From right to left it flowed, crisply, radiantly it trilled and sang and gambolled, it jabbered at the rocks and flung purity at the air. Between Gay and the river lay a surface of baked mud, over which half a thousand birds strolled and milled, digging their long sickle-shaped beaks into the mosaic of crusted scab.

He left Edmond and rushed towards the river. The birds did not move but within ten paces the insects rose up like black felt, covering him and warding him off. So dense was the hostility that he could no longer see and could hardly breathe. He flapped his arms in anguish. He crushed a hundred tiny bodies against his face, smearing them down over his chin; but then he felt immediately the attention of the next wave which came in on the blood of their predecessors.

He thought that eggs were being laid all over his face in open blood, and he ran away from the river. He plunged headlong back into the reeds, and he scoured his face and hair free of the infestation. He shook his comet-tin and rubbed hot ash over his skin and he rubbed his tattered scalp too with hot ash, crying out at the pain.

The insects left him. They went back to the crevices in the mud and waited for the birds to pick them out.

In the middle of the next afternoon Gay came across a moose which had become stuck in the mud. It shook with an epileptic fit, being eaten alive by the insects. All around the moose the quagmire stank. Gay went inland for dried reeds. He collected them, weighted them, and lit them. He meant only to drive the insects away from the tortured creature, but when he lobbed the flagrant bundle the moose exploded. A great hole in its flank burned fiercely and flames raced out along the cracks in the mud.

Gay turned south.

CHAPTER TWENTY-FOUR

Waboshiek Greets Gay – A Fine Howdy-doo

When Gay arrived at the top of the falls, all that he could think of was sleep. Perhaps the poison from the insect bites had accumulated in his blood. Perhaps his stupor was caused by the light dance of the water, or the warm breeze which rose up the falls from the valley to banish the mosquitoes.

He set Edmond's skull on a ledge above the river, and replenished his comet-tin with damp lichen. The place struck him as benevolent, even tender, with its three large and dimpled stones surrounded by the shush of the water. On one of the stones he lit a fire. There was a moment before full dawn when everything around him was the same light grey, the drear calm of spirit. Edmond's skull, water, sky, rock, smoke from the fire – the forest darkness hung back while they all slid into limbo, and the only thing of colour was the suit of the Harlequin. For whatever reason, he suffered a marvel of sleep. He did not hear a sound, his sleep skipped quickly into a sweet blackness, with neither scent nor print nor whisper.

When Catherine complained, Waboshiek waved her away. 'Someone will snuff him out, sooner or later.'

'But the rocks are sacred to me.'

Waboshiek bit off a piece of fingernail. He spat it out and then carefully retrieved it, and put it onto the fire.

'I will find out why he is here.'

He smoked and prepared himself; he saw Gay's pain and poked at the swelling on his head.

Gay was awoken by he knew not what. He was hungry. The shadows of the trees had already compressed the sunlight against the eastern bank of the river. He lit his fire, which blazed feverishly until he moved away from the heat, and then the fire withdrew, even from the driest of wood. He walked along the bank and went after food – fish, rabbit, otter, squirrel – none of which was alarmed by him; all of which kept their distance, as though their domain had been entered by a leper. The day turned its cold shoulder on him. Hopelessly he roamed up and down the river bank.

His world shrank. His dominion over that world was still absolute but its boundaries had closed in until he knew himself as the only creature within a tiny glass cockpit. He was preserved from attack, and might venture where he would, but he might as well try to grasp the grey disc of the moon as arrange himself with the elements about him.

Waboshiek watched him cautiously. He did not reach for the coloured man, and he did not release the animals for they would have been drawn towards the coloured man to feed his power. At this point Waboshiek did not know whether the coloured man was alive, or what understanding he had with his soul. It was the damnedest thing. He could hardly see the coloured man at all, but he could see the power in the coloured man's head. The coloured man lay down beside the fire. He slept. Waboshiek withheld any sympathies, and craned forward.

Gay could not stand. He was convinced that he was weightless. He could not move, but hung in space above a deep gorge. In stasis – land, houses, trees, a river; miles beneath him, no sign of life. If he panicked he would be lost. He was not surprised to see his vomit fall in a long silver cord from his lips, thousands of feet through the air, to lose itself in the ground far below.

His chin tilted forward and he found himself suspended in warm water, staring up at a huge black night, the same blackness which flowed into the pools of his eyes. Over his face blew a strong wind, tepid and consistent, which seemed to arise from a crater behind his head. He could not move. His body stretched before him like a flimsy winding-sheet, spread across the surface of the water, anchored only by the weight of his head on the rock. The wind fled cleanly over him, disturbing neither the water nor the torrents of blackness which swirled between himself and the sky. Across this blackness, stampeding with the wind and thunderous, came the herd; a thousandfold beating surged from the crater over Gay's head, hoofs pummelling the edges of the wind.

The blackness jarred and became elusive. Innumerable nails hammered into the lid of his coffin. Gay choked and fought the dust, unable even to raise his hands to push the weight off his chest. His eyes came out of his head and slithered sideways down the surface of his face. He saw only a flat and compressed horizon of black calm, far away, on either side of him. Snakes burst out of his knees and slithered fast as whips for the closing crevice of day.

The ground rose up. The water drained away until it was wafer deep, gossamer thin as his body. The lid would close and he would be swept away now, any moment now, with the rush of wind and hoofs – were it not for the nail which was driven through his forehead into the rock, like a coat-hook away from which his body fluttered.

His jaw hung open. His skull stretched impossibly, the top of his head strained like wet rope. The stampeding came as bright stars thrown across the sky. One by one they stuck; and they threaded down to the needle pushed through his skull, a thin white-gold cord of eternity.

Waboshiek was intrigued. To finish the coloured man off would be child's play. But the coloured man was innocent, powerfully so. To destroy such innocence would severely diminish Waboshiek's own power.

He wondered how he might find out about this coloured man, this vehicle, this dancer.

Waboshiek alighted upon Edmond's skull.

In his second dream Gay awoke from his dream to find himself lying on a polished whitewood floor. Not three paces away a fire burned healthily, warming even the air at his back. The warmth was real, the fire therefore real except inasmuch as it did not burn the wooden floor.

Edmond served food – rabbit, squash, bear, pronghorn, buffalo, snake, rat, opossum, fox. He ate heartily but had no taste for the buffalo.

Edmond had him laughing at himself. Gay loved Edmond when he was in this mood, the urbanity flowing like fine wine. The neat little mustache remained perfectly level, the teasing dry and laconic. Edmond, it appeared, had not enjoyed the journey west. He had been vastly entertained by Gay's liaison with the Chicago dog, but had been miffed by Gay's failure to strike up any conversation with the owl. As for Gay's attempts to 'run' the prairie; well, Edmond would never again allow himself to be transported by one who mustered all the grace of an enervated duck.

Gay wiped the tears from his eyes. 'It is a skill', he said, 'which I have not yet mastered. Your own attempts to "ride" the ocean were not, as I recall, triumphant?' His eyebrows were already raised, finely supercilious and quite prepared to ward off Edmond's no doubt withering riposte. Yet when he glanced at Edmond, he found Edmond staring at him. The stare was intent, but somehow stupid and desperate, as though Edmond had missed the point of the jest. The eyes slid away.

Edmond smiled boyishly. He made some fatuous and winning comment about heads, which had Gay amused once again.

As long as Edmond spun his droleries he held Gay in the palm of his hand. Edmond, however, made enquiries; initially the lightest of suggestions, but when Gay showed his perplexity Edmond became persistent. Such nagging was most unlike him. What he did not know had never bothered Edmond. Now there was a suggestion of greed, and of an ill-concealed impatience which did not sit well with Edmond's character. Something was out of place. Why should they have need to discuss *Gay's* head? Was not Edmond . . . indeed . . . what was Edmond? His expression was perfectly agreeable but his eyes were completely missing. Narrow, golden circles burned brightly around the circumference of the eyeballs, but the pupils were enormous and matt black; they sucked in all animation from the air surrounding Edmond's head.

This is not Edmond, Gay thought – it being not so much a thought as a feeling of repulsion. This is very nearly Edmond, but it is not Edmond. What is this?

Waboshiek drew a blank. It was the most remarkably stupid conversation in which he had ever taken part. The coloured man told him nothing. Worse, it seemed that the coloured man *knew* nothing about himself.

Cautiously Waboshiek covered his retreat and faded into the dawn.

CHAPTER TWENTY-FIVE

Waboshiek Is Intrigued by the Message from the East – And Goes after the Emissary within Gay's Head – Rennah Wells Retires, Frayed at the Edges

Catherine learned that Waboshiek had dragged Gay's body down to his wickeup; she did not want to have anything to do with him. Her back ached, she felt heavy and not part of the world. She stayed in her own wickeup by the river and there she used the knife, bleeding herself of the malignancy which would otherwise burst from between her legs.

Waboshiek did not quite understand what was going on. There was truth, there was possibility, there was hocus-pocus. Somehow, from somewhere, the coloured man had power. He knew nothing about it and therefore he was sick. In order to understand his story, Waboshiek needed Catherine.

Much to his discomfort, Waboshiek waded through the clear shallows of the river to approach her wickeup. He was still twenty paces away from the woman's pit when her jabbering started. She screamed her outrage at his intrusion. Waboshiek tried to explain, but got nowhere. He lost his temper and issued commands, which floated uselessly downstream. Thigh-high in cold water, up to his head in ridicule and screeched abuse, he tried to placate her. Her insults flapped at him. Waboshiek gave up, flung curses at her and waded ignominiously back upstream.

On his second sortie he let it be known that he had no interest whatsoever in menstrual blood. On the contrary, he respected Catherine's privacy and was grateful that she nursed her malignant self well away from his wickeup. It was, however, of the utmost importance that he seek her advice, for had she not already, and perhaps with her hairy twat, unwittingly, assisted in the destruction of the village, and should he not aid her in limiting such misfortune?

Back came a reply. Catherine would be in her wickeup that night.

Waboshiek should remain outside and only talk to her through the walls.

Waboshiek agreed; and just before midnight he opened the bidding.

'The coloured man has visions. He talks of them in his sleep. I don't understand them.'

'Surely you know what he says.'

'He is your people.'

'I want nothing to do with my people: there is no such people.'

Waboshiek sighed. He smelt fish. He hated fish – stupid, gloomy creatures.

'It is true that there is no such people, that you are rare. Will you not use your power to help me?'

'I will not show myself to this man.'

'No,' Waboshiek agreed, 'no. He is weak and he would be a plaything to any malignant spirit.'

Her ball of spit flopped against the bark beside his ear. Waboshiek retreated hurriedly. She called him back and said that she would do as he asked.

The information was cold and surely dead. Through Catherine Waboshiek learned from the coloured man that the White Father would not stir from Fort Malden, and had ordered that his warriors should wear long dresses as a sign of friendship, though not to the Americans. However the White Father had hit upon the idea of gathering the tribes to his homeland, away from the Americans, where they would dance in front of many whites and be listened to, the whites agreeing to sit in their thousands to see how the tribes lived. It appeared that their emissary, the coloured man, had brought with him the skull of his friend, whose spirit would not settle until the mission was accomplished.

He could not humiliate himself further by asking for Catherine's interpretation. She herself was sorrowful and offered no commentary.

Waboshiek could not make head or tail of it. His mind was dislodged and it took him completely by surprise when, midway through the following afternoon, a small canoe drifted round the promontory to offload the Dungbeetle preacher.

Waboshiek shuddered in disgust.

Rennah Wells wiped his nose on his sleeve, and wiped his sleeve across his forehead, and settled his hat on his brow, and shut his eyes. Then he could see Saukenuk as it had been: a fine warm spray hanging in the air, green slopes of grass waving gracefully and rising in tiers towards a hillscape of thinly scattered trees, the thick perfume of June honeysuckle – and the village itself, sleepy and cleanly ordered, with acres of tended growing-land.

He opened his eyes and saw what remained – two ramshackle wickeups stark amid a field of ash – and saw Waboshiek.

The light was fierce and yet it appeared that the whole of Waboshiek's head was in shadow. His image did not come forward for Rennah. He was quite absent. When Rennah looked into his eyes he saw nothing but repulsive corridors of gloom, down which he was invited to disappear.

Rennah held out his left arm.

Waboshiek ignored it. The Dungbeetle had changed his skin. Perhaps. But it was still the Dungbeetle – packing up shit and rolling it from one end of the prairie to the other. If not shit, then shoes.

Waboshiek had no use for shoes. Nor Hymns, nor Spiritual Exercises, nor Constitutions. Pictures of the Lord God, perhaps? No.

No. Black Hawk and the rest of the tribe had had some use for such things, and had been deceived. He, Waboshiek, had not been fooled, not for a moment. Not by the Dungbeetle, who was, of course, naturally enough, still alive. Same lack of spirit, but still alive. Like fog.

Waboshiek led Rennah up, through the ash, towards his wickeup. Catherine spat at him. Rennah wiped the spit with his sleeve and grinned inanely.

He was astonished to find Gay, but his eyes lit up at the goitre of pulpy flesh which protruded from Gay's right temple.

Waboshiek watched carefully. He had seen the Dungbeetle at work but once before, two years ago, at Saukenuk. There he had seen the Dungbeetle sucking up the air with his voice. It had been a cheap whiskey trick, that voracious surrender to the peddler of a one-horse universe. Waboshiek had understood the insidious comfort that an old and honest man like Black Hawk would have needed in his attempts to fathom the whites. Waboshiek had not been so fond.

He smelt, now, that the Dungbeetle, too, had listened to his own evil. The Dungbeetle understood and was not so foolish. When the Dungbeetle craned forward and his fingers stretched towards the coloured man, the air tensed. Waboshiek felt the movement inside the coloured man's head and saw the pain on the surface of his lips.

It was not the Dungbeetle's place to witness these things. Waboshiek picked up his rattle and prodded at the greed in Rennah's gut.

Rennah retreated.

Waboshiek saw that Rennah would never be powerful and could never hope to be powerful, but was like the black slime which swallowed whole spirits and then set to work rotting them.

Rennah was cunning enough to realise that something was expected of him. He switched his attention to Edmond's skull. He knelt humbly. He knew that Waboshiek understood a few words of English.

'This . . .' Rennah slowly imprecated, 'this is the sacred head of King Charles, the Great White Father of England, our Lord and Chief. And he has been dead these hundred and fifty years.'

Rennah's voice rose to a wail. He loomed forward to kiss the skull. As he did so, his intestines uncoiled adamantly and a jet of blue flame belched thunderously over the docile fire and across the gloom.

Waboshiek roared with laughter. He was vastly amused. Rennah felt that he was getting along fine until suddenly there was no laughter, there was hatred which poured from the shaman's eyes so powerfully that Rennah felt it all around him, at his back even, and cold, so that Rennah was rolled over and swept like flotsam out on to the blackened earth, his arms reaching up in an attempt to grab hold of the sunlight.

Rennah weighed up valour, and opted for discretion. He brushed the ash off his clothes, spat the taste of it out of his mouth, and took to his canoe. He paddled on down the Rock River until it met the Mississippi. Into which broad slow maw he dumped all spiritual and constitutional footwear before working his way cross-current to the island home of a deserted Fort Armstrong.

This much did Rennah achieve: when Waboshiek told Catherine that there was much to be accomplished with the coloured man, Catherine saw that there was no option but to obey him. She, too, hated the Dungbeetle preacher.

In the morning Waboshiek told her not to eat, and he gave her tobacco and a bowl of tea which she should sip to quieten her appetite. He ascertained from her that she no longer bled from her vagina. He gave her a different bowl, from which the coloured man should drink at intervals throughout the day; and he ordered her not to talk with him should he awake. At noon, Gay's body was moved so that it lay north to south, and she washed the ashes from his face and neck.

Waboshiek went upriver, prayed to the willow tree and cut a stick, two arms' length. He returned to his wickeup and tied an eagle's feather to the top of the stick, and planted it in the ground by the coloured man's head.

Waboshiek was uncertain as to the complexities he might encounter. There was no danger to Catherine because she was merely the vessel through which he would gain entry to the coloured man. He himself would approach the coloured man as an innocent, so he might escape at any time. The power, if evil, would burst out, and finding no home it would twist in its own wind, shout loudly and return whence it came. The coloured man would suffer, but he would not be allowed to die. Waboshiek had not made up his mind about the bones. The coloured man would be comforted by the presence of his friend.

It was possible that he derived some of his power by the companionship with his King. But Waboshiek did not believe the Dungbeetle's claim. Waboshiek had brushed with the coloured man's friend, and this friend had no feeling of being a great chief. His spirit was not yet cold and was easy to find; so his soul had not gone far and had certainly not been travelling for a hundred years. He was a great friend to the coloured man, whose own soul was obscured by the illness.

There were a great many complications and not a little confusion amongst them. It would be disastrous to lure the evil and pass it to the coloured man's friend; at best this would be a messy business, at worst it would backfire and let loose Coyote-knows-what beneath the flat earth.

No. Waboshiek removed Edmond's skull to the safety of his own wickeup and prayed to him, made him many offerings, joked with him and otherwise secured if not his aid then his compliance.

For four days Waboshiek wrapped himself in the loud silence. He ate for the first two days, offering plenty to the *damagomi*, communicating with them, testing strength in repartee and vision. He quit the wickeup only at dawn and at dusk in order to bathe in the river.

He talked with Catherine, telling her what foods she should leave at the flap. He himself ate neither flesh nor salt, but the *damagomi* consumed their fill. When his bowels emptied he buried the waste in the woods along with whatever food the *damagomi* had refused. On the third day he administered to himself a series of emetics and, once again, he buried his vomit in the woods. He talked softly to the *damagomi*, rousing them with his rattle, traversing the four layers of the sky and the four layers of the earth with the aid of his drum. He travelled carefully, wary of the storms in the waters below flat earth, concealing himself from the evil shamans which lurked in them. He rose through the four layers of the sky and sought the company of his *manitou*. Together they rode the drum in ecstasy.

When he saw that he would be disturbed – again by the intrusion of the scrabbling Dungbeetle – Waboshiek sang himself, *sotto voce*, back to earth.

Rennah beached the canoe beneath the bluffs. He checked through his burlap bag, running his finger along the axe-blade, and he checked his rifle. He made no fire but he ate dried meat and settled, comfortable enough on a blanket, well above the waterline. To this silent, massive, black glide of the Mississippi, Rennah slept.

He awoke in the night, his forehead covered with sweat. Within him his abdomen thrashed. Pain sprayed like fire around the centre of his body. He urinated helplessly over the blanket, his penis stinging: he drew his legs up and crouched on all fours in his piss, with his head first pressed against the earth and then hauled back to face the stars. He panted strenuously. He threw himself lengthways down on the blanket, he turned and clasped his knees; he rolled like a bale of tumbleweed from one side of the blanket to the other, mewling, the little pleadings spilling from between his teeth. He ran, stumbled, crawled, and ran again.

Waboshiek was vastly amused.

On the morning of the fourth day, a clean and favourable day, he ordered Catherine to strip the coloured man of his colours and to paint him blue, air being the dominant element in his constitution. Waboshiek painted his own face white. Together they built the coloured man a wickeup: Catherine built, Waboshiek was sporadically advisatory on matters of architecture. He helped her to drag Gay's body to its new and somewhat decrepit dwelling.

When he heard that the coloured man was awake, he ordered Catherine to prepare hot stones, which were placed in the coloured man's wickeup an hour before sunset; while he himself prepared the buffalo footbone. At sunset a small fire was lit in the centre of the wickeup.

Midway between sunset and midnight, when the skies had been dark for an hour, Waboshiek entered the wickeup, naked to the waist and barefoot. He sat and sang softly, Catherine taking up his songs. He threw plants on to the stones. Four times the flap of the wickeup was lifted to let the hot air escape.

The coloured man floated in and out of consciousness. Waboshiek followed him in trance, each time leading him back to a wakeful malaise. Eventually Waboshiek rose and walked round the fire. He returned to his place and lit his pipe, puffed on it and offered it to Catherine. He ordered her to turn Gay's body round so that his head pointed to the east, his body lying on its left side. Waboshiek slipped the buffalo foot under his left temple.

Gay faded out. He was drawn quickly into a black hole of sadness and abandonment. A thin whistle summoned him and he was glad to go, to have done with the swirling gloom inside the wickeup. Waboshiek went with him. Gay slowed and hung in the blackness, the wind shrieking past him and threatening to dislodge him. With an uneven pummelling of the wind the stampede rose out of the blackness once more, surging towards him, hoofs thundering through the wind. It hurtled over his back, each hoof a mallet blow; sharper now, like knives. It was as though he was roped under the shoulders. His arms flapped helplessly as the rope dragged him along a line of spears. His flesh was torn, his bones snapped and cracked like twigs. He split into two halves, his body fell away on either side and his heart leapt for safety into his head.

Waboshiek swayed and chanted, his eyes half closed. He ceased to sing. Catherine took up the slack; he felt her warmth and concern. She sang louder, to waken the *damagomi*.

Waboshiek meditated on the blackness. He closed his eyes and listened. Soon he felt his *damagomi* arriving, he felt it fluttering through the night air, in the forest, under the ground, everywhere, even in his belly. He clapped his hands, once, and the singing stopped.

Waboshiek spoke with his *damagomi*, which was confused and excited. They bantered irritably and fervently. They became more confused. He questioned, and repeated his *damagomi*'s replies; the dialogue became faster and mingled until they were one in ecstasy.

The Shaman yawned. He peered blearily at the roof. Catherine made up the fire. He stretched, walked about, and joked with her. They had something to eat. The uneaten food was buried; Waboshiek became distracted and was enticed away.

This time he took no nonsense from the *damagomi*. He harangued it for its idleness and ridiculed its cowardice. He urged it to give up its torpor and go searching. What else would any respectable *damagomi* do? He, Waboshiek, would no longer flatter a *damagomi* that lived only on its reputation.

There followed an interlude of absurd communication, until gradually Waboshiek returned from trance, singing and humming contentedly to himself. When he was quite grounded, he explained to Catherine that he had seen the trouble from which the coloured man suffered. The *damagomi* had ferreted it out. The coloured man having returned with him into consciousness, Waboshiek ordered Catherine to interpret the diagnosis for his benefit.

The coloured man, said Waboshiek, was suffering from false blame. He had unwittingly been party to the death of a young girl, for which he took blame. This blame had dogged him, and had intensified when his best friend had died – again, no fault of his, but something which he saw as a pattern of death for which he was responsible. Therefore the coloured man was sick. He, Waboshiek, would remove the blame. He would first swallow the pain.

He put his bone to the side of Gay's temple, and put his own head against the bone. He rattled. When he pulled the bone away the skin came with it.

Gay cried out. Catherine soothed him. Waboshiek told Gay the story of how he had met his own *manitou*, and Catherine translated it for Gay. Then Waboshiek leaned forward and sucked at Gay's temple.

He spat the blood into his hands, peered at it, and held it up for her to see.

'Black blood. This is bad blood. Its sickness must go into the fire.'

He passed his hand over the fire and burned the blood. He again put his lips to Gay's head, took a mouthful and spat it into the fire. He went back and felt with his tongue around the inside of the hole in Gay's head. He felt the Maggot squirm, but he did not say anything. This was the highest secret, and not one for the entertainment of his helper, indeed perhaps not even for his own use.

He took another mouthful of slimy blood and spat it out on to the fire, and quickly threw a handful of plants over the flames. By the time the smoke had cleared Waboshiek had the Maggot out of Gay's head and into a silver box inside his leggings. When Catherine next saw him, she applauded his skill in having extracted from Gay's head a small piece of bone, which Waboshiek was holding up for her.

'This is the blame. This is the root of his sickness, which is dead.' Waboshiek buried the splinter in the earth between his legs.

He drank down four more swallows of good blood from Gay's head, for, as he explained, the *damagomi* was thirsty and hot and wanted to drink blood. 'This is for him. He has helped me. Now he will be refreshed and will quieten.'

They smoked and talked until dawn. Waboshiek gave her plants to poultice the wound in Gay's head.

It was necessary for Waboshiek to reward himself and Catherine for their services. Waboshiek gave her Gay's black silk mask. He already had what he wanted, but made a play out of accepting Gay's silver knife. After this, he went back to his wickeup and ate ravenously to restore himself.

Waboshiek spent his days with the Maggot. As was usual with such a Maggot, it fed only on flesh. Waboshiek would have liked to have offered it warm human flesh, but there was none to hand. He considered offering it a chunk of Gay, but in the end it had to make do with deer and rabbit. Waboshiek hurried to apologise.

The Maggot was powerful, Waboshiek knew. It was protected from afar. Not that he couldn't have held it between his fingers and crushed it to death; but such intentional, or even casual, destruction of power would rebound upon him, and Waboshiek was convinced that the Maggot was more powerful than he was.

What then was the meaning of this power? What did it want?

It came from far to the east and Waboshiek wondered if it were not a curse, if it would cause numbness to spread upwards through his body and he would die shabbily, like the tribe had died. He summoned his *manitou* and together they built a protective wall.

Waboshiek waited. Nothing happened. He recalled the coloured man's vision of the rushing hoofs and the death facing the young girl, which was the moment when the power had lodged in the coloured man's head for shelter. But he could not see through the fog, and he could not find the origin of the power. The journey it had taken was ceaseless and disrupted; the power forlorn and desperate, seeking kinship.

Waboshiek stirred uneasily in recognition. The *damagomi* refused its assistance, although the power was not evil. He learned only that it was older than countless generations.

He had a dream: a man and a woman were hanging naked by their feet from the branches of a tree. A crow copulated with the man and then flapped to the ground, where it lay with its head facing to the east and died.

Gay had a dream: in which he was the cleverest man of them all. He was lying on his back in a field of wild strawberries, just the tip of his prick poking up through the coverlet of leaves. A moist breeze tickled his prick. The maidens, with their baskets, came closer, laughing at each other's secrets. They picked the strawberries one by one. Gay sniggered with delight at his trickery. One of the maidens came over and tried to pick off the tip of his prick. She called to her friends and they took turns to pluck at him until, suddenly, they succeeded; and they, and he, were gone into the air.

He awoke in fading ecstasy. The room was dark save for a small fire. In front of him a golden-haired woman sat back on her heels and wiped her hand on a piece of cloth. She drank from a cup of water, then pulled his blanket up to his shoulders and murmured him back to sleep.

CHAPTER TWENTY-SIX

*Disenchantment – Gay Returns Empty-headed from the Underworld –
Saukenuk and Catherine Uncovered*

The sun had eased its way over the dark vault and plunged now through another hole, no bigger than a button.

A golden rod balanced against the earth, prodding alight a small ridge of hills, an arid lake bed, dimpled craters of dust. There was a scattering of such rods, drawn like harp strings between the ground and the speckled darkness overhead. This one tiny beam of light slipped a little way across the terrain, as if top-heavy and unable to secure a foothold, until it narrowed to a moment of ghostly whiteness before extinction. The hills fell into concealment; to the east another landscape was thrust into illumination. The strings of light appeared ceaselessly to stalk the lifeless earth in episodes of ungainly and haphazard flourish, dicing it with sudden brilliance before being severed from above.

Thus, as the sun clambered across the elm bark roof, did Gay observe the thousand miniature geographies which spread across the floor of the wickeup.

Above his head hovered a lazy and sweet-smelling undulation of smoke, which quivered up from the flameless fire. At dusk this canopy was darker than the small bolt-hole of sky; at the long haul of night the smoke swirled light grey towards the darkness. Gay lay for hours and watched the sheer veils slither round the edges of the hole. He watched the smoke fluster and crowd back from the opening, until it was sucked out into the clear black night. The fire was left to die. The smoke wisped and lingered. Gay dozed, the door to consciousness kept ajar by the playful scamperings of squirrels across the roof.

Long before the sun pricked the husk with its first pale rods a woman came into the wickeup and set the fire, bringing Gay a bowl of mush and a strong, bitter-tasting infusion. The first smoke clung sullen to the ground, weaving underneath the platform on which he lay, until the blaze was met. The flames were stifled with fresh leaves and the canopy reformed beneath the roof-poles, reluctant to broach the spyhole of dawn.

Catherine came regularly to tend him. She handled him kindly but was no more interested in him than in the fire. Once a day, when dusk had stilled the last brassy indignation of the birds and the sky sometimes slung a diluted bloodstain across the smoke-hole, Waboshiek came and stood over him. His eyes were greedy for recognition, and Gay played dead.

One evening Waboshiek sang to him and anointed the sore on his head. He did not visit Gay again for several days. Gay succumbed to the swathings of torpor, his thoughts and imaginings spun inconsequentially, fizzed and fled. If he suffered from anything – and in this there was no anguish – it was from unaccountable fits of sorrow. He found himself crying sweetly, as though at an arrival rather than at a loss; and this he did not understand at all. It did not occur to him that he was lonely, nor that Edmond was drifting away into perspective. Death had blurred the edges of Edmond's outline while enriching the colours of his soul; so that Edmond was supremely present and yet utterly without influence. Gay's guardianship was no longer of any use or comfort whatsoever.

He was without purpose, purged of purpose; and he did not know how to recognise such a feeling, nor how to present himself, nor what indeed that self might be.

When Waboshiek returned to Gay and peered down at him, Gay stared back. He saw a wide-faced contemptuous man, strong-jawed, with thickly fleshed lips and nostrils. The obvious strength of the face was in its larger, lower portion: the handsome physiognomy of a grandly complacent yeoman. Above the bridge of the nose, however, all was compressed into meanness and suspicion. This effect was heightened by the man's eyes, which threw out a great display of light and then shifted from side to side as if to announce the subtleties of calculation which were passing through his mind. Given that he could not be a ham actor, Waboshiek seemed like nothing so much as an unfortunate clerk doing his best to camouflage his low station in life.

Waboshiek looked at Gay and saw an emptied fraud. This was not a value judgement, for Saukenuk had once harboured many frauds. He noted that Gay was not in the least frightened, a recklessness which could only be due to the removal of his power. Waboshiek assumed that the coloured man was a mere tool of power. The air would fill such a shell of a man and carry him off at its whim. Some respect was owing to him, though, for his carrying of the Maggot. Waboshiek left him where he was.

Time hobbled past. Gay heard no signs of life. He sat upright on his sleeping platform and the room swam before his eyes, the thin sunbeams jangling discordantly. A bar of light struck at his knee and he groped his way to the door-flap. On rickety legs, trousers flapping loosely around his thighs, he took himself up the slope to the borderline of the woods.

He sat for a while to recover his senses. The leaves drooped and the grasses were battened down by the pressure of the sunlight, which flooded upwards from the river. Gay did not know what he had been expecting to see, but his heart sank at the rudiments of survival which merely baked in the cruel white glare of the sun.

He suffered an acute sensation of panic. What lay before him was devastation, to his left a half mile of blackened stubble, in front of him a light grey coverlet of ash which extended towards the river and lost itself amongst the whiteness of stones laid bare by summer. This fine grey blanket was sparsely punctured by charred poles, which jutted forlornly at air that was flat and lifeless and repulsive with the musty odour of consumption. Here and there a freakish weed lurched up and splayed a ragged dusty costume over the sulliage. The ruination was casual and established.

There were two other cabins besides his own, which had been cobbled together out of bits and pieces of tree and scorched animal hides. One of these was down by the river, itself shallow and unadventurous, the bared rocks lending it the appearance of a boneyard, from which the water seeped. Upriver, patches of hardly cultivated land had thrown up a screen of ugly stalks, their foliage hung yellowish like flayed skin.

A sinuous ripple spread through this small plantation. The tall stalks swayed, their leaves fluttered out like streamers. Gay waited to see an animal or a human being, but the ripples spread like a tide quickening across the strand. The waves rose acrobatically, one upon the shoulders of another. A first current of air lapped at Gay. It fell back, somersaulted and broke across his face, the air warm but charged with cool moisture, lifting the dull and cindered atmosphere.

Gay walked light-headed down through the ash towards the river, and was surprised to find that the bank was much higher than he thought, and that it hid a substantial width of deep and sturdy-flowing water. This was not the only deceit. To his left, further upstream, lay the mounds of tumbled rock through which, he realised, an enormous volume of water filtered constantly. The river turned sharply and rose steadily over a distance, so that the remains of the Indian village lay not in the abrupt shadow of a plateau but at the foot of a long and graceful stairway, at the end of which the river gathered its skirts and glided solemnly out of sight behind a rocky promontory, the breeze dancing attendance on its departure.

The earth was dry and crumbly, and provided no foothold. Wading upriver, his legs weakening, he came upon a pile of stones and crawled to the top of the bank.

He saw that he was beneath the scorched cultivations.

Twenty paces away a large magpie beat into the air and settled down again. Such was its agitation that Gay wondered if the bird might be wounded; he stood still, not wishing further to inflict it with terror. It hopped and fluttered as if anguished by a poison, its head switching left and right in a panic of non-comprehension. Suddenly it leapt into the air and landed not ten paces away.

Gay lost sight of it. He walked forward, and again the bird sprang up and fluttered to one side. Out of the grass and across the open scrub crawled a young rabbit, hunched and lame. The magpie saw Gay see the rabbit and erupted in a possessive fury. It roistered over to the poor creature and hopped around it, stabbing sharply with its beak into the rabbit's head.

Gay had never before witnessed such vicious frenzy. The rabbit sank down stunned as the sharp black beak drove into its skull. Gay advanced as quickly as he might, but in a trice the magpie had pecked out the creature's eyes and flown off.

The punctured, gouged thing was alive when Gay reached it, blood oozing through the soft hair around its ears, the empty sockets lying still in ghastly scarlet. He picked up the small handful of blind misery, unable to decide how to end its life. Fear trembled through the grey down, the creature protested feebly with its legs as Gay clenched it, every bit of warm life strained in perseverance, the heart pumping anxiety. When he placed the rabbit back on the ground it sat still for several minutes. Its nose searched, and then it crept slowly back towards the field of maize. Gay waited until it had disappeared, and then he walked stiffly back towards the wickeups.

The first one that he entered was but a little way above the riverbank. At first Gay took it for a place of storage; pieces of skin and cloth, pots, dried plants were all littered over the floor as though victim to a frequent and haphazard rummaging.

There was an element of the macabre in the thin sheath of faded yellow hair which hung from the cornerpost, and there were other trophies stockpiled – a hatpin skewering the stomach of a child's doll, a silver buckled belt, a lace handkerchief smeared with blood. A range of thighbones – from chicken or turkey or grouse; many sizes – were preserved in a large dish of oil. Mats and rugs hung from a thick rail which ran down the centre of the room. Under one of the mats there was a light saddle. Strong thongs were tied to the stirrups and pegged into the ground. Set amongst the colourful rugs the contraption resembled Hone's rocking horse. But what with the display of a second pair of stirrups – hoisted overhead like spoils – this structure took on the sinister aspect of an altar, capable of loosening within the savage breast every reserve of triumph and contempt for the white man. Gay covered the gruesome totem and stepped away.

The other wickeup lay not far from where Gay himself had been lodged. Here was the horde of a peddler, an Autolycus. Here, from a thickly furred platform, the Regent of Trifles might survey his treasury of teeth, feathers, jawbones, beads, quills, ribbons, crucibles, pestles and paraphernalia. Gay was struck by the seeming superfluity of objects. The first wickeup had suggested a brisk harshness; here, by contrast, he intruded upon the home of a pernickety spinster. This habitant exerted custody over – amongst the remains of other departed pets – Edmond.

Gay did not loiter. Such ambient greed and personal deprivation repulsed him. He rescued Edmond and carried him off, past the drawing of the military man which was pinned near the door-flap.

The sun was almost overhead and beat down through the layered breeze. Cushions of hot air swelled from the baked earth up across the village. Gay was stronger on his legs, but fatigued. He made something out of his own abode, with a skull, a costume, a baton, a shirt and two pairs of shoes; forlornly aping the natives' creation of significance.

He was momentarily perturbed the next morning, when Waboshiek appeared to berate him, and he flinched when Waboshiek squeezed the skin at his temple. He guarded his belongings, but Waboshiek did not seem to care. He merely observed Gay, unsmiling, arms crossed, hands clasping his elbows. He twice flapped with a feathered fan, although Gay neither saw nor heard the movement of any fly. Gay thought that he might show some distaste for Edmond's skull, but he did not. Gay dithered with the skull. He had no wish to offend Waboshiek, nor his customs, whatever they might be. He turned away from Waboshiek but for a second, and when he turned back Waboshiek had gone.

The shaman greatly admired Gay's Harlequin costume, especially the row upon row of sequins. Gay washed the costume and laid it on a flat rock to dry. It was marvellous. It went missing at midday. Gay found it hanging from a tree. It appeared that Waboshiek did not want the sun to fade the colours.

From Catherine there was food, and nothing else.

Gay became much impressed by Waboshiek's lofty secrecy, having himself frequently sheltered in such detachment. He realised that Waboshiek's occasional officiousness and agitation, though genuine, could be set aside at will. His sulks and explosions of anger were highly theatrical, and Gay mimicked them. Waboshiek relished such monkeying.

However, there were times when Waboshiek was seemingly emptied of any emotion: a superfluity of light hugged the bowls of his eyes and Gay chose to remove himself from his presence.

Catherine and Waboshiek disappeared without any ceremony. The air was hot and heavy and sank down close on the margins of the river. For several days there had been an invasion by tiny green flies, which clung in clusters to the tops of wooden poles. Gay walked away from the wickeups, back through the thin border of forest, looking for food.

A half mile to the north the woodland dwindled into scrub, an untraversable terrain of dry tussocks, stiff dead grass and arid streambeds into which a horse or man might tip and break a bone. The plain did not support any trees. It stretched further than the eye could see, rudely scorched, the air above it congested and soupy orange in colour; the sun, depositing itself on the western edge of the land, melted the horizon, which quivered and shook as the earth accepted its weight. The air concentrated into dusk and there was not a sound.

Dumbfounded, Gay turned away from the fat red belly and his mind stretched thin into the twilight, so taut that he feared it would break free of him. He retreated into the woods, the faint sound of the falls hissing through the trees, the final birdsong wept lullingly as he started back to the wickeups. He thought that the forest was settled, but in that strange interlude between day and night he first saw Catherine copulate; Waboshiek standing straight-backed, she bent forward to embrace the forked trunk of a tree. They performed quite silently. When they had finished, Waboshiek folded himself away into the darkness, Catherine sank down unassuaged and rubbed her belly along the ground.

Her face was warped and buckled by sun and winter winds, her body had endured and was sleek. Her breasts were like eggs, her belly like the unstretched snow-white belly of a virgin vixen. She crouched for several minutes and then began to croon to herself. Continuing to chant in a stately and Romanish prayer, she stood up and walked a few paces, timorously, as if feeling her way across a bed of splinters. To Gay's surprise she stretched and felt down for her belly and began to dance in a slow three-step rhythm, not without grace although she was constrained by the narrowness of a native skirt. It was incongruous and pathetic and resolute against the close-ranking gloom. After she had gone, Gay waited, not wishing to admit to his intrusion.

CHAPTER TWENTY-SEVEN

Party Tricks – Rennah Sniffs – Gay Struts, and Shows a Fine Pair of
Heels to Waboshiek

One hot midday, when Gay was dozing through the high sun, he was awoken rudely by constant shouting and a stamping of hoofs which shattered the heavy silence. Waboshiek's voice answered. Gay pushed aside the flap and looked out. In the middle of the ruin a young Indian boy wrestled to control his pony, which cavorted wide-eyed amongst the ash, frighted by the clouds of acrid dust rising around it. Outside his wickeup Waboshiek stood grinning. The rider was unable to keep the pony still, but when it bolted he guided it up towards the woods, and Gay, shielding his eyes, saw against the trees a line of Indians, some on ponies, some walking, mostly women and children, a dozen or so men whose horses dragged litters, and behind them a party of four, shepherding a dark monster, bulbous and hairy and hump-backed.

The procession guarded the tree-line and turned into a grassed clearing, spreading themselves around the circumference.

They wailed. Thin lamentations spread from the clearing down past Gay towards the river and multiplied until the air stabbed and jangled and the noise rebounded shrilly from the far bank.

Waboshiek walked up towards them and when he reached the clearing the noise subsided, and Waboshiek sang.

'They won't harm you,' Catherine said. 'This is where they lived, and that is what's left of them.'

Gay walked with her to the edge of the clearing and saw them closely; deformed creatures, mutilated and scarred, burned and withered flesh clinging to their bones like varnished fruit, their faces coloured like maps. They sat silently while Waboshiek sang out his greeting, and the buffalo stood alone in the middle of the clearing, its belly ensconced in the grasses; two birds perched on the hump behind its head, pecking at the cloud of insects which milled around the shaggy bulk.

Waboshiek advanced, and sang. Gay wondered if the creature were

197

not deaf, for it took no notice of him. Its head was magnificent and untroubled, swinging heavily from side to side, flattening the grasses, a snort rising from the buried snout. Waboshiek sang. The hours passed, time stood immobilised, hobbled to the sound of his voice.

At the first fall of the day the men sent arrows into the buffalo's body, behind the front legs; and the buffalo recoiled, and sat. Its head lifted. Its long beard dripped cud and soil.

The powerful shoulders trembled, beneath a thick mat of curls the eyes gazed mournfully. Waboshiek sang to it, sang to its soul a serenade which brought tears of calm to Gay's eyes and streams of blood from the buffalo's snout and lips. It turned its head once more. Its tongue hung askew. The birds flew away. The buffalo groaned a long and contented commentary as its shoulders sank forward and the life skipped out of its mouth.

Waboshiek sang. His small rattle collected the sounds in the air. He approached the corpse and with his knife he cut out the buffalo's heart, holding it up to the fading sun, honouring the creature. He slit its throat and cut out a steaming tongue. Traces were attached to the buffalo's legs, and with a cracking of sinew the buffalo was drawn apart so that it lay spreadeagled on its belly. The first cut was from above the hump to the base of the back, and from each side the flesh was prised away in a long slab, sweet-smelling steam rising from the gore, the bones revealed through a skein of slippery mucus.

When the fire was lit Catherine said, 'It is their celebration, not ours.' She turned away, abruptly. Gay stood watching for a moment longer, astonished at the solemnity and dignity of these miserable people, and then he bowed his head and walked back towards the darkness of the river.

Passing Catherine's wickeup, he climbed along the rocks at the edge of the water, climbed upwards until he came to the top of the falls, and from there he watched the fire waver towards the evening sky with its smells of cooking meat.

He waited there for several hours, until his senses were called by the repeated striking of a drum, to which was joined a sharp and fast clatter of hardwood sticks – stirring an urgency within him. Gay stood and looked down at the valley. Three men were capering about beside the fire, but they quickly sat down and barked like dogs, patting their hands against their faces. This happened perhaps five or six times, each time with a different group of people. There was no applause. And then, inside the circle, one of the savages set himself up as the master of ceremonies. He lashed the ground with his stick, he hopped and shouted and turned to a post and thrashed at it; and the circle filled with people and confusion.

Gay sighed. Such a display would be jeered off the stage in London.

He made his way cautiously down the falls and back along the riverbank. He sang quietly to himself, to the stars, to the fluting gurgle of the water until the shadow in front of him spread and fattened and moved independently of his own body.

'Gay!'

Who turned, and saw Rennah Wells in the moonlight, below the bank and just underneath Catherine's wickeup.

'John Gay!'

'It is. What brings you out here, Rennah?'

'It's a free country.'

'So what's your interest in it?'

'No different to anyone else's.'

'Then make yourself known.'

'Up there?' Rennah nodded towards the fire. 'If you go up there, you're never gonna come back alive.'

With this he retreated. He kept staring at Gay, treading backwards, glancing fearfully up the slope, until he disappeared into the shadows beneath the bluffs.

Gay did go up there.

It was a concoction of fundamental frenzy, mindless, frantic, an indulgence in compact madness. Gay perched on the edge of the chaos, his spirit horrified by the ugliness, his senses beaten upon from every quarter: by the caterwauling, by the labyrinthine composition of identities, by the harsh determination of the music. Here a shuffling bear, there a demonic scarecrow, a crippled bird, a stubby lunatic with the face of a gargoyle, a wailing crone. There seemed to be dozens upon painted dozens, a crazed universe circling precisely against the clock.

The ground wobbled. Sparks floated free off the fire and soared upwards, spraying the blackness with hot spume. Gay recoiled backwards and then there was a stick jabbed into his back.

He turned and faced Waboshiek, who swayed from side to side and held out a jar of whiskey for Gay to take. His eyes were steady; the fire threw light down into those depthless pools but nothing rose to the surface. He was drunk; his face was seamed with oily sweat. Gay tilted the jar and swigged.

Waboshiek motioned that he should drink more, and Gay did so, the whiskey tumbling into his belly. Waboshiek grinned. His right arm went back to his side and before Gay knew it Waboshiek pulled out a knife and pushed it into Gay's belly until the hilt pressed against his skin.

Deep within himself Gay felt the cold of the metal. He felt no pain, just the cold of the steel beneath the warm sparkle of the whiskey. Waboshiek kept on grinning. Gay did not dare to move, feeling that the life would fall out of him if he stepped away. Waboshiek swayed. His eyes took in Gay and then glassed over, as if Gay would never again disturb the surface of his being. He pushed heavily against Gay, pushed and twisted the hilt of the knife and lurched back a pace, withdrawing a handful of white intestines from Gay's abdomen. The smell of rancid blubber steamed gently.

Well, thought Gay; well indeed. Fine trick.

He sank to his knees, coughed, and thought that he might vomit.

He whistled the first bars of a slow, quiet tune. Waboshiek swayed above him. Gay winked. With his right hand he loosened the drawstring at his breechclout. He rose up and lunged at Waboshiek. He grabbed the offal and turned half away, raising it eagerly to his lips. His cheeks swelled; his throat rose and fell. He downed the gummy intestine in a trice, the whole mass sliding easily unseen along the inside of his right arm into the open maw of the breechclout. He smacked his lips and belched and reached down for the whiskey jar. He offered Waboshiek the old Grimaldi swagger.

Waboshiek spoke into the darkness. He watched Gay drink. He watched, over Gay's shoulder, as the circle cleared. Catherine approached, her slender white wrists showing against the edge of her cloak. She handed the Harlequin costume to Waboshiek, and he passed it over to Gay.

'Waboshiek will see your dance.'

'What dance?' Gay begged.

'Of what you are. Of your history. Of your life, Mister Gay; you are dancing for your life, as is everyone else here.'

'And Waboshiek?'

'Waboshiek does not dance as Waboshiek, he dances as Fox. He dances for Fox's life. There is no need for you to be so ambitious. You are not obliged to perform your paltry conception of the secrets of the universe, Waboshiek merely wishes to understand who you are.'

Bollock-deep in animal tripe, unrehearsed and addled by the onrush of the whiskey, there wasn't much Gay could do other than match Waboshiek at his own stage-trickery. He retired into the darkness, made himself vomit up the spirit, and dressed.

Waboshiek, as Fox, approached with cautious courtesy.

Gay cartwheeled across the circle, pinpoints of firelight scattering from his spangles, and crouched at Fox's feet. Fox froze. Gay rose and bowed deep, mockingly, seizing his hat from his belt and flourishing it before putting it on his head. There were cries of anger, almost of pain, from around the circle. The music stopped. Gay whistled the first line of 'What'll Missis Grundy say?' The audience fell quiet. Gay put his hand to his ear. He heard nothing.

A *fouetté* cross-stage into an attitude: disturbed by the rippled whistle of a thrush. Gay cocked his ear. He heard nothing. *Fouetté*, repeated to the east. Repeated to the west. And north. The thrush accepts his invitation.

Harlequin lures the thrush back to Fox. He offers it to Fox. Fox is too slow and the thrush escapes, its whistling pesters Fox and Harlequin. They are both annoyed. The thrush falls silent. They both stand still.

Harlequin searches for the thrush. Fox looks around him. The thrush whistles again, very close. Fox and Harlequin jump. Harlequin bats about with his hat. The thrush settles on the edge of the circle. Harlequin stalks it, hits out at it and misses. His head follows it as it flaps around the circle and settles again. Stealthily Harlequin tiptoes towards the thrush, hushing at the audience (whose mood, Gay notices, God bless 'em, is at last beginning to change). Harlequin hushes furiously at them. He creeps up to the thrush, hat raised – and some inspired drumster alerts the bird, and is applauded by those sitting near to him. Harlequin pretends fury, and the stalking begins again. The bird settles near Catherine. It whistles sadly. Harlequin tiptoes closer.

Catherine's lips are yielded to the most sublime and innocuous smile, her eyes complete with remembered wonderment. Gay smiles at her. The thrush hops and whistles. There, in front of her lap, lies the Harlequin's mask. He leaps and catches mask and thrush. Down he sits and swallows the elusive bird. Down he sits and swallows. He belches. The expression on his face is one of triumph, of satisfaction; of perturbation, of querulousness, of agitation.

He sneezes, he whistles, he trills. The thrush is flapping up and down inside him and he hops and flutters like a marionette, back to Fox, drummed in. He presents his predicament to Fox, who howls, and stamps his feet, and raises his stick, and whacks Harlequin in the stomach.

Gay saw the blow coming. He could anticipate it but he could not avoid it. He crouched in pain.

Waboshiek sang lustily above Gay's head, his feet thumping the dust. Gay would have had him there and then, with a swift butt to the man's groin; but stage etiquette demanded no taking of vengeance.

Fox circled him victoriously. Harlequin looked back through his own legs and watched the pattern of the feet. Fox danced in the smallest of slow hops sideways; four at a time facing outwards — no doubt soliciting the admiration of his audience — then four facing inwards, asserting his supremacy over Harlequin.

Gay pulled the mask over his head. Fox's feet turned away. Harlequin ran eight steps to the post, one step up it for thrust, two steps back, two flip-flaps, up, and a twist; a shout to the sky and he came down astride Fox's shoulders as Fox turned to crow over his missing victim.

Waboshiek was strong and his reactions were quick. He held the weight without falling. Gay had no wish to humiliate him. Arms outstretched, Harlequin followed the directions of the momentum and escaped down Fox's back, hand-standing gracefully into an attitude, holding it momentarily in order to recover his breath and to see what he might have to fear.

Waboshiek was undecided. Gay had little time to gauge the feelings of his audience, but this was not the moment to settle.

There were no props, no traps, no sprung walls or windows through which he might exit.

He prowled around the edge of the circle, waiting for his body to lead him on. He turned inwards to bow to Fox on every tenth step, more to keep an eye on him than anything else, but reaching for his poise, preening himself, realising that he had not the energies for any great display.

He began to mock himself, mincing and hopping and plucking at his hair, like a cockatoo. The women laughed amongst themselves and he exaggerated his movements, strutting and crowing and shaking his spangles, intermittently leaping towards one or another group of women, who jeered and waved him away. The men chose not to see him; they kept their eyes on Fox, who had resumed his interminable clod-hopping in the centre of the circle. A fierce malevolence provoked Gay. Little by little he unlaced the flap at his groin and eased a coil of pale intestine out between his legs, where it hung and swayed suggestively.

This was precisely the type of cheap and tasteless exhibition which he and Edmond loathed, but Gay was possessed by the urge to desecrate. Spritely he pranced to and fro around the circle, lugging the ponderous and glistening member forward for inspection, as though searching for some acquiescent depository. He persisted, shrieking birdsong, his upper lip curling against the black silk mask, his tongue lapping furiously at the air.

There were wails of displeasure. The animosity beat against him. He had trapped himself within the masked creation. Shaking with violence, he spun on round the circle, the painted faces flashing past him. He stopped, but there was no way out. He snarled. He offered himself and his contempt. He spun. The music beat on, and into the music came the repetitive plaint of a woman's voice. The lamentation rose and fell, unsorrowful, almost comforting. He was drawn towards the centre of the circle, where Fox stood and where Catherine swayed from side to side. The drums stopped. He stood in front of her, he didn't look at her; he shook, feebly, the intestine forward.

'You go too far,' she hissed at him.

'Tell me what to do!'

She saw two eyes, wild and pleading, behind the slits in the mask. She reached and took hold of the warm intestine and withdrew it and fed it into the crown of the Harlequin's hat, which she held in front of her waist. Raising the hat high, she spat three times at Gay's groin.

Then she turned her back on him and offered the hat to Fox, who took it and sang and danced and scattered dirt inside the hat and placed it a pace away from Gay's feet. Fox carried on with his dance. Others came forward.

Gay returned to his wickeup, and lay down, distressed by the contemptible idiocy of his performance. What had they understood? What had *he* understood? There was nothing there. There was nothing in such cold balletic gesture, nothing in empty attitude; there was nothing to understand. 'Twas hollow vanity, all that he had ever known. He did not want to create anything, nor have anything attributed to him. The whistling still terrified him, the whistling in the Green Room and the whistling in the air. He felt that he was protecting a valuable possession – perhaps himself, perhaps his sanity – something which would leave him at the slightest opportunity. He felt threatened above all by himself. He was shocked at his lack of substance.

CHAPTER TWENTY-EIGHT

Geography and History and Shadows – Waboshiek as Courier – His Hospitality towards Edmond – Rennah's Bolthole

The next afternoon a group of horses stopped behind Gay's wickeup and Waboshiek summoned him. Catherine was amongst the riders and she indicated that he would be escorted out of the village. He gathered his belongings and accepted the horse which Waboshiek offered, and when Gay took Edmond's skull on his lap, the shaman nodded approval.

They rode behind the ruins and away from the heavy sun, which gave Gay the strangest sensation of travelling over an ice-thin surface, the occasional cries of children rising from another world beneath him.

'I wonder', said he to Catherine, 'if there is anything I might do for you. Perhaps pass on a message? There must be some who fear for your safety.'

'*I* fear for my safety.'

'You fear Waboshiek.'

'Waboshiek? No. I fear Rennah Wells, as does Waboshiek. Not for himself, you understand.'

'And therefore he fears me?'

'Why should he fear you? He has what he wants from you. If he feared you, you would be dead; as dead as your friend. Waboshiek has healed you; you are beholden to him. More so than I am.'

They rode through the woods, leaving the women behind them to carry full bladders of food. Divested of this year's fruit, the trees and bushes were hung about with vines and creeper, the leaves were gilding and fragile, the sun fell disreputably upon younger, stripling growth. There was no sense of urgency and no caution. The forest floor was dry, the undergrowth sagged sadly when brushed by the horses. They lost sight of the Rock River, the woods thinned and they rode through a natural clearing, the land rich, the late-seeding grasses horseback-high. Gay smelt moisture and earth and an exhilarating scent of distance, wide distance. It was as much like a sound, like the silence of the ocean.

The clearing was perhaps three miles wide, the trees stretching in an arc to the north. They turned south-west, five of them, towards the one open face, they rode fast; Gay, encumbered, followed as best he might. They stopped in a line; against the sun they sat motionless, their horses breathing heavily and sneezing. His own horse joined the line, the grasses swishing against its chest.

Gay saw for miles – across the great river Mississippi, beside which the Rock River was a mere stream; and beyond, over the vast sheet of prairie which dipped and rumpled towards the sun.

There was not the place within him for such immensity. He might better have taken in some comprehension of the heavens – aided by centuries of cliché – than he would ever account for the magnitude of the panorama which stretched away from him.

They sat in silence, Gay dazed by the aweful vacancy of the land, until the horses became restless and Waboshiek grunted and Catherine pointed and Gay saw a small figure dragging a canoe up towards the Fort on that island in the middle of the Mississippi.

Waboshiek slid down and stood staring out towards Rennah. One of the men spoke to him. He answered abruptly and two of them wheeled away and galloped back through the russet waves of grass. Waboshiek spat.

'Where is the rest of the tribe?' Gay asked. 'Are there any others?'

'There.' Catherine pointed. 'On the beach.' Gay looked but could see no Indians lining the bank. 'They were buried there, alive; those who didn't drown. The militiamen cut razor strops from their bodies.'

'And did Rennah Wells have something to do with that?'

'He was their preacher. They listened to him, and they trusted him. Until he abandoned them. By then Waboshiek was powerless; he understands that.' She sat back; in a tired voice she asked Gay, 'Why has he come back? What more can Rennah Wells want?'

Gay knew.

He dismounted and pinned Edmond's skull under his arm, his horse wandering off to join Waboshiek's. He stood quietly, surrounded by grasshoppers. Waboshiek prayed and rattled and rolled until the rim of the sun touched the horizon and a lone shout sounded from the island fort in the middle of the Mississippi. Waboshiek called to the horses. He held Edmond's skull while Gay mounted, then raised it up to catch the sun and handed it to Gay, and nodded cursorily over his shoulder.

They rode down the slope into the shadows of the woods, the air gathering a moist chill. The women had stopped to tie bundles of sticks. They rode on through the field of stubble, black wisps sticking to the horses' shanks, over the light grey ash which lost itself amongst the whiteness of stones. Past these stones the men dragged bundles of wood, throwing up trails of fine porcelain white which hung defiantly still and left the air ghosted in emptiness. Gay looked for some expression of unhappiness in Waboshiek but there was none. Waboshiek stared at the destruction, his eyes drugged, the lower half of his face heavy and settled, almost contemptuous.

They left the ruin and rode into the deeper darkness. The ground rose steeply, the river widened beneath them and disappeared to the south. The track narrowed. There was little covering for the rock. They waited patiently each time a horseman passed them, hauling his bundle of wood up the hillside.

Waboshiek left the track. He returned with four freshly cut saplings; and they continued, winding their way upwards. Looking back, Gay saw the trails of dust streaked across the grey dish beneath him, and beyond that the Rock River trickling free of the forest, a last balm of sunlight stroking the tops of the trees.

They broke out upon the surface of the bluffs and circled around to the north, where the broad black avenue of the Mississippi swept past, many hundreds of feet below. They stood then at the end of a thin bridge of ebbing sunlight, the boiled pate of the sun drowning in the darkness of the prairie, a fanfare of scarlet and indigo blazing across the sky. Gay's breath quickened as at an enormous sorrow. He waited for the darkness to swallow him; he wanted to hang, now, in the great drop of blackness. He wanted to push aside the curtain of sunlight and rid himself of his self; there was nothing at all to fear from Death, from a slow calm flight down through the darkness, the air whistling about him.

Then the sunlight was gone and Gay found Waboshiek staring at him, light gushing from the sills and lintels of his eyes, darkness sinking within. Waboshiek turned to face over the river and Gay saw with him the unhurried flight of an eagle, dipping from sunlight into shadow, cruising the slender parapet of dusk.

Waboshiek led him away. Gay did not know how long he had stood at the edge of the bluffs, nor how long Waboshiek had been with him. Small fires were burning all over the plateau. The smell of warm food scraped at Gay's nostrils and set his stomach churning. He mimed his hunger to Waboshiek, who shook his head and pointed to Edmond's skull.

The sun had long gone but the dusk was spacious, night lazing beneath the bluffs. The women were on their hands and knees between the fires, plucking out spears of grass and clearing the ground of any other vegetation. Waboshiek had stuck his four staves into the earth. He walked carefully around the circumference and took Gay a hundred paces away to the north, to where a hole had been freshly dug down to the rock. There he motioned to Gay that he should bury Edmond's skull, and without hesitation Gay entrusted Edmond to Waboshiek's care.

Throughout the hours of darkness the fires shimmied and the voices of the women rose melancholy in enquiry and lamentation across their burial ground. Waboshiek returned but once through the teeming night, bringing a small platter of food which he set above Edmond's grave. When sunlight first bit through the dawn the ragbag remnants of the tribe filed away north, Waboshiek watching them leave.

'Will he not go with them?' Gay wondered.

'No,' said Catherine. 'They have no use for him. He failed them in life, and his last duty is to protect their dead.'

'Will you not go with them?'

'No.'

Gay bid farewell to Edmond. At a distance of fifty paces Catherine followed Waboshiek down the path off the bluffs, and Gay followed them both back to what was left of Saukenuk.

CHAPTER TWENTY-NINE

Winter Quarters — Catherine's Central Heating — Gay's Depths Are Plumbed

The first clouds grew out of the north-western horizon like a magnificent fungus. In the early afternoon the sun lay down on thick bolsters of white and threw tales of resurrection eastwards across an emptiness of sky. A sudden keening wind, a thickening gloom; and then — with a flurry, with a pause, with a military solemnity — the rains came to curtain off the day.

Saukenuk was sealed not so much by the rain as by the wind, which slid violently from the north-west in a remorseless flush of acrimony. It did not pause to bite. It drove thousands on thousands of needles across the land. This was no frolicking wind, this was a sustained and vindictive taskmaster, harrying south the rain without leniency or respite. Whether the sky held off in occasional blue innocence or sagged thick with surrender, the wind replenished its retribution, slashing across the surface of Saukenuk until it seemed to Gay that everything was flat and should become flatter, and even to stand up was an act of the most absurd defiance.

Neither of them could live through it in solitude. Gay sheltered with Catherine. He had no wish to impose; she had no wish to be imposed upon. She drugged him. She told him that she was doing so and he drank what was offered. He felt no hunger. They lay dormant, their senses stretching towards the wind and clinging to their bodies by the finest thread. Their hearing was numbed by the constant shriek, their touch fragile and credulous. He stared for hours at her face, the dry and scorched and ridged skin, the delicate mouth. She hardly seemed to breathe, but had shut herself away, an odourless exhalation eddying around her lips as if unable to settle in her. With her fingers she coaxed him, she accustomed him to a gentle frigging; she ringed him firmly lest he spend his heat. Long after he fell into a fitful sleep she lay on his shoulder, staring up at the ever-changing dimensions of the grey hole in the roof, attending to her source of heat. Beneath the rugs her body touched his like tepid water, the skin so smooth and indistinct that she seemed to be bodiless, her head lying like a rock beside a pool. Occasionally she would reach for food and place it between his lips without concern, her fingers dangling over his open mouth as though she were feeding a slothful dog.

When he was thus readied, Catherine wrapped up and went to fetch Waboshiek.

It struck Catherine as a wilful eccentricity that Waboshiek should have chosen this time to dry his laundry, to all intents oblivious to the storm outside. He himself stood and sang quietly, rather jovial and contented. He then appeared to declare a minor irritation with the weather: after which he laughed and mumbled away to himself and pottered about his wickeup. In a dilettantish fashion he went about his chores and tidied up, arranging this, that and the other, picking things off the floor, laying out a bowl of food, for all the world looking as though he were cleaning out a large kennel. Then suddenly Waboshiek was standing beside her, clutching a ragamuffin bag and his rattle and an assortment of sticks, blinking rapidly, barely concealing his impatience.

Outside, the rain pattered at her face. The wind had slowed. It came in mutinous gusts, resentful and unwilling to settle. Waboshiek stood beside her, either demanding or according respect, Catherine could not tell which. He poked her in the back with a stick. She set off, and Waboshiek followed like a helpless potentate, insisting that Catherine should clear his path.

When they entered Catherine's wickeup, Gay was still asleep. Waboshiek sniffed at the food and dropped it on to the fire. He told Catherine to throw the drink outside. He pushed stones into the base of the fire.

When Gay awoke, he found that he could not move although his restraints were invisible, the bands being constructed of compressions of air which amounted to terror. These strips of terror held him across the tops of his legs, around his neck, and from his armpits to his shoulders. He sweated, and urinated feebly.

He watched the girl's delicate mouth. Unease became confused with sexual excitement. There were many levels of feeling, and he did not know which way to trust. The terror furrowed into his flesh. He desired the girl not with any potency, but for the potency she would give him; he trusted her, and yet she was repulsive.

Something was perhaps not right; yet he saw that it was wrong to procrastinate. She was so definite in her actions, and so sure of herself. She held his hand and smiled at him, and quite cleverly cut off his hand, and held the hand up for him to see – he still felt the sensuous touch of her fingers on his.

This is wrong, he thought, this is not Catherine. And there was a smell of burning hair.

Gay felt nauseous and he screamed, pain stampeded through his body, the earth tilted right and left. His body hung from his backbone as if tied to a beam which was being thrown in jolts from beast to beast. He glimpsed his soul, pale, hiding in the shadows.

He called for help, and a slender white arm reached towards him with his own hand, in which there crawled a tiny maggot. The smoke set fast. He lost sight of everything and hurried to sever the rope, which caught fire and blazed and whiplashed him towards the line of iron teeth.

Bang!

Time stood still. Up rose Gay, a flash of shredded silk. Five hundred spangles shattering. Up and over. Tucked. The first somersault. In thin air now. Roll. Still tucked. Roll again.

Now came Waboshiek's chequered expression against the boards. Now falling towards Catherine's eyes, Catherine's voice – 'There is nothing to fear. There is only fear itself and that is nothing.'

Gay straightaway looked up and saw with pleasure the cornflower blue eyes streaked with gold, her skin the pale colour of an unripe peach. Without a doubt, *this* was Catherine. Gay observed the lackadaisical affection in her voice; a true affection, without irony. Around her eyes the skin swelled and hardened, but her eyes scarcely faded. Gay laughed, for nothing impinged upon his confidence in her.

Waboshiek held up Gay's hand. Gay laughed. Waboshiek placed it on the blanket on the floor. He took his little wooden knife and cut off Gay's arm and placed it beside the hand. He laughed at Gay and Gay laughed back. He cut off the other arm and put it on the blanket; he cut off the legs one by one, at the thigh, and placed them by the arms, and he stood and laughed, and he saw that Gay was still laughing. Lastly he cut off Gay's head, and he held the head out in front of him. He laughed and Gay's head laughed back at him. And Gay looked into his mirror, and saw his soul, and laughed.

Then Waboshiek took all the parts and cleaned them and put them back together again, whistling cheerfully.

CHAPTER THIRTY

Gay Has Problems with his Soul – Coyote Does Not

The air had him now. The air had everything he had ever known or was likely to know. He only cupped a small ball of light to his chest, very small and in need of protection.

He wanted his soul near to him. Unimpinged upon and deprived of distraction, his soul might coalesce and find a home in his body. Thus confined, it would be unable to flee. Undisturbed, it would see no reason to escape. He would not interfere with it, nor alarm it, nor provoke it, nor treat it lightly, nor be so foolhardy as to regale it. In time his soul might accept him and consider to live with him, but he could not force this issue.

He stood for hours, staring at the river, that long black fissure in the grey mud. He watched a line of ducks swimming in a surge with their necks stretched forward, like a disease fighting its way up through the bloodstream. He watched the ducks dabble and bob, and in the open water revolve in a packed circle. There were perhaps a hundred of them, and yet he saw each one distinctly. He felt the pressure of each separate life. He knew this as a conceit, yet he was helpless to distance himself from the overwhelming confusion caused by so many unique beings. His soul cowered away. There was no unanimity, and no security of such.

Run, he thought to himself, run and abandon your soul. It will not mind. You will never live in harmony. Leave your soul here amongst the ashes. Take Catherine for company and propriety and solution and go before you become mad.

At night the coyotes came. He heard them snuffling and yapping and snarling around the wickeup while his soul hung whitely, close by the smoke-hole, out of reach, as Catherine slept by his side.

Waboshiek came again, in sunlight, singing nothing but fiddle-cum-fee. He sang and he danced. He and Gay and Catherine tramped through the mud up to the bluffs where Edmond was buried, and Gay looked down and once again saw the beach of deserted souls.

The swollen river had rushed and scoured. And now the white tops of skulls lay like eggs embedded in the sand.

The Mississippi fled past them to the south, spreading itself curtly around the island and its drenched-black fort on whose wall Gay was just able to pick out the figure of Rennah Wells.

At one point Catherine laughed and a shower of bright crystals cascaded higgedly-piggledy home, into Gay's heart, like the hundred warm pinpricks of sun off the surface of the puddles. He shut his eyes and cupped his hands over his ears. On the way back to Sauk-enuk, he urged her to come south with him, but she would have none of it, not without Waboshiek, and Waboshiek would never leave. 'Tell him to leave. Tell him that I am leaving and that you will follow me.'

When she told him, Waboshiek's eyes feasted on the light and Gay felt a wave of desolation suck in at his own back, which was then repulsed. Waboshiek grinned and gabbled and sang.

'What does he say?'

'He hasn't made up his mind.'

'There isn't time,' Gay pleaded. 'Rennah Wells will come, as soon as the river falls.'

Waboshiek laughed. He nodded agreeably and patted his stomach.

Gay came upon the fort from the north, his canoe scuttled against the rocks by the force of the current. He arrived half drowned; and Rennah, who from the walls had seen him coming, reckoned that Gay must damned near have used up his nine lives by now. He dragged Gay into the guardroom, which was heated by a small woodstove, and he left Gay to make up his own mind about life or death.

Around them the fort rotted from the massive damp. Pools of water lay about the parade ground, troughs and ponds hid beneath drenched sedge. Gay shrank from the pervasive morning mist and the green slime which covered walls, beds and floors. A clammy moisture stuck to his belt, a thick damp rose from his bedding, and steam nightly ridiculed every attempt to dry his clothes. The fort stank of corruption. Gnarled goitres of mushroom reached up the walls and discharged clouds of putrid green dust over the hordes of lice. A dainty tracery of white decay fanned across the roof of the guard-house, speckled poxily with pinpoints of red.

Each in his own cell, Gay and Rennah waited, each man defending himself as best he might, feeling himself trickle away amongst the enormous volumes of water which drained from the land. Behind the sodden papery walls the Mississippi swelled past, brown and silent, until it seemed that the surface of the earth was abandoning them and fleeing southwards with indecent haste, leaving a bleached and gutted debris.

Gay lay and listened to Rennah, who remembered times when both of them preached for food, when they had nothing save wagon and Venn and hard toiling across country with darned books and those copies of how every man had a right to happiness, and Rennah sniggered and edited and omitted and lapped at the jug of whiskey.

Many times Gay awoke suddenly somewhere in the long night, and it was as though he had been interrupted when he was about to speak. Yet now on his awaking he had nothing to say. The night was thick and black but he couldn't bring himself to light a candle, for the blackness was a parent who would be angry if disturbed. He lay still and listened as Rennah informed him as to how extraordinary the savages were: their purity, their nobility of spirit, their distinctive bearing, the pride in the carriage of their heads. Rennah claimed that the frontal lobes were bigger, that there had to be a supplementary cord of supply from one of the essential organs.

Rennah interpreted. Rennah explained. Rennah constructed.

Rennah's long dirty fingers enfolded an orb of air, and smoothed its circumference: until Gay turned his head and stared, and saw a hollow, floating skull. As Rennah's fingers circumscribed small rings of light, caressing frantically the black emptiness, so Gay shuddered with disgust.

When the mist lifted, Rennah took up his position on the walls. Gay kept an eye on him.

The birds came. Thousands upon thousands. Lark, duck, snipe, goose, crane settled on the land like unfurled carpet, crying, fighting, searching for food. Hour after hour the birds fell out of the low grey sky, sweeping in from the north to plunder insects from the swampy beach. When the sun came, it rode through the afternoon like a wan and reluctant knight, in and out of puffball clouds. The birds lifted off, screeching ingratitude. They wheeled and quietened and went on south in stark formality, leaving the beach for other transients.

As the light faded they went below to their cells. They had nothing to say to each other. Gay lost Rennah in the gloom as Rennah sat on his pallet tilting at the jug of whiskey: he never lost the feel of Rennah's eyes, and that feel was for his body, and Gay knew that he might for a time hold Rennah in the palm of his hand.

One night Gay felt Rennah steal into his cell, and he got Rennah's palms resting on the crown of his head, the long fingers hanging down like spider's legs, probing and slithering around his temples, hot and damp.

'What is it, Rennah?'

'It's nothin.'

'What do you want?'

'Nothin.'

In the morning Rennah was up early, and Gay hurried to join him. There was but a light mist over the far shore. Rennah's red and addled eyes strained to see across the river, his dunghill breath clouded into the air. They stood for an hour, and then, from the mouth of the Rock River there came a canoe, indistinct but for a flash of golden hair. Rennah grunted approval. The golden hair was at the front of the canoe, there was another shape at the back. Rennah hungered after them.

He climbed down from the walls, and when Gay caught him he was packing his burlap bag.

'Don't go,' Gay murmured from his own cell. 'Not yet.'

He danced. He danced until, exhausted, he spun supine along the bars which divided them, and Rennah reached through with both hands to clutch at Gay's head, squeezing at the temples.

'Who did that?' he demanded. 'Waboshiek took that, didn't he? You tell me now!'

'Why?'

Their faces were but a few inches apart; Gay stared into the maddened eyes. His own eyes portrayed a doeish innocence. He took Rennah's face between his hands and pulled him forward. He kissed his lips. And, in a trice, Rennah's tongue snaked into his mouth.

Gay danced, and Rennah hung on the bars. He moaned in prayer. At the end Gay stripped and washed himself – torso, fingers, lips – free of Rennah's eyes.

From the walls, in the evening light, he watched Rennah push out his canoe, like a rat quitting its hole in the riverbank, downstream, and past the mouth of the Rock River.

That clear cold night. The landscape once again pinioned by moonlight, everything static except for the flow of the river, the prairie on either side spangled with frost. He had, now, what he wanted; a perfect solitude. His skins had shed themselves and burned like so many sparks in the darkness through which he had passed. Here he stood astride both time and place, and might represent himself in strong, unhampered purity. This was the only thing worth living for, this beauty which he might perfect in isolation. To perfect himself as a statement, with whose beauty he might confront the world. This was possible. This was all possible.

He knelt and wept.

For it was not possible. It never had been possible, and his soul cried out at his own destruction.

He knelt at the rotted wall and prayed. He prayed for Catherine's safety and for Waboshiek, for Edmond's soul and for the life of Elisabeth, for Ann, for his mother, for his father. He turned everywhichway to face God; God all about him, but silently super-cilious; his soul writhed and moaned and yearned to no avail. He prayed for himself. For himself. But there was no still, small voice of calm. His own soul would not answer him, it echoed his words disdainfully, winking and spitting from the night sky.

He went down to his cell and warmed himself, and his soul screamed abuse at him; frenetic with malevolence it sneered at him. Ignorant he had been, and wilful; his soul was cold unto death and did not seek his protection.

Death urged him to think about this, but he thought about Death and that particular silence, aweful when the curtain fell across the stage, like the silence of a skirt come to rest beside his head when he lay on the boards as an infant imploring.

And had he then longed for Death, all this time? Was that the trick?

Was that what he was trying to tell himself? Was that what came out of the fog, which he neatly avoided? The air as his enemy.

He leapt at it, he struck it, he unbalanced it.

He weaved from side to side of the cell, he darted at the air. He clapped and he sang and he shouted; and when the cell was cleared of Death, he took his vengeance out under the sky, weaving across the fort, scuttling halfway up the sides of the walls until they cracked and splintered, there were a dozen John Gays rampaging through them, screaming the Harlequin's scorn at their decay.

Waboshiek grinned, put the little silver box to his lips and swallowed the Maggot.

Gay stopped. Carried by the moonlight over the Mississippi came the tinkle of a small bell, and on top of the bluffs there was a fire.

His own fire at his back, Gay sat and watched.

The moon hovered starkly, throwing a silver cloth along the wide dish of the river. Fox opened his weakness and the moonlight burned him like acid. He concentrated, he searched. His senses flapped like stranded fish. He screamed abuse at Coyote, the dark holes of his eyes opening like pits towards the silver cloth. He cursed Coyote for his slyness, his ignorance, his childish irresponsibility. He urged Coyote to show some respect. Coyote laughed, and Fox cuffed him on the side of the head, shattering the air in Coyote's ear and knocking him dead. Up jumped Coyote, grinning. Fox pointed Coyote to the beach; together they sauntered amongst the skulls, Fox shed tears like patchwork. Coyote made bad jokes and Fox knocked him dead once again. Up jumped Coyote and Fox felt better, light-hearted even, with skin hardening over his weakness, as though he were being born. Coyote grinned, and Fox stepped from the bluffs and ran off along the moonlight.

For two days and three nights Waboshiek danced, singing of the world and its souls, of his pain, singing to the flat earth and the sky, across the river to the burning fort. On the edge of the bluffs he sang and he prayed, as Waboshiek, as Fox.

Gay watched. Until on the morning of the third day the numbness crept up from Waboshiek's toes and he lost his footing and fell to his death, the air sweeping through the holes in Gay's body.

Gay stood up then, and stretched. He went to his cell and slept the sleep of the dead. When he awoke he torched the cells and made himself a raft which carried him south; not far, a day later he was back at Saukenuk. He climbed the bluffs and retrieved Waboshiek's rattle and his own comet-tin, and set fire to the three wickeups.

Gay found Waboshiek. He dragged Waboshiek to the beach and buried him, and lit a fire. Throughout the night he danced, and Fox danced down through the hole in the sky to keep him company.

They sat, and they talked; and then the earth fell silent, and they waited.

Gay was perfectly calm.

The morning rang wet with mist, which the sun scraped cleanly from the bowl of the earth.

Gay tested the reach of his limbs and the balance within his back. The line led from his coccyx, along his spinal column and up through his neck, until it was controlled within his forehead. At such a moment his mind was a perfect blank, his soul in mere harmony. He meditated. He waited.

At midday Rennah came.

He did not at first see Gay, who sat in the shadow of the trees some four hundred paces upriver.

Gay smelt him; and watched him, calmly; as with a small spade and axe Rennah chopped and dug. Five spadefuls of sand, the single chop, and the head held aloft in stasis.

Rennah started in a fever of indiscriminate greed. He severed a dozen heads before taking some account of what he was doing. He paused then, and arranged the heads in a line; with a pair of calipers he measured them and compared them.

Thereafter he scraped the sand away from the bodies and took his measurements where they lay, severing but occasionally, disdaining what did not please him.

He passed quite close, and was delighted to find the embers of Gay's fire. Off he went to his canoe and brought back Catherine's head, tied by its golden hair to a folded iron tripod, and there was a small cauldron which he filled with water and set to boil over the replenished fire. Then he walked away up the beach.

Gay waited.

At sunset the land on the far bank of the Mississippi shimmered inside a violet mist.

It came like an old dream from childhood. It was a gaunt, shabby figure, stumbling from side to side in triumph, the collection of human heads flapping at his waist. In place of his own head it wore the smiling skull of a bird.

The air poured hotly down into Gay's stomach, pulsing with power. He drew in the air and controlled it. He stepped out of the shadows, startling Rennah.

'Have you found what you're looking for?'

'Some. I ain't found Waboshiek.'

'That's because you don't know where to look. He's here. I saved him for you, Rennah.' Gay extended his hand. 'We'll go halves. We both have to make a living, somehow.'

Rennah stared. He saw Gay smile in a friendly and helpful fashion. There was something both alluring and repulsive about the actor, like a cur seeking affection with a sly glance. But he was the only friend Rennah had ever had.

Gay led him over to a patch of gore which had seeped up through the sand. Rennah looked down.

'I heard tell that Waboshiek is still alive.'

'From her?' Gay smirked across at Catherine's head.

'Yep.'

'Why believe her? Look and see for yourself.'

'And you ain't caring?'

'Care? No. I don't care.'

Rennah put down his chopper. He untied his belt of heads and laid them on the ground. He knelt, and took the spade and leaned forward and began to dig: two, three, four, five – and the stasis.

Gay took Rennah's hair and pulled it back so that he should see the dying sun, and he sank the chopper into Rennah's throat. Blood sprayed red and dribbled down off the sides of the sun.

Far worse than the blood was the stink which gushed from Rennah's windpipe – of sewage, of rot, of decaying meat, of burnt hair – a hideous stench. Gay struck again, at Rennah's midriff, and out of his stomach came the maggots, tumbling and squirming in their hundreds. Rennah's neck sighed. Gay dragged him over to the fire. With the spade he shovelled the maggots into the cauldron. He pulled the cauldron over, and the boiling water flooded across Rennah's body.

Gay somersaulted.

The snows come. The grey slack bag of heaven falls apart and thousands upon thousands of snowflakes rove above the land, baffling the sky with myriad flits of perspective. The wind comes in rebellious flurries, truculent and loth to expire, a spew of snow tumbling and rolling like chaff. So the world is clothed and pure, its white lies accepted, the land is undisturbed by the smell of footprints. All's well that ends Wells and buries saintly Edmond.

Time flips the year up into the air like a silver coin; up and over – glittering in thin air now – over again and Death's a dime a dozen on the boards; the year falls and lies buried in the snows, undisturbed, both past and future under cover. The sun perches on its flimsy shelf, and with a sudden crack the resilience of a bare forked tree is ended.

No-one meddles.

The midmorning temperature lifts itself to zero and stays that way, day after day. The snow creaks loudly; nothing else splits the silence. The snow wet-nurses the land; it wraps up the noise of footsteps and hands them back to the air. There they coalesce and hover safely like souls, hanging whitely, respected guardians. Such a display would be jeered off the stage in London.

It is time to shed that last skin.

The great white snows stretch for many hundreds of miles – an ethereal gift; which in turn commands respect for the air, now wandering thin over the prairie, its playful demons scuffling with the stillness of Time.

Gay somersaults.

This is *our* Time, Fox and Coyote.

Time was: when Fox sang to the sky and met Coyote, who took away his loneliness. And together they sang and danced and made a clod of earth which they threw into space. Fox sang. Coyote danced. The land grew bigger and finally they jumped down onto it, their fall cushioned by the snows. They stretched the world on all sides with their paws, and that's how they made the world, bit by bit.

It was quite some trick.

And one fine incisive morning, when the frost had hardened a rind over the snow, they upped and set off westwards; Fox grumbling about maggots, Coyote armed with a prayerbook and intent on creating mischief. They both had to make a living, somehow.

AFTERWORD

Both London and New York newspapers document the essentials of this story. John Gay and Edmond Parsloe did take *Mother Goose* to New York, and Edmond died there. The Victorian *Gentleman's Magazine* reports that John Gay walked west, until encountering wise men from an Indian tribe, who were so impressed by his gestures that they made him a chief for a year. Natives on both sides of the Atlantic reckon this as a white man's supremacy myth. Adding myth to myth, Celtic Magic takes credit for introducing to the Northeastern American continent its magico-mystical archetypes: Sow as Buffalo, etc. The bare bones of the story were passed to me by Edward Abelson.

I have played hard and fast with the possibilities, and have curtailed historical event. It is not clear, and after three years I could not clarify, what part the 'mad prophet' Waboshiek played in the massacre of the Sauk and Fox tribes, to whose chief, Black Hawk, he acted as an independent spiritual adviser. Rennah Wells suffered grave misfortune at that time, and has not fared much better in these pages.

Chrissie Broomfield established that, as far as Islington civil and theatrical registers go, there was a three-year gap in John Gay's life. Flora Tristan provided the most vivid picture of London. Bill Dudley, Claire Hudson and Francesca Franchi fitted Gay into the Sadler's Wells.

Paul Foster shipped him across to New York, whence Peter Matthiessen and Peter Nabokov ran him across the prairie. Howard Reid suggested what he might find at the other end, George Horsecapture undercut some of his pretensions, and Mircea Eliade altered his structure of thought.

To these sources I am particularly indebted, as to Jaime de Angulo.

I always wanted this story to be a film, mostly because I wanted to see a brilliant dancer against a vast and wild background. And indeed, in this book, while there is more concern for the set than for the character, there is most concern for movement.

I would not have had the money to move anything whatsoever had it not been for the generosity of Bernard Crick and the trustees of the George Orwell

Award, who graciously called *Coyote* a project. This project has consumed an enormous amount of time, and I have been unacceptably reliant on the kindness of my parents, Edward and Eileen Thornley, and my wife, Sheila, who has coped with more than her fair share of vicissitude and exasperation and incomprehensible moaning.

Coyote set off seven years ago, and proved astonishingly difficult to domesticate. James Campbell and Hilary Rochford-Dyer befriended the beast, Robin Robertson beat some sense into it, Pascal Cariss picked out its fleas.

To all the afore-mentioned, alive or dead, my respect and gratitude.

Richard Thornley
Astley, May 1994